Palma Harcourt

# AT HIGH RISK

WALKER AND COMPANY
New York

C.1

S

First published in the United States of America
in 1978 by the Walker Publishing Company, Inc.

ISBN: 0-8027-5382-5

Library of Congress Catalog Card Number: 77-91361

Printed in the United States of America

10 9 8 7 6 5 4 3 2 1

BL   MAY 15 '78

For Elizabeth

# Contents

# Rosemead's War

# Chapter 1

The first person I ran into when I arrived at the Embassy was Julian Rosemead. It was scarcely a surprise. As soon as I knew I was posted to Paris I had looked up the list of my colleagues-to-be and seen his name. But the warmth of his greeting was unexpected.

Julian and I had known each other a long time. We were exact contemporaries; we had been at school and university together, and had joined Her Majesty's Foreign and Commonwealth Office on the same day. This, however, gives a pretty false impression. We had little in common.

I remembered Julian from our Ampleforth days as a small, slight boy with colourless hair, weak blue eyes and a *basso profundo* voice. He was a brilliant scholar but hopeless in every other way. If anybody wanted him, which wasn't often, he was usually to be found in the library or the chapel; for a Papist who wasn't a convert, he was extraordinarily pious. In the holidays he disappeared to some dreary Midlands town where his widowed mother lived. He was not one of the boys I had to stay with me; we simply weren't on those terms.

And once at Oxford, he at Balliol and I at the House, we rarely met. As far as I know, Julian, determined to make sure of a First that can never have been in any doubt, spent most of his time working. I had other ideas. Following in the footsteps of three elder brothers I gathered rosebuds while I might, a Blue – mine was for golf – and, somewhat incidentally, a First in Modern Languages.

With these advantages I decided my chances for a diplomatic career were good, but it surprised me to hear that Julian Rosemead had opted for the same choice, and been accepted. If I had thought about it, which I didn't, I would have imagined him as a potential mandarin in the Treasury or in one of those strange research establishments administered by the Foreign Office. Yet here he was, almost a decade later, doing quite nicely for himself in the Rue du Faubourg St Honoré.

Inevitably, during working hours, I saw a fair amount of him. When I arrived, the Chancery was having a face-lift and people were being shunted from one place to another, dependent on the painters and the electricians and other varieties of workmen. I found myself at the end of a corridor until someone, doubtless believing that Julian and I were old friends, suggested I should be moved into his office, and there I stayed while the chaos of redecoration continued. I was comfortable enough for the moment and Julian appeared happy with the situation.

Out of the office I didn't see him at all, except briefly at a couple of official receptions. Apart from my relations in the Paris *banlieue* I had come with a sheaf of introductions, and several of my colleagues, more compatible than Julian, were extremely generous. I had no lack of entertainment. But it did cross my mind that Julian wasn't exactly hospitable; he never even suggested that I should visit him.

Then, at the beginning of my seventh week, he asked me to dinner. The invitation was for Thursday and, after some confusion, I realized he meant the day after next. It was not only unexpected, it was very short notice. Frowning anxiously at me, he apologized.

'It's a – a rather sudden party, I'm afraid. But Johnny, our son, has been – ill, and Jean and I thought we'd take the opportunity to have a few friends in while he was feeling better. Do come, Piers, if you possibly can.'

I wasn't doing anything so I thanked him, said I'd be delighted and made a note in my diary. Thursday morning I regretted it. Charles Grail, who is our political Counsellor and my line boss, pleaded that a dinner-guest had let them down and Mary would be extremely grateful if I could fill in. Since both he and his wife had been more than kind to me and they gave wonderful parties – I had known them before in London – I refused with reluctance.

'Of course I understand, dear boy,' Charles said, playing with a pencil on his desk. 'Do you know where you're going?'

'The Rosemeads live in the *huitième*, near the Parc de Monceau.'

'You're dining at their flat?'

'Yes. You sound surprised.'

'No – no! I was forgetting you and Julian were old chums. The Rosemeads don't entertain much as a rule.'

Charles's secretary was in the room at the time and she must have spread the glad news. After the second person had made some crack about my being highly honoured to be invited to the Rosemeads', I seized a chance and asked Charles what it was all about.

He gave me a long look over the top of his half-specs. 'I wish I knew. When the Rosemeads arrived – about a year ago – they found themselves somewhere to live, they settled in, they began to do their duty. Maybe they followed the French custom of taking people out to restaurants more than most of us do. Even with a representation allowance, that can come extremely expensive in Paris. But, apart from that, they behaved like everyone else. Then suddenly they changed.' Charles mimed bewilderment. 'Now, on a rare occasion, Julian will stand someone lunch. Otherwise they're anti-social. They refuse invitations or, if essential, Julian goes by himself. Jean never appears or helps with any of the things the other Embassy wives do. And nobody, but nobody gets asked to their flat. So you see, Piers, you are being highly honoured.'

'Yes, but – but why? Have you asked him about it?'

'Mary and I have each made gentle probes but they've not been well received. It's a pity, a great pity. Julian's brilliant, hard-working and, I would have thought, ambitious, but there's no room for hermits in the Foreign Service.'

'Perhaps they're just going through a bad patch,' I said. 'He told me their son's been ill.'

Charles laughed. 'That's their standard excuse, I'm afraid. Nobody believes it any more.' He leaned back in his chair and clasped his hands behind his head. 'Look, dear boy, you brought this up. I didn't. But if you could have a chat with Julian on the subject, you'd be doing him a real favour.'

I didn't want to do Julian a favour. To be honest, I didn't even want to have dinner with him. As I shaved, bathed and dressed, the temptation to telephone and say I was ill grew stronger, but I put it firmly behind me. This was a date I couldn't cut. And better now than when Margot was here.

My spirits soared when I remembered that Margot was arriving at the weekend. I sang with the radio all the way to the Place des Ternes, where the flower stalls were closing for the night. I bought an armful of pale pink tulips and deep blue irises. I hoped that Jean Rosemead would like them; I couldn't visualize Julian's wife. I thought again of Margot and wondered if she and I would ever marry. I had asked her before I left the States but she had turned me down, saying that she couldn't stand the starchiness of diplomatic life. Nevertheless, she was joining me in Paris!

My spirits still high, I parked on the Rue Murillo, a short dead-end street lined with tall, cream-coloured buildings, their windows blind with shutters. This was a *très snob* part of a *très snob arrondissement*.

Going through a black iron gate into a courtyard, where the scent of new-mown grass and wallflowers mingled together, I pressed the bell. Immediately there was the buzz and click of the Paris *entrée* that one finds in older apartment blocks. The doors opened into a marble hall. The lift, a mixture of glass, gilt and crimson carpet, took me majestically to the second floor. Julian was waiting for me.

Smiling through his thick spectacles, he offered me his hand, which was slightly moist. 'Glad you could make it, Piers.'

He led me through the apartment into the drawing-room. This was large and high-ceilinged, both elegant and comfortable, its distant wall a width of heavy brocade curtains. So far I was the only guest. But Julian made a great fuss about where I should sit and what I would drink and whether or not I would like a window open, until I felt like some aged relative who might be about to cut a fond nephew out of his will.

When everything was at last settled, he said: 'Piers, there's something important I want to – '

And then Jean Rosemead came into the room.

As soon as I saw her I knew she was what I ought to have expected. Probably a year or two younger than Julian, she was an athletic-looking girl, with wide-set brown eyes in a pleasant, intelligent face and long brown hair caught back at the nape of her neck. I got the impression that she was charming, sincere, efficient and, like Julian, nervous.

Yet it wasn't me that was making her nervous. Having regarded me for half a minute, her head on one side, she said: 'Julian was right. Black hair, sallow skin, aristocratic nose – you do look like a Spanish grandee, Piers.'

Slightly taken aback that she had been summing me up – which was precisely what I'd been doing to her – I said: 'If Julian had warned me I'd have been in character and kissed your hand, Jean.'

She gave me a wide smile. 'I'm afraid my hand isn't very kissable. Too much housework.'

'Piers brought you some flowers.'

The buzz of the *entrée* served to cover Julian's irritability. Other guests were arriving. He excused himself and went to greet them. Jean thanked me for the tulips and irises and took them into the kitchen to put them in water. I was left alone.

I drank half my whisky and helped myself to some nuts. Clearly the evening was going to be tricky. I hoped the new-comers might improve the situation but when Julian introduced them it seemed unlikely. There were three of them, a middle-aged lawyer and his wife, who turned out to be the Rosemeads' neighbours from the ground floor, and a plain, rather shy English girl, a friend of Jean's and a secretary from some Paris-based international company.

Julian said: 'Piers has just been posted to our Embassy,' and at once I became the conversation piece. As a subject I lasted through our pre-dinner drinks. I told them I had just completed three years at the United Nations in New York, that previously I had been *en poste* in Madrid, and that I knew Paris quite well. I demonstrated my excellent French, ex-plaining that I had a half French, half Spanish mother. I said that I was living in an apartment in Neuilly lent me by a cousin, whose *femme de ménage* I had inherited so that I had no domestic problems. I said that I was unmarried.

'But,' I added, suddenly remembering the joyous fact, 'my girl-friend's coming to stay. She's flying into London from New York today and on to Paris on Sunday. I haven't seen her for one hundred and six nights.'

'To stay? You mean, with you? In your apartment?' The lawyer's wife sniffed.

Her obvious disapproval amused me. 'Most of the time, I hope. She may spend a day or two at the Residence with the Pavertons.'

'With Sir Timothy and Lady Paverton?' In spite of herself she was impressed.

'Is she a friend of theirs?' This was the first interest Julian had shown in what we had been saying; most of the time he seemed to be lost in his own thoughts.

Wishing I hadn't mentioned Margot since now I had to explain, I said: 'No. She's never met them. But Lady P, who's also an American, as you know, saw a portrait that Margot had done and liked it and was interested and she's asked Margot if she would paint her.'

'Margot? Not Margot Ninian?'

'Yes.' I was surprised. At twenty-nine Margot was beginning to make a name for herself in the United States, but she hadn't an international reputation and I certainly wouldn't have expected an English girl working in a Paris business firm to have heard of her. 'Do you know her work?'

'One of our American clients left a magazine in the office.' She flushed. 'I – I'm interested in art – I try to paint myself – and I looked through it. There was a long article on Margot Ninian with about half-a-dozen illustrations. I thought they were marvellous.'

'You must bring her to visit us,' Jean said. 'We'd love to meet her, wouldn't we, Julian?'

Julian didn't answer. There had been no need. A woman in *bleu de travail* had appeared in the doorway and announced that dinner was served. Immediately Jean hurried from the room again. She wasn't a restful hostess. She had been bouncing up and down like a yo-yo while we were having our drinks. And I think we were all relieved that it was time to move into the dining-room. Here at least we had a chance to relax.

Dinner began. We had a rough *pâté de la campagne*, veal stuffed with mushrooms and truffles, green salad, cheese; the food and the wines were excellent. The woman served us unobtrusively. Conversation turned to politics and we had a heated discussion in a mixture of French and English. Perhaps for the first time that evening we were really enjoying ourselves.

Then the scream cut through the apartment, shrill, astonished, angry. It was followed by banging doors and pounding footsteps, and the most appalling sound, a high keening that was terrible to hear.

Jean reacted almost instantaneously. She was on her feet, knocking over her chair, running from the room while the rest of us were still set in suspense. In the doorway she collided with a girl, whom she thrust out of her way with careless violence. The girl screamed at her, the same shrill, angry scream as before but now it reanimated us.

'I'm sorry,' Julian said. 'I'm most terribly sorry.'

But this wasn't a broken glass, or soup spilt on a dress. It couldn't be dismissed with an apology and the social minimum of attention. The girl demanded more than that.

She stood there, her eyes round with shock in a paper-white face. A tear trickled down the side of her nose and she snuffled loudly. Her right arm was outstretched towards us, her hand held stiffly at an awkward angle. A thin trickle of blood fell from her fingers on to the carpet. She ignored it.

'He bit me!' she said in English. 'The little bugger bit me!'

'*Ah, la pauvre! Elle est blessée.* She is hurt.' The lawyer's wife, full of sympathy, would have gone to help.

Julian forestalled her. Thrusting her aside, he reached the girl first and, by determination rather than physical strength, propelled her before him out of the dining-room. I got up and shut the door behind them. At least I had muffled by another degree that heart-rending, hideous keening that I thought would never stop.

Immediately the lawyer and his wife began a violent argument. He was for going at once; they could be of no help to the Rosemeads in their trouble. She was for staying; the Rosemeads would be hurt if they just walked out. The shy girl surprised me with her decisiveness.

'Of course we can't go,' she said firmly. 'We can't desert them. We must behave as if nothing had happened.' She turned to me for support. 'That'll be best. Won't it, Mr Tyburn?'

The three of them, expectant, were looking at me. The final decision was mine. I hesitated and, suddenly, the keening was cut short. Its absence hit me like a blow.

'Perhaps you'd tell me what this is all about. You obviously know.' I sounded far more detached than I was.

'It's Johnny, poor little one. That dreadful baby-sitter must have upset him somehow.'

'He doesn't often cry like that. I am a neighbour, Monsieur Tyburn, and I would know. He is a good boy.'

The women had sprung to his defence but they had told me no more than I had already guessed, and there was a lot they hadn't told me. That undulating wail wasn't the ordinary crying of a child, as they wanted to pretend. I might be a bachelor but with three sisters and two brothers married – my second brother was a priest – I had an abundance of nephews and nieces of various ages; I knew something about small children. And what of the girl with the bitten hand? Was she unmentionable?

'It is simply that the child misses his *grandmère*.'

The lawyer nodded his head several times as if he had made a definitive statement, and not added a further complication. I opened my mouth to ask. But Julian had come back, carrying a tray on which were a stack of glass plates, a bowl of chocolate mousse and a jug of cream. To say the least, it was an unexpected sight.

'Jean and I offer you all our apologies,' he said. 'We didn't mean to precipitate you into a family crisis, but Johnny isn't well tonight and what with a strange baby-sitter . . . I'm sure you'll forgive Jean. She doesn't feel she can leave him again and asks you to excuse her.'

His guests chorused their sympathy and understanding. I added my murmur too. Obviously young Johnny was a spoilt brat with an uncontrollable temper – which was something unexpected. Julian and Jean were both competent, sensible people. I wouldn't have imagined them as doting parents.

Rather tactlessly I said: 'Is the baby-sitter's hand – '

Julian chopped off the end of my question. 'She was quite useless, quite useless. A stupid girl! Our *femme de ménage* – the woman who was serving dinner – has taken her home. Which is why I'm having to be *jeune fille*.'

'Now that's an interesting thing,' the lawyer said, as if on cue. 'In England, when you want someone to pour the tea or cut the cake, you say: "Will you be Mother?" But in France we always turn to the youngest member, the *jeune fille* of the family.'

A minute later, Julian having served the mousse and refilled our glasses, they were deep in a philosophical *cum* philological discussion – the sort of thing the French love. And, except for Jean's empty place, there was nothing to suggest that our dinner-party had been so rudely interrupted. Nonplussed myself, I gave them full marks for imperturbability.

We had coffee in the drawing-room. Everyone refused liqueurs. Then, after a minimal interval, the lawyer took out a fine turnip watch and regarded the time. At this obvious signal we all stood up. My relief, however, was premature.

'Piers, you don't have to go yet, do you?' Julian said. 'Stay and have a night-cap. There's something important I want to talk to you about – an Embassy matter.'

'But – ' I didn't believe in Julian's 'Embassy matter' and the last thing I wanted was a heart-to-heart with him. 'Surely it can wait till tomorrow.'

'No!'

I couldn't argue, not after that incisive negative. I shook hands with the lucky, departing guests and sank into an armchair, swearing to myself that never again would I have dinner with the Rosemeads. I heard the chorus of goodbyes in the hall and the front door shut. There was a long pause. I assumed Julian had gone to check on Jean and his son.

When he still didn't come, I unfolded my length from the armchair and poured myself a whisky. Taking the glass with me I strolled to the far end of the room where earlier I had noticed what, at a casual glance, was an unusual painting. It was a portrait of a tennis player, a girl in a short white dress; poised on her toes, her head flung back, her racket arm upstretched, she was on the instant of striking the ball to serve an ace. The artist had caught her vitality and her confidence. It was a good, professional job. Margot would have approved.

'Do you recognize her?' Startled, because I hadn't heard Julian return, I didn't answer at once and he went on. 'That was painted just after Jean won Junior Wimbledon or whatever it's called. She was a fine player. Of course it was more than ten years ago, when things weren't nearly so organized. Tennis wasn't such Big Business then, and the rewards weren't so great. Nevertheless, she was doing well. It was quite a sacrifice.'

'She gave it up to marry you?'

'Yes. Ironic, isn't it?'

'Well – it would be a bit difficult to combine the diplomatic round and the tennis circuit, I suppose.'

He ignored my feeble joke. He poured himself a weak whisky and added a lot of soda. 'Here's luck to you, Piers! Not that you need it. Everything's always gone as it should for you, hasn't it?' He gave me a wistful smile. 'One of these days you'll be ambassador in a top post.'

'What about you, Julian?' I wasn't quite sure what he was getting at. 'Charles Grail was saying only this morning that you've got a brilliant career in front of you. It's my guess I'll end up serving under you somewhere. Talk of things going as they should, you're way ahead of me. You're happily married and you've got a son – '

'For Christ's sake!' It was more a prayer than a blasphemy.

'Julian – ' I gritted my teeth.

I wanted to go home. It had been a frightful evening and this conversation was taking us nowhere fast. Yet he looked dreadful, his skin the colour of mushrooms, his eyes redrimmed, his hands shaking. I wouldn't have left him alone, but Jean was here. They could mourn the disaster of their dinner-party together – if they really thought it all that important.

'I'm resigning from the Service, Piers.'

'What?' I had been half way out of the armchair, but I let myself down again, very gently. 'You're joking. Why should you resign?'

'Because I've finally decided I'm not the sort of person the FCO wants. The Rosemeads aren't suited to the required way of life. I ought to have realized it years ago, and, of course, I did – but I couldn't bring myself to face up to the fact. You see, Piers, I'd always set my heart on going into the diplomatic. Even now I find it difficult to conceive of any other future. But . . .' He sighed.

I didn't know what to say. I hadn't asked for his confidences and I didn't want them. On the other hand I felt desperately sorry for him. Silence, not altogether companionable, stretched between us. I murmured something about not making any hasty decisions and he laughed at me.

'Forget it!' he said. 'I didn't mean to bother you with my private affairs. Unfortunately they're a bit apt to obtrude at the moment. And – there is a problem that I'd hoped to discuss, but it's too late now. Piers, will you do me a favour?'

'What?' I was wary.

'Will you lunch with me tomorrow on the Île de la Cité?'

I don't know what I had expected but an invitation to lunch was the last thing. 'And – ' I prompted.

'I – I want to go to the Memorial for the Deported. After-wards we might eat at La Perdrix d'Or. Have you been there? It's not cheap but the food's superb. I'll explain then.'

'Has this got anything to do with your decision to resign?'

'Look – I said I'd explain then. Will you come?'

'All right.' I was reluctant but it was a small favour. I wasn't committing myself to anything.

'Good!' Julian glanced at his watch, and stood up. 'Piers, I don't want to put you out but I'm a bit worried about Jean and Johnny.'

To my annoyance I found myself apologizing for having, as it seemed, outstayed my welcome. Yet Julian's rudeness wasn't intentional. It was more that, since he had achieved what he wanted, his mind was on other things. He hadn't time to spend on niceties.

Personally I saw no reason to forego them. At the door – he wasn't going to see me to the lift – I stopped, wished him goodnight and offered him the conventional thanks. He didn't respond, except to my goodbye.

'And thank Jean for me, will you? I hope Johnny will be better soon.'

Julian, who was shutting the door before I had turned away, swung it open. Two spots of angry colour had appeared on his cheeks. Gradually they faded as he stared at me.

'They didn't tell you,' he said slowly.

'Nobody has told me anything,' I said, not bothering now to hide my irritation. 'And that includes you, Julian. All anyone has done is make a lot of enigmatic remarks that I've failed to understand.'

'I thought you knew, Piers – not about the other thing, of course – but about Johnny.' He passed a hand over his face in a hopeless kind of gesture. He said, his deep voice sounding deeper than ever, 'My poor Johnny! He's a strong, healthy eight-year-old – too strong sometimes. He may live till he's eighty. But he'll never be well. He's a mental defective – a true moron. It's a tragic, hopeless case.'

I murmured something incoherent. He shut the door and I didn't wait for the lift. Outside, the May night was full of beauty. I was glad to be away from the Rosemeads.

# Chapter 2

Next morning when I arrived at the Chancery Julian was not at his desk, though he had been in because the top was littered. I assumed he was with the Ambassador; H.E.'s Private Secretary was recovering from an operation for gallstones and Julian was helping out.

I got down to work. There was more than usual to do. The Prime Minister and the Foreign Secretary were expected in Paris the week after next for meetings with the French President, and London was inundating us with demands for information to complete their briefings. The concomitants of the flap had percolated through even to me. Charles Grail had passed on a couple of knotty problems and I was fully occupied.

It wasn't until around noon when Julian shadowed the file I was trying to gut that I recalled his invitation to La Perdrix d'Or. I looked up, swallowing my irritation. This wasn't the day for a long lunch hour. With Margot arriving on Sunday I had no desire to work over the weekend.

'Good morning, Piers. We have a date, you remember?'

'Hullo, Julian. Yes, I do remember but, as you may observe, it's not the most convenient time.' I gestured at the papers scattered round me. 'Couldn't we possibly postpone it?'

His mouth set. 'No. The – the arrangement was for today and you promised. Please don't back out now.'.

He was taut as a mainspring. But a night's sleep had improved his appearance and he no longer looked so harried. I thought how glad he must be to escape to the office; at least during the day he was free of Johnny.

'Half a minute and I'll be with you,' I said, doing my best not to sound resigned.

Some of the stuff I was working on was classified and I had

to lock it up. Not bothering to sort it – which would mean extra work later – I bundled the lot into a wire basket and shoved it all into the safe. Julian showed no gratitude for my haste. On the contrary he objected when I insisted on having a pee before we left the Chancery. One would have thought that the bomb was due to go off any second!

'Shall we take my car or yours?' I asked brusquely.

'Yours. I always leave mine for Jean. I come on the Métro. It's not the most convenient of journeys but I'm used to it. And I enjoy the walk at either end.'

'You only run one car?'

'Yes. One's enough for me, even at diplomatic prices. What with upkeep and French insurance rates, I can't afford two cars. Our modest Ford does us very well.'

We had arrived beside my new Jag, of which I was rather proud, and I saw his lips twitch. For a moment, resentful of the comparison he was making, I felt a positive dislike for him. Then he deflected what had really been only a touch of spleen on my part.

'You don't have my responsibilities, Piers. I have to save every penny I can for Johnny. It's all right now. I – I'd scrub shit to keep him from going into a home. But if anything happened to me . . .' He left the sentence unfinished.

'You haven't any relations?'

'No. We're both only children and very much alone since Gran – Jean's mother – died last year. Johnny was terribly upset when she had to go into hospital. He couldn't understand it. She'd always lived with us, you see, and he was devoted to her. He's beginning to get over it, but the sort of life we're expected to live in the Service is impossible without her. She made all the difference to us.'

'Couldn't you get a – a nurse?'

'No, it would cost too much. Even financially we're worse off since Gran died. Her annuity was a big help. To be honest we hadn't realized it would die with her.'

'Why don't you tell Charles about it? He'd be sympathetic. He'd do what he could for you. You should have told him long ago. Perhaps, if you're really set on resigning, you could get a transfer – to the MOD, for example. Then you wouldn't lose your Civil Service rank or your pension rights, and it ought to suit Johnny better.'

'Fancy Piers thinking of pension rights!' Julian laughed without humour. 'I was going to have a talk with Charles when this other thing blew up.'

'What other thing?'

He didn't answer. Instead he looked at his watch and frowned. 'Can't you go any faster, Piers? If we don't get there in the next fifteen minutes we might as well not go.'

It was my turn to ignore a question. I was edging my way around the Place de la Concorde at a fair speed considering the amount of traffic. I had no intention of risking my brand new Jag for the sake of some unspecified mystery. As far as I was concerned we were going to the Île de la Cité for lunch. I was prepared to visit the Memorial for the Deported, which I had never seen, and lend a sympathetic ear to Julian's problems, but that was it. To be honest, the sooner I was back in the office the better I should be pleased.

By this time we were driving along the Quais beside the Seine. In erratic bursts of stopping and starting we passed the Tuileries gardens and the Louvre, and at last we reached the Place du Châtelet where I could turn right over the Pont au Change on to the Île de la Cité, the old heart of Paris. Now I had to find somewhere to park on the narrow, cobbled streets not too far from the blunt end of the island, which the Memorial occupies.

Luck was with me. On a second go round, with Julian getting more and more impatient, I waited in the Rue du Cloître while a tourist – an Italian to judge by his licence plates – studied a map. When, without any warning, he bounced his Fiat into the middle of the road, I parked neatly in the place he had vacated, locked the Jag and hurried after Julian, who was already half way across Square Jean XXIII.

The Square is, in fact, a little park with trees and flowers where people walk their dogs and mothers bring their children and visitors take photographs of those fine flying buttresses along the east front of Notre Dame. It is neat and civilized and domestic. Beyond it lies the Square de l'Île de France. Washed by the Seine on two sides, this 'Square' – like Jean XXIII, the French call it a Square and not a Place – is rough-grassed and treeless. On a fresh May day with the wind coming off the river, it was not very inviting. Julian, who had waited for me – his eagerness seemed suddenly to have evaporated – shivered as we clanged through the iron stile one after the other.

'And there's the Memorial,' he said, pointing to a low stone and concrete structure, featureless except for two small slits, and an inscription between them. 'What do you think of it?'

'It looks rather like a gun emplacement,' I said, unimpressed, and read aloud the words cut into the wall: ' "*Aux deux cent mille martyrs français morts dans les camps de la déportation*" But that's affecting enough.'

Julian wasn't listening. I saw his Adam's apple bob up and down as he swallowed saliva. He passed his tongue nervously over his lips. Then, straightening his slight shoulders, he said in his sepulchral voice:

'Well – better get it over. You take that entrance, Piers. I'll take the other one. We'll meet at the bottom.'

I couldn't help laughing; we made such an improbable pair of boy scouts. But Julian was deadly serious, and obediently I made for my entrance. I saw Julian run across the grass and disappear into his. I remember thinking that if he didn't meet me inside and was never seen again, we'd all have a problem.

Then my mood changed. I was descending a steep flight of stone steps whose enclosing sides seemed to press against me. Each of the twenty steps was so deep that I had to look down to keep my footing; correspondingly the walls loomed higher and higher about me. I'm not over-imaginative, but I had a sudden sense of loneliness and desolation that I hadn't experienced since I was a child. I yearned to turn, to go back, to escape, to resume everyday living, and equally I knew this to be impossible.

At the bottom of the steps I found myself in a roughly triangular courtyard. The walls rose steeply about me, but there was no roof. I could look up. I could see the sky. But somehow the scudding clouds and the blue brightness only emphasized that I no longer belonged.

Instinctively I made for the apex of the triangle, where a grille was inset at the bottom of the wall on the prow of the island. I got as near to it as I could, but the floor – I couldn't decide if it was stone or rough concrete – ceased some four feet in front of the grille. There was a drop, not great; I could have got down and up again easily, but the space before the grille was protected by the bottom spikes of a wrought-iron sculpture, a sort of forbidden gate, which stretched yearningly as high as the wall itself. And from where I stood, or even if I crouched, I could see only the muddy green waters of the Seine.

'Piers!'

I started. Julian was standing by what seemed to be an entrance to an inner chamber, beckoning to me. Reluctantly I went to join him.

'Have you seen anybody?'

'Seen anybody? No – not a soul.'

'Not when you were coming down the steps?'

I shook my head. Julian passed a hand over his face, a nervous habit he had. I heard voices, footsteps; this appalling prison was about to be invaded by a bunch of tourists.

I followed Julian through a narrow passage between two claustrophobic blocks into a dim, hexagonal crypt. A single ray, trapped from the sun, shone from above. Immediately ahead a long, narrow gallery stretched into the distance, its barred shutters closed, a light at the far end reflected from its faceted walls – the tomb of the Unknown Deportee. For my taste it was too theatrical and the murmur of voices, the shuffling of feet, the clicking of cameras – there were some half-dozen people in the crypt – made the place ordinary. Or would have done. The names etched on the walls – Dachau, Ravensbruck, Belsen, so many names of horror, and the quotations from Sartre, Aragon, Saint-Exupéry – these made me choke.

' "*Ils allèrent à l'autre bout de la terre et ils ne sont pas revenus*",' somebody read aloud and, for the benefit of his companion, translated it into German. A guard came from one of the side galleries and offered to sell us brochures about the Memorial. A Japanese looked at his watch and took one more flashlight photograph – the bulb seemed to explode in my face. Julian put up his hand in protest. The Japanese and his girl departed.

'Let's go,' I said. 'I've had enough.'

'Not yet. Give me five more minutes, Piers.'

'I'll wait for you in the Square.'

'All right. But keep your eyes open.'

I made a strangled noise to express derision and left him. It was good to be in the open air again. I raced up the stone steps and took in great gulps of air. Everything looked splendid, from the glorious east front of Notre Dame to the houses across the bridge on the Île St Louis, the trees, the cars, the dirty waters of the Seine, a boat, children playing with a hoop, a woman carrying some flowers, even a paper bag blowing across the rough grass. The Japanese and his girl, both bestrung with cameras, had got no further than the stile, where they were having an earnest conversation. I loved them too.

Cold in the wind, I walked up and down. Soon I was impatient. Time was wasting. I was hungry but there was that pile of work at the office. If Julian didn't come soon we'd have to settle for a sandwich and a beer, and I wanted more than that. He'd promised me a good lunch.

At last he appeared, his face screwed up as if his thoughts were hurting him. 'I don't understand it,' he said. 'I was sure . . . Piers, have you seen anyone?'

'Lots of people,' I said, 'and they were lucky. They were all going to eat.'

'Have you seen anyone whom you know, whom you recognized?'

'No. Should I have done? Does this mean we won't get our boy scout medals?'

Julian sighed. 'I wish you wouldn't be so facetious. It's no laughing matter.'

'I'll do better after a whisky and a bowl of onion soup,' I promised. 'And, my dear Julian, after that explanation you were talking about.'

He nodded his agreement. 'I booked a table at La Perdrix d'Or.'

'Good. Lead me to it.'

Accommodating my long stride to suit Julian, I told myself that I must also control my tongue. Julian was no fool. If he believed something was important it probably was. And he was right that I was being facetious. I was over-reacting to those steps, that courtyard, that grille over the river. Because of my French grandfather? I'd never known him, of course, but my mother often spoke of him. He'd not been deported. He'd not been in one of those hideous camps. But he'd been caught sheltering British airmen and he'd come to a hell of a sticky end.

We went back across the Squares to the Rue du Cloître and I checked that the Jaguar was safe in its slot before we turned into the narrow Rue Chanoinesse. Here, where Abélard and Héloïse once walked, we pushed our way through the locals hurrying home to lunch with long loaves of bread in their hands, past leisurely tourists with their cameras and shop-keepers putting up their shutters for their afternoon siesta, past children, dogs, cars. The air was redolent with petrol fumes and the smell of good French cooking.

La Perdrix d'Or was painted brown and gold. From the outside it appeared chic and shut, its windows heavily curtained so that only a glow of light was to be seen from the street. Inside there was more brown and gold and an enormous menu with a partridge on its cover. The waiter looked hurt when I said that unfortunately, most unfortunately, we couldn't linger over our meal and what would he suggest. The whiskies came while we were discussing his suggestions and we settled for onion soup, a *filet* with a wine sauce, salad, cheese. To assuage the waiter's disappointment at such a plain meal we ordered a whole bottle of good Beaujolais; I hoped it wouldn't make me sleepy for the rest of the afternoon.

Julian nibbled a breadstick and stared suspiciously at the other customers, none of whom was in the least interested in us. In fact our table was in a corner and nicely sited for a private conversation. We wouldn't get a better opportunity to talk. I decided to jolt him.

'Julian, are you going to explain what we were meant to be doing at that Memorial, or shall we discuss something else? For example, why somewhat suddenly you asked me to dine with you and Jean last night.'

He blinked and gave me a weak smile. 'They're not two completely separate subjects, as of course you've perceived, Piers. We were having these people in to see if Johnny – They knew about him.' He stopped, sighed and started again. 'I asked you on the spur of the moment. It seemed a good opportunity to tell you what had happened – away from the office. As things turned out . . .'

'No matter. Tell me now.'

'Sorry. I'll try to explain.' He sipped his drink and, still nursing the glass, said: 'Last Tuesday morning, at the Chancery, I picked up the telephone and heard part of a conversation that I wasn't meant to hear. There's a lot of new wiring being put in, and some extra instruments, as part of our general face-lift. Perhaps the lines got crossed. I don't know. I didn't mean to eavesdrop – but I was so surprised I just listened. Believe me, Piers, I wish I hadn't.'

The arrival of the soup saved me from comment. I tasted the rich, delicious liquid and wished I could have enjoyed it in other circumstances. Julian was playing with his spoon.

'I can't remember the exact words but there's no doubt in my mind, no doubt whatsoever, Piers. The chap who was speaking was threatening one – one of our colleagues. He was telling him he had to keep this appointment at the Memorial for the Deported on Friday; he would regret it bitterly if he didn't come; he had no choice – in fact, it was either doing what he was told or facing unfaceable consequences. It was no sort of joke, Piers.'

'And what did our man say to all this?' I heard my own scepticism.

'Scarcely anything. There was something about it being impossible, and that if the chap was in earnest he'd better come to the Chancery. That just made the first chap laugh. It wasn't a pleasant laugh.'

'I'll bet it wasn't. It wouldn't be, would it?'

'Piers, for God's sake, be serious. Don't you understand? Someone at the Embassy – and I – I suspect it's someone quite senior – is being blackmailed. Or he's about to be.'

32

The waiter interrupted us. Our soup plates were removed. The steak was served, with the salad as we had asked. Our glasses were refilled and we were once more left in privacy.

This had given me a moment or two to think, to try to separate the wheat from the chaff. I was inclined to believe the broad outline of Julian's story, but I certainly didn't swallow it whole. He was a poor actor and I was sure he was lying, that some of the facts were askew. I also suspected that he knew or guessed far more than he'd told me.

'Suppose the unfortunate character had turned up,' I said, 'what had you planned that we should do? Confront him and his blackmailer? They'd have denied everything, laughed in our faces, sworn it was something to do with a girl or none of our business, which it probably isn't.'

'A girl? No.' He dismissed the idea. He leaned across the table and regarded me solemnly through his thick spectacles. 'Piers, I've given this a lot of thought since Tuesday, and if we'd been able to identify anyone today I was going to refer the matter direct to London. That's if I was right and he was a – a senior man.'

'Direct to London? Over the Ambassador's head?' I was horrified. 'You mean you'd have expected me to back you up in a crazy accusation for which we'd no evidence, no – '

'Yes, I would. I realize, Piers, it would have been our word against his and there's no – no actual proof. Which is why H.E. might have believed him – a – a senior colleague – and not taken it any further. But whatever London said they'd have had to look into it. They couldn't afford to take a chance.'

A bit of steak stuck in my throat and I swilled it down with Beaujolais. One thing was for sure: Julian might not have made a positive identification of the voice on the telephone, but in his own mind he was convinced that he knew who it was. And he kept harping on the chap's seniority, which suggested he must be at least a Counsellor. A Service Attaché? A Minister? But there could be all sorts of explanations.

Without thinking, I said: 'Thank God he didn't turn up. You may be going to resign, Julian, but I've still got a career ahead of me – I hope.'

As soon as I had spoken I wished the words unsaid. Of course Julian was in no position to start such a wild hare. But nor was I, and because we happened to have known each other at school was no reason . . .

He read my thoughts. 'I'm sorry, Piers. If it had been just for myself I wouldn't have taken advantage of – of – ' his mouth twisted – 'an old acquaintanceship, to involve you like this, but your family does have influence in government circles, doesn't it, and I hoped perhaps . . . It seemed to me a question of duty. There could be such – such dire results.'

I looked at him in exasperation. He had made me feel guilty and slightly ashamed, which was annoying because it was unfair, and, though I hated to admit it, he had made me feel apprehensive. Knowing how over-scrupulous he could be, I was half afraid that he might not be content to let the matter drop. And I wanted no part of it! He exaggerated the amount of clout I carried. My career was far from gold plated.

'Julian, I appreciate that our profession is particularly susceptible to blackmail,' I said slowly, 'and I agree the consequences can be horrendous. However, since our man didn't keep this appointment, I don't see that there's anything more we can do.' I paused to give him a chance to admit his suspicions but, when he didn't take it, I went on thankfully: 'I suggest we forget the whole thing. What do you say?'

He nodded his head in miserable agreement. He wasn't happy with my proposal but he was painted into a corner. The waiter brought cheese, poured us the last of the wine and asked if we would have coffee. We finished lunch in silence. It had been an excellent meal. As he paid the bill, I thought what a shame it was that Julian had prevented me from enjoying it as it deserved.

About six o'clock I returned from Charles Grail's office to find Julian tidying up his desk. 'Hullo,' I said. 'H.E. let you off early tonight?'

'He's gone to Chequers to stay with the Prime Minister. Actually he left soon after three – he was catching a four o'clock flight – but I've just finished in there.' He sounded fraught. 'I've not had a moment for my own work. I'll have to come in tomorrow and try to catch up. Will you be in over the weekend, Piers?'

It can't have been the very ordinary words so it must have been the false intonation that jarred on me. I gave Julian a sharp glance but his back was turned, his face half buried in a filing drawer.

'Tomorrow? No! I'm going to Versailles for the day to visit some cousins. I intend to get through this little lot before I leave tonight – however late it may be.'

I hoped that Julian would take the hint. Instead he came and sat on the edge of my desk. Ostentatiously jabbing my thumb into a reference book to keep my place, I looked up at him. I was about to make some cutting remark. Then I remembered what he had said about our 'old acquaintanceship'. I swallowed hard.

'Okay, Julian. What is it?'

'Piers – this morning I didn't tell you the – the whole truth.'

'No. I rather thought not.'

He gave me a lop-sided smile. 'There's more to it. The chap on the telephone – '

I took a deep breath. Julian was going to name the potential blackmailee. I thought of the Ministers; surely they were both beyond reproach. And the Attachés? The Counsellors? What about Charles Grail? Was there anyone who wasn't vulnerable, one way or another?

Julian said: 'He made an alternative appointment. When our man jibbed at the Memorial for the Deported, he – he gave him a second choice – the Parc de Bagatelle on Sunday afternoon.'

Slowly, very slowly, I began to let the breath out of my lungs. Not that I was pleased with this turn of events; Julian, like a keen hound, was set on a fresh trail and it wouldn't be easy to dissuade him from it. I wondered why he hadn't mentioned anything about Bagatelle at lunchtime and what else he might be concealing. I still didn't believe he had told me all he knew.

'Our man didn't go to the Île de la Cité; why should he go to Bagatelle?'

'He won't – probably. But we must, Piers.'

'Not me, Julian. And if you take my advice you'll give it a miss too.'

'No – no, that's not possible. I'll have to go. Why won't you come with me?'

'I can't. Sunday's the day Margot arrives. I shall be out at Charles de Gaulle meeting her plane. She'd never forgive me if I weren't there.'

'Of course not. I'd forgotten she was coming on Sunday.'

He sounded angry with himself, and he didn't argue any more. He slid off my desk, locked up the rest of his papers and said goodnight. I thought of the weekend ahead of him – office, helping to look after Johnny, worrying about the future – and compared it with what I was planning for myself. I had to make one more effort.

'Julian, leave this blackmail business alone – please. It's probably all a misunderstanding.'

But I was whistling on the wind. He didn't bother to reply. He sketched a vague salute, said goodnight again and shut the door. I sighed and turned back to my work. There was a great deal to do if I wasn't going to come in tomorrow.

# Chapter 3

The sun shining on my face woke me. For a minute I lay luxuriating in the warmth of the bed, the breeze from the open window, the talk of birds. It was a beautiful day, Sunday.

Sunday! I bounced up like a jack-in-the-box. The time was five minutes to nine. Yesterday I had enjoyed my Versailles cousins so much that, invited to lunch, I had stayed to an extended supper. And, getting home late, I had forgotten to set the alarm. The result – I had over-slept, on this of all mornings!

I leapt out of bed, pulled on some slacks and a sweater, put a comb through my hair. Without bothering to wash or shave, I dashed out of the apartment. It was quicker to walk than to take the Jag. I raced along the Rue de Longchamp to the Avenue – once the Avenue de Neuilly, now renamed after Charles de Gaulle. Here, at the little kiosks near the Métro entrance, I bought the *Observer* and the *Sunday Telegraph* and an armful of flowers, including a dozen yellow roses – wild extravagance. On the way back I stopped at the bread shop and added to my purchases two *croissants* for my breakfast and a *petit parisien*, that lovely crusty bread that goes so well with cheese. I was home by nine-thirty.

While I waited for the coffee to perc, I made my bed, tidied around and arranged the flowers. My *femme de ménage* doesn't come in on Sundays, but everything had had an extra shine yesterday and the apartment gleamed. Telling myself that Margot would approve, I mocked my own nervousness; I had never felt like this about a girl before.

Though not really hungry I made a brunch of fried eggs, *croissants* and coffee, and with it read the Sundays. As usual they were predicting gloom and doom. But the Anglo-French meetings in Paris the week after next had got some space. There was a picture of H.E. strolling along the Faubourg St Honoré, which must have been posed for the occasion, and an article on the Woman's Page devoted to Lady P. I tore it out for Margot; she liked to know something about her sitters in advance.

I should have been watching the clock. In a mad scramble I hid the breakfast things in the dishwasher, showered, shaved, dressed. I was still late for mass; the priest finished reading the Gospel as I came in. Hurriedly I said a prayer and tried to concentrate but my thoughts skittered. Margot would be on her way to Heathrow now. I visualized her in the airport bus and discarded that for a taxi and the taxi for somebody's private car. In her last letter she had written that she would be in London from Thursday; there were one or two potential patrons whom her agent wanted her to meet. She hadn't mentioned where she was staying and I hadn't heard from her since; she was too damned independent. But she would be on Air France Flight 843, arriving at 13.30 at Charles de Gaulle today. I joined lustily in a hymn of praise and thanksgiving.

I arrived at the airport with fifty minutes to kill. I checked that the flight was on schedule, wandered around the shops, had a whisky at the bar, wandered around the shops again. At last I could station myself by *Sortie 34*. A trickle of passengers carrying bags emerged, grew to a stream, flowed past me and died. Margot wasn't among them. Another trickle and another stream but no Margot. As time passed I became more and more pessimistic. Then, when I was at my lowest ebb, I saw her.

Tall, slender, long-legged, bursting with vitality, she strode towards me. She was wearing a burnt-orange suit with a cap to match, and had never looked more beautiful or more desirable. Beside her walked a grinning porter – nobody else on that flight had managed to get a porter – who was pushing a wire trolley loaded with bags. As soon as she saw me she waved. I waved back. Filled with a mixture of love and lust I was weak at the knee – but determined not to show it.

'Darling, I hope all this luggage means you've come to stay for months,' I said, kissing her hard on the mouth.

She had a wide mouth, no lipstick. In fact she wasn't wearing any make-up except around the eyes, which were green and angled to her high cheekbones. It was a very sexy face. I wondered how I had survived these last few months without her.

In the car, she said: 'I wanted to call you from London, Piers. I tried yesterday at noon, and Thursday and Friday nights, but you were never in. It made me wildly jealous.'

'Good!' I said, happy that – contrary to what I had thought – she had tried to get in touch with me. 'But unnecessary. I spent yesterday with some cousins at Versailles. Friday I worked late at the office so that I didn't have to go in over the weekend. We've a flap on at the moment. And Thursday – '

I thought of Julian. It was past two o'clock. He would be walking with assumed unconcern along the paths of Bagatelle. In quick flashes I saw him beside the lake where the black swans lived, in the sunken garden among the irises, in the rosarium. He had told me nothing about the set-up for the meeting, and my imagination could colour it as I pleased.

'Thursday?' Margot prompted. 'You took out your new girl?' She put her hand on my thigh.

'Don't do that!' I said sharply. 'Darling – I'll drive off the road.'

She laughed, until I told her about the Rosemeads and Johnny . . .

When we reached the Rue de Longchamp, I parked the car in its place under the apartment block, and we carried the bags along to the lift. One, rectangular and heavy, turned out to be a folding easel, which reminded me of Margot's main reason for being in Paris; as soon as we got inside the apartment, I showed her the article about Lady Paverton. She insisted on reading it at once.

Her verdict: it made Lucy out to be ultra ghastly.

Lucy? I wasn't on those sort of terms with our Ambassadress. Soon Margot would be addressing H.E. as Timothy! On the lip of laughter I thought what fun the next few weeks were going to be.

'Darling Margot, I love you.'

Pushing me away, she read aloud: ' "When I asked Lady Paverton what she admired most in her husband, she said, in her husky, American voice, 'His integrity. The fact that he's an honourable man. In these days when people are ready to break rules to suit themselves Sir Timothy wouldn't even bend one.' " He must be a stuffed shirt.'

'He's not. He's extremely able – and charming, or so all the women say. Doubtless he's honourable too. As a matter of fact he's got quite a reputation as a man of principle. But let's forget the Pavertons, Margot, and everyone else, shall we? I haven't made love to you for months. And I've missed you horribly. Have you missed me?'

'Horribly, my dearest Piers.' She teased me but now she came willing to my arms. 'We must make up for it, mustn't we?'

We weren't doing too badly, as a beginning, when the doorbell rang – and rang and rang. It was impossible to ignore it. I turned my head in order to see the bedroom clock. It was exactly four, an odd time for an unexpected caller on a Sunday afternoon. Cursing him and his persistence I slid reluctantly from the bed, seized a robe and made for the front door.

I put my eye to the little spy-hole and looked into the hall. The light was on. There was nobody outside my door or the door opposite. Whoever had been leaning on the bell had gone. Simultaneously the *minuterie* dowsed the light and I heard a gate clang. I ran into the kitchen, to the nearest window overlooking the Rue de Longchamp.

I caught a glimpse of someone – a small grey figure at the wheel of a blue Ford as it spurted away from the curb. I wasn't able to read the licence number, but I was almost certain the plate was the diplomatic green. And I had no doubt about an extra CD plate on the bumper. I found myself staring at the road long after the car had gone.

'Piers! Where are you?' Margot called.

'Coming, darling.'

'Who was it?'

'I'm not sure – possibly someone from the Embassy. But no matter. It can't be important.'

Julian Rosemead, I thought, could wait until tomorrow. With Margot here tomorrow would come too soon.

On Monday morning – a day of grey sky and fine mist – I

went, reluctant, to the office. I was busy at my desk until eleven, when I had to attend a meeting of the political staff. I expected Julian to be there, but he didn't appear and Charles Grail asked if I had seen him.

'No. I assumed he was with H.E.'

'I don't think so. H.E.'s not back from his Chequers weekend yet. Anyway, we can't wait.'

The meeting ended. Charles kept me to discuss a short paper he wanted written. From a casual remark I gathered he had intended the chore for Julian – I was second choice and, slightly piqued, I asked him if there was any great urgency.

Charles looked at me over the top of his half-specs. 'Why the question? Have you got something better to do?'

'It's twelve o'clock. If I go home to lunch now I'll miss the rush hour.'

'My dear boy! And you a bachelor. Why are you dashing home to lunch like an ardent bridegroom?'

'My girl-friend's come to stay.'

'Oh, Gawd! Couldn't she have waited until the PM and His Nibs have been and gone?'

I explained about Lady P's portrait and he told me to get out. The paper had to be completed by noon tomorrow and there would be dire consequences if it weren't finished then. I fled. This was a bit of luck. Margot, who had been too busy in London to recover from the jet lag of her flight from New York, had said she was going to have a lazy day in and around the apartment. Lunch together would be a bonus.

Blessing old Charles, I nosed my Jag through the Chancery gates and, with the help of the guard, edged into the road. Annoyingly the Rue du Faubourg St Honoré is *sens unique*, so I had to turn right instead of left, and head away from Neuilly. But once on the Champs Elysées I made good time until, having missed the turning to the underpass, I found myself at the Étoile – and in trouble.

A large space had been cleared in front of the Arc de Triomphe and gendarmes, whistles blowing and white batons waving, were directing the flow of traffic around its perimeter. I thought at first that a party of VIPs was expected; there were several cameramen running about. Then I caught sight of the line of police cars, the ambulance, the fire trucks. Obviously there had been an accident of some sort. A group of men, several of them in uniform, moved into the centre of the road and gazed up at the Arc.

As if at a given signal the whistles stopped blowing, the batons stopped waving and the traffic, which had been creeping along, ground to a halt. Like everyone else I wound down the car window and poked out my head. The great Arc de Triomphe rose above us, dwarfing us all, as Napoleon had intended it should. I was slightly to the side of it and had an excellent view.

After an elongated moment in which nothing happened, I saw people on the very top of the Arc, gesticulating widely. To be precise I could see only two-thirds of each figure above the irregular stone parapet, so that they appeared like glove puppets moving unnaturally up and down.

Without warning one of them began to climb over the edge. There was a gasp from those below as he swayed outwards, but he was in no danger. He was roped and he hung in space, like a spider, before he settled gently on a jutting ledge decorated with lions' heads that runs around the Arc. Here he seemed to busy himself about something, but not for long. Suddenly his companions began to hoist him up. He rose in the air, was seized under the shoulders and helped back over the coping to the safety of the platform.

The show was over. I pulled my head into the car. The mist was turning to rain and my hair was damp. I wound up the window. Somebody opened an umbrella and tried to hold it over the cluster of men in the road. Somebody else, having turned to survey the stacked traffic, issued an order.

And the film began to roll again. Whistles blew, batons waved, the more curious who had got out of their vehicles hurriedly climbed back in, the cars eased forward. I was nearest to the Arc on the inside lane – if in this chaos there was such a thing as a lane – and I didn't have the right of way. Nevertheless I accelerated, determined to be aggressive. My lunchtime with Margot was dwindling fast and I had to make some yardage.

Out of the corner of my eye I caught sight of a gendarme

sprinting in my direction, but I didn't connect him with myself or the Jag until he began to run beside me, mouthing through the glass. I stopped the car and wound down the window again.

'Monsieur! Monsieur!'

The rain blew in, wetting me.

'Look, I'm sorry if I've done something wrong,' I said, 'but it can't be very important and I'm in a great hurry.'

'It is I who am sorry, monsieur, but you must come. Over there, monsieur. Please to park behind that police car.'

There was no point in arguing. I said a mental *au revoir* to Margot and did as I was told. The gendarme trotted beside me. When we arrived and I had brought the Jag alongside the curb of the island on which the Arc de Triomphe stands, he once more bent down to the window.

'*Merci, monsieur.* Wait here, if you please.' He saluted smartly and left me.

Swearing to myself, I looked out of the rear window to see if any other cars had been stopped, but it seemed not. The traffic was now moving with fair speed around the Étoile, and only I had been singled out. Why? Why me? I was riled.

'*Bonjour, monsieur.*'

A man had opened the Jag's door and was sliding himself into the bucket seat beside me. He was of medium height and build, in his middle fifties I would have guessed, a *poil de carotte* with a military moustache that matched the flame of his hair, and a ram-rod back. His voice, unexpectedly soft, took obedience for granted.

'*Vos papiers, monsieur.*'

I produced my papers – passport, *carte d'identité*, all the bumph for the Jag. I waited while he glanced through them. He was quick but thorough. He gave them back to me and I thanked him.

'Now will you please tell me, monsieur,' I said, 'why you have made me late for an important appointment.'

'My apologies, Monsieur Tyburn, but it was necessary. Permit me to introduce myself. My name is Henri Le Gaillard.'

He bowed his head sharply and offered me his hand, which

was warm and dry. I caught the faint echo of countless heel clickings in his past.

'I am honoured, monsieur,' I said, 'but I should still be grateful to know the reason for my delay.'

'I needed help, Monsieur Tyburn. I looked up and saw your beautiful car – and its licence plate. I knew immediately that it belonged to a member of the *corps diplomatique*, and I also knew from the number "45" that its owner was from the British Embassy. So I had you stopped.'

'That sounds very logical, monsieur,' I said, and indeed it was – the French licensing system identifies countries or organizations by the first two or three digits of their CD plates. 'But I'll rephrase my question. Why, at this moment, do you need the help of a British diplomat?'

'Do you know someone called Julian Rosemead?'

In the last quarter of an hour I had experienced frustration, irritation, resignation – even surprise and mild interest. Now I couldn't put a name to what I felt. It was an extraordinary mixture of apprehension, guilt and an emptiness in the pit of the stomach.

'Yes, I know Julian Rosemead. He's a colleague and – and a personal friend of mine.' I can't think why I added that. 'Is something wrong?'

'Come, Monsieur Tyburn. *Je vous en prie.*'

That lovely French phrase which can mean anything or nothing, whatever one damn well wants! In this case it was part convention, part imperative, part apology, but most part a gentling. Monsieur Le Gaillard was basically a kind man and he knew himself a bearer of bad news.

The burst of rain had eased. I got my mac from the back of the car and followed him. We didn't have far to go. Stepping over one of the loops of iron chain that link the hundred stone pillars round the Arc de Triomphe, we scrunched across the gravel to where a gendarme stood, feet apart, hands behind his back, chin sunk on his chest. He seemed regardless of what was going on, but at Le Gaillard's approach, as if someone had flung a switch, he sprang to attention and saluted. It made me want to laugh.

The grin was still stitched across my face when Le Gaillard knelt. Gently and reverently he drew back part of a waterproof covering that had been tossed over some shapeless object on the ground.

And I found myself staring at Julian Rosemead's body.

'Jesus!' I whispered. 'Dear Jesus!'

The next thing I knew Le Gaillard had me by the elbow and was marching me across the gravel and underneath the great Arc. Roughly I pulled my arm free from his grasp. I turned to go back but he stood in my way.

'*Non, non*, Monsieur Tyburn. There's nothing you can do for him. He was dead as soon as he hit the ground.'

'Hit the ground. You mean he fell? Julian fell off the Arc de Triomphe?' I heard my voice crack. 'But that's – that's bizarre.'

'I would like to show you, if you are not too upset.'

I took a grip on myself. 'Of course, monsieur.'

He nodded approvingly. 'We will go up in the *ascenseur*, though it is not the way Monsieur Rosemead went. The staff have all been questioned. Nobody actually remembers him, but we are fairly safe to assume that he walked up the stairs. You know the arrangements here?'

I shook my head and he explained. 'Visitors buy tickets over there and have a choice, either to go up in the *ascenseur* or to mount the stairs. On a clear day in summer there are big queues. Today is misty and sad and there have not been too many people. The man who runs the *ascenseur* and gives a little talk on the way up studies his clients because he hopes for a tip when they leave; he is definite that Monsieur Rosemead did not ride with him. The woman who collects the tickets by the stairs says that at one point there was a rush of students and, possibly, Monsieur Rosemead pushed amongst them.' Le Gaillard shrugged. 'It isn't easy to count the numbers so as to compare them with the tickets and I don't suppose she bothers too much. Most people are honest and the odd one doesn't matter.'

His words were flowing over me but I was only half aware of what he said, and he stopped talking as we got into the lift. We went up in silence except for the creaking of the cage. It was a shorter journey than I had expected; I hadn't realized that the lift doesn't go right up to the platform. We had to walk up three flights of steep metal stairs before we emerged on the roof of the Arc.

Thankful to be in the open, I took great gulps of cold, damp air. I still couldn't accept that Julian –

'Where did he fall from?' I asked abruptly.

'Over here. He would have been looking between the Avenue des Champs Elysées and the Avenue de Friedland.' Le Gaillard gestured towards two of the twelve spokes that radiate from the Etoile. 'Now we are standing exactly where he stood. Lean over, Monsieur Tyburn. I will hold your arm. It will be quite safe.'

I was ashamed to refuse. I bent forward from the waist and looked down. Far below me was a toy world with miniature cars and doll-like people – unreal, unimportant. I felt Le Gaillard's grip and the pressure of the coping which, tall as I am, reached my knees. Reassured, I leaned further out. Directly beneath me was a row of flood-lights, but because of the angle of vision I couldn't see the broader ledge below on which the roped man had landed and which Julian must have hit. I drew back.

'Did anyone actually see him go over?'

'No. I don't think so. There were twenty to twenty-five people up here. That's all. And the Arc is vast, as you appreciate, worthy of Napoleon. If Monsieur Rosemead had chosen a fine day it might have been different.'

'Chosen?'

My eyes met Le Gaillard's. I knew exactly what he was thinking. Thousands of visitors walked safely around the platform every year, looking at the view, taking photographs. It was possible, but highly improbable, that Julian had just toppled over that stone coping to his death. Even if he had been suddenly overcome by vertigo it would have been too easy for him to step back. And anyway what the hell had he been doing on the top of the Arc de Triomphe on a dreary Monday morning when he was supposed to be at the office?

'What sort of person was he, Monsieur Tyburn? Was he

foolhardy perhaps? Might he have dropped something important to him and have climbed over to retrieve it?'

'No. I shouldn't think so. I can't imagine him taking such a
stupid risk. He's a – was a sensible chap. If anything he'd be
over-cautious.'

'You speak with assurance. You knew him well? He was your
*copain*?'

'I was at school and university with him, Monsieur Le
Gaillard, but until the last couple of months I hadn't seen him
for years. We were at different posts.'

'So you wouldn't know if he had some reason for taking his
own life?'

I had expected the question since Le Gaillard had made me
appreciate how unlikely accident was. But suicide? I thought of
Jean and Johnny. Julian had said he 'would sweep shit sooner
than Johnny should go into a home'. I couldn't believe that he
had deliberately deserted them. He had spoken of the future
with purpose, if not with joy. Yet if his death had been neither
accident nor suicide . . . My mind shied.

'Monsieur Tyburn.'

'Sorry. I was thinking.' And about time, I told myself; I
had been behaving like an absolute fool. Le Gaillard had
drawn a trump when he plucked me out of the traffic. Stunned
by Julian's death – and what a death – I had cooperated too
fully with this policeman. 'To answer your question, monsieur.
As far as I know there was no reason why he should have taken
his own life.'

Le Gaillard diagnosed the sudden reticence in my voice at
once, because his manner altered. Stroking his bright moustache, he nodded consideringly and, as if there was no more to
be said, led the way to the exit. But, with his hand already on
the metal rail, he paused.

'Monsieur Tyburn, now we go down these stairs and through
the little museum back to the *ascenseur*. In the museum you
will see a group of people, mostly foreign students. They were
on the platform when Monsieur Rosemead fell and are being
questioned by the police. Of course there may have been others,
but the guards were very quick. Please will you look closely at

47

them in case you recognize anyone.'

He didn't give me time to answer or to ask him why. He clattered down the stairs ahead of me and into the museum, a long, high-ceilinged room, dominated by a colossal statue of the Unknown Soldier. I gazed about me, at the statue, at the objects on the display tables, at the stall where postcards and booklets can be bought, but especially at the miserable, disgruntled visitors who had unwillingly got themselves involved in Julian's death.

A few chairs had been brought, but most people sat on the floor. There was an homogenous bunch of what I took to be Scandinavian students and near them, as if for warmth, a young Japanese couple. The rest were typical middle-aged tourists: a pair of blue-haired American widows, some French from the provinces, a man and wife – probably English.

'I've never seen any of those people before,' I said, as we waited for the lift. 'Did you expect me to, Monsieur Le Gaillard?'

'No, monsieur. But, if you had, it would have been interesting, wouldn't it? After all, there are only three hypotheses. Either Monsieur Rosemead fell, or he jumped, or – he was pushed. Unless I'm mistaken you don't like the idea of the first two. Is the third more acceptable to you?'

I had no intention of answering that. Instead I gave what I hoped was a Gallic shrug. Luckily the arrival of the lift prevented Le Gaillard from pressing the point and we descended, as we had ascended, in silence. He escorted me to my car. Julian's body had been removed, the ambulance had gone, the media had arrived. Someone tried to take a photograph of us, only to have his camera confiscated by a gendarme. Nobody approached us.

'*Au'voir*, Monsieur Tyburn, and thank you for your help. My apologies for detaining you and causing you to miss your appointment. You'll be returning to your Embassy now?'

'Yes, of course. I must report to the Ambassador. And somebody will have to break the news to Mrs Rosemead.'

He nodded sympathetically. Then he pointed at the line of police cars. 'The inspector has left, monsieur, so I think you'll find that you have been forestalled. His Excellency will already know.'

I frowned. I hadn't met any inspector, only a Monsieur Le Gaillard. And somehow, with his last remarks, he had managed to dissociate himself from the police.

He read my mind. As we shook hands through the window of the Jag, he said: 'Please give my compliments to His Excellency. Monsieur Henri Le Gaillard – from the Ministry of the Interior.'

It was quite obvious in which branch of the Ministry of the Interior he was employed. As he walked away I was left wondering – amongst a host of other things – just why the French Security Service should be interested in my old school chum, Julian Rosemead.

# Chapter 4

'Good morning, Piers. Sit down, will you.'

'Good morning, sir.'

H.E. gave me an encouraging smile. 'I'm sorry I wasn't here yesterday when – when it happened, but my plane was delayed by some damned strike. Still, I'm sure the Minister coped admirably.'

'Yes, indeed, sir. But there's one point – ' I hadn't told anyone at the Embassy about Julian and the blackmailing business. At the time I reported to the Minister he had seemed exasperated rather than sympathetic, and anyway the whole thing was so nebulous. Later, I'd talked it over with Margot, and we'd decided that the Ambassador at least ought to know. But for the moment I was forestalled by the intercom.

The disembodied voice of H.E.'s secretary said: 'Monsieur Le Gaillard from the Ministry of the Interior would like to see you when it's convenient, sir.'

'Very well. But he'll have to wait, probably about half an hour. Apologize for me. Meanwhile, no interruptions unless essential, please.' The Ambassador switched off the intercom and turned to me. 'You heard, Piers. We have half an hour before I have to see Le Gaillard. You appreciate who Le Gaillard is, don't you?'

'I assumed he was from the DST, sir, though why – '

'That's right. And he's one of their big guns. He's responsible for the safety of all visiting VIPs, and naturally that includes our PM and the Foreign Secretary when they're in Paris next week. This means that at present he's interested in anything untoward connected with the Embassy or its staff, particularly since the Directoire de la Surveillance du Territoire has received information that there may be some sort of attack on us while the PM's here.' H.E. sighed. 'I must admit, Piers, I wish Julian hadn't chosen this moment to kill himself.'

'Is it definite that he did, sir? I know the other possibilities seem equally improbable. But – '

'I'm sorry, Piers.'

The Ambassador put his elbows on his desk and made a pyramid with his well-manicured hands. His grey eyes stared into the distance. His expression was sombre.

'I know you and Julian were friends. You were at Ampleforth together, weren't you? Which means you share the same faith and RCs hate the idea of suicide, so his death must be a great shock to you. For that matter it's a great shock to everyone, especially such a spectacular death – not a bit like Julian.' He shook his head. 'However, I'm afraid there's little doubt that he did kill himself.'

'But why, sir? Religion apart, he was so devoted to his family.'

'I'm about to tell you why, in the strictest confidence. Except for ourselves, only the Ministers and Tom Chriswell know.' Chriswell was the Embassy Security Officer. 'You're being told because we need your help.'

'Yes, sir. Of course. I'll do whatever I can.'

It was the formal answer. I couldn't think of anything else to say and H.E. clearly expected some response. He nodded his thanks. Then he picked up a brown manilla envelope which was lying beside him and slid it across the desk to me.

'It seems that Julian – unfortunate man – was being blackmailed.'

'*Julian* was being blackmailed?' This was a complete turn-up; I couldn't accept it. 'Are you – are you sure, sir?'

'Well, there's the evidence. That packet was waiting for me – sent *par exprès* – when I got back from London yesterday. Fortunately it was marked "Personal" three times so nobody had opened it.'

I picked up the envelope, regarded it with distaste, tried to rearrange my thoughts. The name and address had been written in block capitals with one of those felt-tipped pens. There was nothing unusual about that. What was perhaps unusual was the elegance of the lettering. Since knowing Margot I had become conscious of such things. I noticed at once how beautifully each letter had been formed. But my mind was on Julian.

I spilled the contents of the envelope on to the desk top. There were five photographs and, after what H.E. had said, they were more or less what I had expected – nudes in erotic attitudes, always the same two men and one of them Julian. I looked at each carefully. The photography was of excellent quality and there was no question that it was Julian and that he was taking an active part; his happy, dreamy smile showed he was enjoying himself. The other character was a youth of medium height with long fair hair and a splendid athlete's body that made Julian look pathetic.

Poor wretched Julian! He must have told me those lies because he hoped to meet his blackmailer at the Memorial for the Deported and wanted someone he could trust as a witness, or for some kind of protection. Presumably the meeting at Bagatelle had been equally abortive. And perhaps another had been planned for the Arc de Triomphe. God knows what had happened there but, whether or not the blackmailer had turned up, it must have seemed to Julian that there was no hope. In the long run, I told myself, it would have made no difference if I had gone to Bagatelle with him – or answered the door on Sunday afternoon.

But I wasn't sure I quite believed it.

Suddenly conscious that H.E. was watching me, I shuffled the photographs together, put them back in the envelope and gave them to him. I remembered something Julian had said about not being the right person to be in the FCO; I had assumed that he was referring to the difficulties that Johnny caused, but equally he could have meant his own homosexuality.

'. . . asks oneself what the blackmailer wanted. Piers! Are you listening?'

'I'm sorry, sir. I was thinking about Jean, Julian's wife.'

'Ah, yes. Poor girl. It's a tragedy for her. But, and this is where you come in, Piers, I'm afraid she could cause us something of a problem. She wasn't exactly responsive when the

53

Minister's wife and Mrs Grail went to break the news of Julian's death to her. In fact, as soon as the police had gone, she asked them both to leave. Of course she was upset, but she expressed herself very – er – forcibly, I gather. Have you seen her since yourself?'

'No, I haven't, sir.'

Margot and I had had an argument about it. Margot had said that I owed it to Julian to do everything I could for Jean and Johnny, that some flowers and a note of sympathy were inadequate, to say the least. But I had had an awful day myself and I had no reason to think that Jean would welcome me. I knew that Mary Grail had gone to her and, if anyone could help at such a time, it would surely be Mary, not me.

'Well, I'm hoping you're prepared to go and see her now, Piers. I'd hate to cause her more distress than necessary, but Tom Chriswell needs to search the Rosemeads' flat. In fact, it's essential. And we thought it would make it easier to get Mrs Rosemead's agreement – and perhaps less disagreeable all round – if you, as – er – a friend of the family, were present. What do you say?'

I took this as a rhetorical question. H.E. knew that it was the last thing I wanted to do, but he also knew I couldn't refuse. The rotten job had to be done, and I had been elected. It was useless to plead that there was no reason why Jean Rosemead, whom I had met once – this 'friend of the family' line was ludicrous – should be more responsive to me than to anyone else from the Embassy. Then an awful thought struck me.

'Do you want me to tell her about the photographs, sir?'

'No, not unless she's – difficult.' H.E. heaved a sigh. 'I know that sounds brutal, Piers, but we have no choice. With these Anglo-French meetings scheduled for next week there couldn't be a worse time for the Embassy to have any sort of scandal. So, the less publicity over Julian's death, the better. I have no doubt Monsieur Le Gaillard and the Sûreté will cooperate with us. On the other hand we can't ignore the fact that Julian may have been set up for blackmail for political reasons. After all, as you're fully aware, any diplomat is at high risk. And if this is what happened in Julian's case we have

54

to know about it. Do you understand?'

If I hadn't understood before I certainly did by the time Tom Chriswell had finished with me. He was a big, untidy man with a bluntness of speech that sometimes bordered on the offensive. Briefing me in the staff car on the way to the Rue Murillo, he left no doubt about what was expected of me when we reached the Rosemeads' apartment. Given no choice, I cursed the position in which I found myself.

A growing hope that Jean wouldn't be at home — she had been given no warning of our arrival — was disappointed. She was waiting in the hall with the front door open when the policeman brought me up in the lift. He had demanded to see my papers and explained that he was there to protect Madame Rosemead from the Press or anyone else she didn't wish to see. She wanted to see me.

'Piers, I'm so glad you've come. I was going to phone you.'

I was taken aback by the warmth of her welcome. She held out both her hands as if I were a dear friend and drew me into the apartment. Then she thanked the policeman, shut the front door and turned to smile at me. It was a brave attempt, not wholly successful. Although she had done her best to disguise the consequences of her grief her eyes were violet-shadowed and there was a pulse beating in her temple. I doubted if she had slept much last night.

'Jean, I can't tell you how sorry I am.'

There are no words for these occasions and, since I didn't think Jean Rosemead was the sort of girl who went in for empty phrases, I left it at that. But I took her by the shoulders, gave her a brief hug and kissed her on the cheek. It was what I might have done with one of my sisters.

'Come and meet Johnny. Then we can talk. You're not in a hurry, Piers, are you?'

'Jean — '

'It's all right. Just treat Johnny as if he were a baby or a – a friendly dog.' Her voice broke.

'Later – if you still want me to. I have to tell you something first. And it's not exactly pleasant.'

'What is it? If it's any more nonsense about Julian committing suicide, forget it.' She was suddenly fierce. 'He'd never take his own life.'

'Outside in the car there's a man called Tom Chriswell. He's the Security Officer at the Embassy. He and his minions want to search your apartment.'

She was shocked by my directness. 'But – what for?'

'It's possible that Julian has left some – some sort of clue as to what he was doing on the Arc de Triomphe yesterday. Jean, once that's known everything can be explained. He could so easily have fallen. The mystery is why he was there on a dismal Monday morning when he should have been in the office. And the security people don't like mysteries, as I'm sure you know.'

'Yes. All right. Why not? We've nothing to hide.' She nodded her head, accepting my lies. 'Those women yesterday. They just took it for granted that Julian had – had jumped. I – I hated them.'

For a moment the seeming irrelevance puzzled me. Then I understood. By chance I had used the one argument that would appeal to Jean. I had implied that the Embassy was trying to find some explanation for Julian's death that excluded suicide. And, after that, everything was easy. Jean was happy to let Chriswell search the place while she and Johnny went for a walk in the Parc de Monceau; it was part of Johnny's routine and wouldn't upset him. Jean was doing her best to cling to normality.

Tom Chriswell wasn't so happy about the arrangement – I think he had visions of them burying incriminating papers in a shrubbery – but I didn't care. I made him and his men stay in the car until we saw the two figures disappear through the wrought-iron gates at the end of the Rue Murillo; Jean, straight-backed and defiant, pushing a low, canvas and aluminium wheelchair for when Johnny got tired, and beside her the boy, who walked in a queer, disjointed sort of fashion.

'All right,' I said roughly. 'Here are the keys. You've got half an hour before they come back.'

'Thank you.' Chriswell's smile was ironical; but he didn't waste time.

I waited in the drawing-room while the apartment was

56

searched. There was nothing for me to do. I walked up and down, looked at the books, which were an uninteresting lot, studied the painting of Jean about to whack that tennis ball, stared out of the window. The wall, which on Thursday night had been a width of curtains, was now a width of window and beyond it a balcony overlooked the park. I opened the french doors and went outside. In the distance I could see between the trees a bridge over a lake and, crossing it, two small, solitary figures. I recognized Jean in her green suit and Johnny from his ungainly movements. And I swore.

'Piers!'

I swung round angrily. For some while I had been conscious of sounds behind me as the search extended to the drawing-room, but I hadn't gone in. I wanted no part of it. Now I stood in the window, still reluctant.

'What is it, Tom? Have you found anything?'

'Possibly. Come and look at this.'

As I stepped into the room I noticed immediately the blank space on the wall where Jean's portrait had hung. One of Chriswell's men had removed it and laid it, face downwards, on the carpet. He and Chriswell knelt beside it. Curious, I joined them.

The portrait had been painted on board, not canvas, and attached to its back by Scotch tape was a large manilla envelope, which Chriswell carefully removed. From it he extracted three photographs. They were nude poses of a young man with long fair hair, the same young man who had appeared with Julian in the photographs sent to the Ambassador. There was nothing indecent about these. He could have been modelling for a group of art students. But on the back of each had been written, again with a felt-tipped pen and beautiful lettering, in English: 'For Julian from his always loving Boy.'

'Don't touch,' Chriswell said sharply as I stretched out my hand; and I realized he was wearing gloves. 'We'll want to try them for prints.'

'Is that all you found?'

'Yes.' He sounded tired. 'Poor devil. Why didn't he come to me. I'd have dealt with his "loving Boy" for him. Rosemead would have been sent home, lost his security clearance, sacked maybe. But, Christ, it wasn't worth his life!'

For the first time I felt some sympathy for Tom Chriswell. I didn't envy him his job. 'You think it was just an affair that turned sour?'

'Something like that, yes. Certainly sending those photographs to H.E. seems to have been an act of pure spite. What could Boy gain from it? Probably he's a queer who's also a small-time blackmailer, and Rosemead either wouldn't or couldn't pay. At any rate H.E. should be relieved. There's certainly no evidence to connect it with any security trouble at the Embassy, as far as I can see.'

I hoped that Chriswell, having reached this conclusion, would go before Jean returned to the apartment, and when he sent his men to wait in the car I expected him to follow. But he sat down, saying that he had to ask Mrs Rosemead some questions. I was arguing with him when we heard sounds in the hall, voices, Johnny's clumping foot-falls along the passage, and Jean's light step outside the door.

Jean came into the drawing-room. She showed no surprise that Chriswell was still there, and brushed aside my apology. She told him, with a little prompting, what Julian himself had told me – about her mother's death, which, because of Johnny, had made their life impossible, and Julian's decision to resign from the FCO. She said that the decision had been hard, that Julian had been depressed and that of course he had been worried. She even admitted they had money troubles; Johnny was a great expense. I could sense her challenging Tom Chriswell to suggest by one false intonation that Julian had had reason to take his own life. But he was as bland as butter; Jean, though she was unaware of it, was confirming that Julian had every excuse for someone like Boy.

At last Tom Chriswell thanked her and stood up. He had the manilla envelope in his hand. He had been fiddling with it as he talked and he had edged out a photograph so that the head alone was visible. He showed it to Jean.

'Mrs Rosemead, would you have any idea who this chap is?'

'No, none. Should I?'

58

'It's possible your husband knew him.'

'Let me see.'

Jean took a step towards Chriswell and he took a step back. She reached for the envelope, pulled – and the photographs were lying on the carpet. Chriswell and I dived for them simultaneously, but Jean was quicker. She retrieved two of them. She looked at them, turned them over, read what was written. Whey-faced, she handed them back to Chriswell.

'No, Mr Chriswell, I don't know who Boy is and I can't explain these photographs.' Her voice was dead level. Her head was high. Only the pulse in her temple betrayed her. 'However, I assure you, though I doubt you'll believe me, that the obvious explanation is – is utterly inconceivable.'

If it hadn't been for the photographs that had been sent to H.E. I might almost have believed her. I wanted to believe her. But all I could do was respect her loyalty. Chriswell's reaction was much the same. I saw admiration for her, albeit a little grudging, reflected in his glance as he said goodbye.

Jean turned to me. 'You'll stay, won't you?'

Somewhat obviously Chriswell looked at his watch. 'I'll wait for you in the car, Piers.' He was giving me an out, which was generous; I had cooperated with him, but I could have been more pleasant about it.

'Thanks, Tom. But no. Don't bother. I may be some time.'

I saw Jean relax and was glad I hadn't hesitated, though why she should want me to stay I couldn't imagine. I sipped the sherry she brought for us and waited. To my surprise she began to talk about Johnny.

'He often understands when nobody expects him to and he can communicate things to me that he couldn't to anyone else. I suppose it's because we're so much together. Even Julian didn't realize.'

'Have you told Johnny yet – about Julian?'

'No. I said he had to go to London unexpectedly.' She sighed. 'Piers – last Sunday Julian took Johnny to the Parc de Bagatelle and something – something happened. It was to do with meeting someone and hiding, and finding something. Then they drove home very fast. Julian never drives fast.

Johnny was terribly excited about it all.'

'And – and you think it was important?'

'Yes. Yes, I do, Piers. I want you to come to Bagatelle with me and Johnny.'

'What? But why?'

'I've got to find some evidence for the Embassy, for Chriswell, for those bloody wives – so that they'll stop believing Julian committed suicide because of Johnny and me – and that odious Boy. Which is what they believe now, isn't it? I want to know and I want them to know what really happened.'

'All right, Jean.' I forced myself to smile at her. She was clutching at straws and the last thing I was going to do was drown her. 'When would you like to go? After lunch?'

'No, we can't. I have to take Johnny to a therapy class. Could you manage tomorrow?'

I thought of the work piling up at the office. Unless I were lucky I would have to stay late tonight, as I had done yesterday, and as I would have to do tomorrow, if I went to Bagatelle with Jean. It all added up to less time with Margot.

'Okay, but may I phone you in the morning to arrange when?'

'Of course, and thank you, Piers.' She looked at me earnestly. 'I'm not imagining things, you know. Nor is Johnny. Julian was horribly on edge last week and when I asked him why he said there was trouble at the office – something to do with one of the senior people – that he couldn't talk about.'

At this point I would have been prepared to tell her any lie I thought she might have believed. But, truth apart, I couldn't think of a plausible story. Instead, though I was yearning to leave, I suggested she introduce me to Johnny. Her face lit up with pleasure.

We found Johnny sitting on the floor in his room; he had the best bedroom in the apartment, with an adjoining bathroom. He was doing a jigsaw puzzle. When we came in he staggered to his feet, like an eight-year-old drunk. Then, with the utmost care, he picked his way around the puzzle and put his hand out towards me.

He was a big, strong boy, as Julian had said, and not bad-looking. What differentiated him physically from other children of his age was the way he held his head to one side and frowned, as if he had to concentrate very hard because everything was difficult for him – that and his lack of coordination.

'Friend of Da's,' he said; at least that's what it sounded like to me. He had a speech impediment too.

'Hullo, Johnny.'

His worried face suddenly uncreased and he smiled at me. It was the most angelic smile I have ever seen.

'Friend of Da's,' he repeated, pumping my arm up and down, and this time there was no doubt as to what he said. 'Friend of Johnny's.'

And, managing to return his smile, I nodded my agreement.

# Chapter 5

I'm neither more nor less observant than other people. If anyone had asked me what vehicles were parked in the Rue Murillo when Tom Chriswell and I arrived in the staff car, I wouldn't have known. Yet now, as I said goodbye to Jean Rosemead and began to walk towards Avenue Ruysdael, I was aware of the yellow Toyota. I wasn't sure if it had been there earlier but I remembered seeing it as I waited with Chriswell for Jean and Johnny to go into the Parc. It had moved up some twenty-five yards.

I can't say I paid it much attention.

Jean had asked me to stay to lunch and offered to drive me back to the Embassy afterwards, but I had had enough of the Rosemeads for the moment. I gave the valid excuse of a mountain of work and she didn't press me. She explained that if I cut across the Parc de Monceau I could get a taxi on the Boulevard de Courcelles or take the Métro. It was the way Julian had gone to the office every morning.

It was the way he had gone yesterday, through the black and gilt gates on to Avenue Ferdousi, which bisects the Parc in a straight line. When he reached a certain point, before the trees hid him from view, he had always turned and waved to Johnny, who would be standing on the balcony. It was part of the Rosemeads' ritual. Yesterday had been no different from any other day – except that it had been the last.

I glanced over my shoulder. Behind me a woman dawdled along with a pram, a small boy pedalling his tricycle by her side; two old men argued as to which bench they should snooze on in the pale sunshine; a Japanese girl in a yellow trouser-suit seemed suddenly to slacken her pace. And, still further back, the scarlet of Johnny's shirt made a bright patch against the cream-coloured building.

I slowed, hesitated, turned round. I waved casually. Johnny waved in return, but there was nothing casual about it. His two scarlet shirt-sleeves semaphored pleasure. He was jumping up and down. I had to respond. Both arms in the air, I trod ground like a victorious boxer.

Gradually I realized that I had become an object of interest. The old men, about to sit down, had moved closer to me. The woman with the pram walked carefully around me but her small son stopped and, thumb in mouth, regarded me from his tricycle. A couple of boys who had materialized from behind one of the ruins in the Parc began to imitate me. A passing priest looked at me disapprovingly. Only the Japanese girl ignored me; she was half kneeling on the grass verge, doing something to her shoe.

Wiping the idiot grin from my face, I gave Johnny a final salute and hurried on. I reached the Rotunda, which forms the main entrance to the Parc, and went out through one of the twin wrought-iron gates on to the Boulevard de Courcelles. There were the usual newspaper kiosk and flower stall beside the Métro entrance and, parked close to them, a yellow Toyota.

I stood at the curb, waiting for a taxi. A lot of traffic flowed past me, but no unoccupied taxi. After a while I gave up. I don't like underground transport and on the whole would sooner walk than use it, but this time there was no alternative and I clattered down the steps of the Métro.

As my head descended below street level I caught sight of an arm withdrawing into the open window of the Toyota – its owner could have been making a signal or dropping an apple core into the gutter – and the car took off in a racing start. It made me think longingly of my Jag.

I pushed past the metal doors at the Métro entrance and heard them clang shut as I ran down a second flight of stairs. I bought a single, first-class ticket at the *guichet*, inserted it in the slot of a turnstile and, when the machine accepted it, thrust my way through. I met nobody in the passages except a man sweeping up paper, but, as I reached the platform, I heard running footsteps behind me.

Immediately they were drowned by a deep rumbling and a train debouched from the tunnel. I got in but didn't bother to sit down; it was only one stop before I had to change.

Propping my length against a stanchion, I looked idly through the open doorway. A girl in a yellow trouser-suit – it had to be the one I had noticed in the Parc de Monceau – walked along the platform and got into the next carriage. There was that extraordinary mooing noise, as if from a cow in pain, which warns that the doors are about to close; then they banged together. The train moved off.

Jean had said I should go from Monceau to Villiers – in fine weather Julian had usually walked to Villiers – and from there to St-Lazare, where I should change for the Madeleine, a short walk from the Embassy. The Métro, Jean assured me, was foolproof. I don't know what that made me. At any rate, as we drew into the next station, I found myself accepting the fact that I had reached Courcelles.

Courcelles! I was going in the wrong direction. Angry with myself I got off the train and strode down the platform. Somehow I had to get to the other side of the tracks. And this, it seemed, was not simple. After an altercation with a stout woman guard who refused to let me go down the obvious passage, which she said was absolutely *interdit*, I had to buy another ticket and start again.

Talk of the blind leading the blind. At some point I realized that the girl in the yellow trouser-suit must have made the identical mistake, and was depending on me to set her right. Certainly she was following on my heels. Together we arrived at the same platform, got on to the same train – though in different carriages – and set off in the direction from which we had just come.

By the time I had changed at Villiers and was on my way to St-Lazare, however, I had forgotten about the girl. I was thinking of Margot. She had said she would be downtown doing some window-shopping, and I wished I had arranged to lunch with her. Later in the afternoon she was having tea at the Residence with Lady Paverton. I smiled to myself; Margot, like so many Americans, never drank tea.

I got out at St-Lazare which, because of its *correspondance* for the railway terminus, is a very busy station, and walked for what seemed miles underground. There were a lot of people about. But only one was wearing a bright yellow trouser-suit. When, having gone wrong again, I abruptly turned to retrace my steps, she also stopped, hesitated and stood still as I passed her, pretending to search in her shoulder bag. I didn't believe it.

The girl was following me! She had followed me all the way from the Rosemeads' apartment. Which meant it must be something to do with Julian. But I couldn't conceive what. Perhaps I was wrong.

Thoughtfully I waited in the middle of the platform where the first-class carriages would stop. I got into the train. The carriage was crowded, but there were two spare seats. I took one and the girl sat down opposite me. She didn't look at me, which at least gave me a chance to look at her. She was a pretty girl, dark-haired, almond-eyed, tall for a Japanese, and either I had seen her somewhere before or she reminded me of someone.

I glanced at our fellow-travellers consideringly. They were respectable bourgeois types, the odd student, a couple of tourists. No. If I spoke to the girl, asked her why the hell she was following me and she protested, they would be on her side to a man. And it wasn't worth a scene.

The warning hooter sounded. Several more people hurried into the carriage, but they had to stand. The doors shut, and the train began to move.

'M'sieur! M'sieur!'

A fierce old woman, dressed in peasants' black, was leaning over me. She held a card under my nose, so close that I couldn't possibly read it, and jabbed with a dirty finger at the back of my seat. It was clear what she wanted. I was in one of the *numerottés*, the seats reserved for the war-wounded, people injured in industrial accidents, pregnant women and so on. I jumped to my feet, apologized for my slowness and helped her to sit down.

I moved along the aisle and stood near the further exit, hanging on to a strap. The train decelerated for the next station, which was Madeleine, the one I wanted; but I showed no interest. I waited while a flux of passengers poured into the carriage, so that I was well separated from the girl. I didn't move. The warning hooter sounded. I counted to ten. Then, muttering *'pardon, pardon'*, I suddenly pushed my way out on to the platform. The doors slammed shut behind me. I felt their suction on my back.

I had made it. The girl in the yellow trouser-suit was still struggling from her seat. She had been much too slow and, if justice had been done, the train would have glided away leaving me to thumb my nose at her, metaphorically at least. In the event, however, all my efforts were vitiated. For some reason the train lingered, the doors opened again and the girl stepped unhurriedly on to the platform. Stalemate.

This had become absurd. The only answer was to ignore her. If it gave her any pleasure she could damn well follow me to the Chancery. Why not? Considering that I had been visiting the Rosemeads and had arrived in a British Embassy car, my present destination would scarcely be a surprise to her.

In fact, she didn't bother to come so far. The yellow Toyota picked her up on the Rue du Faubourg St Honoré, a hundred yards or so from the Embassy gates. I stopped and watched it drive off, but the two Japs were busy chatting and I might not have existed.

Furious, I met Tom Chriswell in the courtyard and poured out my story to him. It was gratifying to see the Cheshire cat grin with which he first greeted it gradually fade. He was frowning when I finished.

'Peculiar,' he said. 'Very peculiar. Of course, she may just have taken a fancy to you, Piers, though it seems unlikely. On the other hand, why do you connect her with the Rosemeads? They're not the only people with an apartment in that block.'

'They're the only Brits. I think the Toyota was waiting there when we drove up in the Embassy car, and the girl assumed, fairly enough, that we'd come to see Jean.'

'But neither she nor her boy-friend in the Toyota followed me. They followed you. Why you?'

'Search me.'

'And if you're thinking, as I presume you are, that all this has something to do with Rosemead being blackmailed, how do you explain the continuing surveillance now that he's dead? They couldn't fail to know. It was in the papers and on the radio.'

'I wish you'd stop asking me unanswerable questions, Tom. I'm beginning to be sorry I ever mentioned the bloody girl. But I thought you might be interested.'

'I am. I am. I'm fascinated.' He nodded his head like a mandarin and I noticed that, though he wasn't much older than I was, he had a balding patch. 'I was just thinking aloud.'

'And have you reached any conclusions?'

'No. However, I'll give you a piece of advice. In the unlikely event that Rosemead's blackmailer had any political motives, he may, having failed with Rosemead, be looking for another First Secretary from the Political Section of the Embassy. So if I were you, Piers, I'd avoid all Japanese birds. He may have decided they'd be more in your line than fair-haired boys.'

'You're joking!'

He didn't bother to contradict me. He grinned, sketched a salute and strode off. I stared after him. I hadn't the faintest idea if he had meant what he said or not.

Compared with my morning, the afternoon was an oasis of peace. Nobody came into the office and the telephone didn't ring. It was a splendid chance to get down to work. Three hours of concentration reduced the stuff on my desk to more than manageable proportions. I read memoranda, telegrams, articles marked for my attention, initialled them and threw them into my out-tray. I wrote answers to three or four queries, checked some statistics and prepared a short paper. I forgot about the Rosemeads and Tom Chriswell and Japanese girls in yellow trouser-suits with Toyota cars.

It was getting on for five o'clock when I realized that there would be no need for me to work late tonight. Margot and I had the evening to ourselves. We could park the Jag on the *contre-allée* of Avenue Georges V, have a drink at Colette's, stroll down the Champs Elysées – stopping for another drink at whatever sidewalk café took our fancy – and have dinner at a small restaurant I knew in the Rue Marbeuf, where almost all the clientèle would be French and the food superb. Afterwards we could stroll back, pick up the car and go home together – to bed. It was my idea of a perfect evening.

A tap on the door disturbed the dream; I should have known it was too good to be true. Lady Paverton's social secretary came in, pulling an amused face at me.

'Piers, I don't think you're going to like me.'

'How can I help liking you?' Indeed she was charming, tactful and highly efficient, as she needed to be at an Embassy of the size and stature of Paris.

'I bring an invitation to you for dinner tonight, eight o'clock, black tie. There'll be a mixed bag of guests. You mayn't find it unentertaining.'

I groaned. 'Does it have to be me? Can't you find anyone else? I've already got plans – wonderful plans.'

'I rather suspected you might. But Miss Ninian assured Lady Paverton that you'd be delighted.'

'What?'

'The Canadian Ambassador has expressed interest in having his wife painted, and Lady Paverton thought this would be a good opportunity for Miss Ninian to meet them.'

'A Ninian in every Residence!'

She laughed. 'Count yourself lucky that this leaves us a man short, or you mightn't have been asked.'

'Commanded, you mean. Do I have a choice?'

'Oh yes! Lady Paverton made it very clear that neither she nor Miss Ninian could commit you. As Lady Paverton pointed out, you may well have a prior engagement, and duty must come first. Diplomats are dedicated people.'

I groaned. 'I hope you're not serious. Margot's already convinced that the diplomatic life is a *danse pavane*. And that's not her thing.'

'Poor Piers! Maybe we can change her mind in the next week or so. Persuade her how exciting and unstuffy it all is.'

'Maybe,' I said. I wasn't optimistic.

Yet, later, sipping my whisky and watching Margot mingle with the other guests in the long drawing-room of the Residence,

I thought how right she looked in the setting. She was elegant and self-possessed, but charmingly natural. She could listen with attention, though I guessed she was bored, and I noticed the casual ease with which she drew a dumpy little woman into the group she was with.

'Kind as well as beautiful,' a voice murmured in my ear. 'One of these days she'll make some ambassador a wonderful wife.'

'Hullo, Charles. Mary, how nice to see you. Have you met Margot?'

'Not properly. A pleasure to come, dear boy.'

'Piers – ' Mary Grail put her hand on my arm – 'tell me about Jean Rosemead. Is she all right? I asked her and – and Johnny to come and stay with us but she wouldn't.'

'That's because she wants to keep things as normal as possible for Johnny, and it's better for him in their apartment,' I said, producing a half-truth. 'I'm sure she was grateful to you for thinking of it, Mary.'

'Are you talking about the Rosemeads?' Lady Paverton joined us. 'How is Jean, Piers?'

'Behaving admirably, Lady Paverton. But of course she's under a great strain.'

'And has been for some time. They both were,' Charles said. 'Poor old Julian! I knew Johnny was retarded, of course, but I had no idea how impossible their life had become without Jean's mother. If only Julian had told us. I'm sure we could have done something.'

Lady P caught my eye and glanced away. Her mouth twitched unexpectedly, leaving me in no doubt that H.E. had confided in her about Boy and the blackmail. She said:

'What's important presently is Jean and her son. When she's gotten over the worst of the shock she's going to be faced with a whole heap of practical problems. Piers, you must make it clear to her that all the facilities of the Embassy are at her disposal, and she has a right to them. Do you understand me?'

I nodded. I understood. Lady Paverton was a clever woman. She had realized that Jean Rosemead would accept help only if it were impersonal. Jean was too proud, too hurt to do anything else. Yet, for some reason, she had made an exception of me. And now, it seemed, I was the official go-between.

It was with pleasure that I heard dinner announced. I knew I had no chance of sitting next to Margot but I did hope that among the dozen women guests I would be partnered by someone who had never heard of the Rosemeads. In fact, I was lucky. I found myself between the daughter of the Canadian Ambassador and the dumpy little woman whom Margot had earlier befriended; her name was Mrs Wintersham.

The Canadian girl was pretty and very young and having her first love affair with Paris. She couldn't decide whether I was trying to seduce her or was as uninterested in sex as she presumed her father to be. In the end we stuck to culture, with a capital 'C'; it was a moderately safe topic.

Mrs Wintersham, who was three times the girl's age and had never been pretty, was much more fun. I began the conversation by asking her if she had ever had her portrait painted.

'I have indeed, Mr Tyburn. I was eight at the time and my sister was six and we were painted with my mother. How I loathed that portrait. It haunted me for years. In the end I had it sold at Sotheby's and spent the money on riotous living.'

'Why did you hate it?'

'Because it proved what I knew but didn't want to believe – that my sister took after our beautiful mother and I would always be a plain Jane, who looked as if she didn't belong. It was little consolation that I inherited my father's brains and my sister was a fool.' She dabbed at her lips with her napkin and took a sip of wine. 'Between you and me, Timothy's been a lot better off with Lucy. She's made him a splendid wife.'

'What?' I nearly choked over my avocado salad.

'My dear, I'm so sorry,' Mrs Wintersham said. 'I thought you knew. I'm the Ambassador's sister-in-law. My beautiful brainless sister was Timothy's first wife – and the mother of his only child, on whom he dotes. Luckily for me, as the boy's aunt I come in for some of the reflected glory.'

'I did know H.E. had a son. Isn't he at Oxford?'

'He's going up in October. He's won a scholarship to Christ Church. Lucky boy, he's got brains and beauty!' She laughed at herself. 'He's just gone off for a trip across Canada and the States – part of his education, Timothy says.'

Mrs Wintersham chatted on about her nephew and I learned more about the Paverton family than I might have done during the whole of my three-year posting. It was very entertaining. Glancing down the table I saw that Margot too was having an animated conversation and appeared to be enjoying herself, which was a relief; she had hated some of the UN parties I had taken her to in New York. The evening, if not exactly what I had planned for us, was turning out quite well.

But with the port and cigars I was back with the Rosemeads. I'm not sure who brought up the subject but it was someone in a group of older and more important men sitting near H.E. I was seated below the salt, as it were, and only caught the tag-end.

'. . . sympathize over that mysterious death of your First Secretary.'

'How very kind of you,' H.E. murmured in the sudden silence. 'A most unfortunate affair but, thanks to the efficiency of the French police – ' he bowed towards the Minister of the Interior – 'no longer a mystery. They have been able to trace exactly what happened. It seems Julian Rosemead went up the Arc de Triomphe to take some photographs – '

'In that weather!' The German Minister pretended to stifle a belch in order to hide his amusement.

'The sun shining through mist gives a most – poetic appearance to our beautiful city,' the Frenchman said coldly, 'such as would appeal to any ardent photographer.'

'Ah so! And he fell – taking his poetic photographs?'

'No,' H.E. said. 'He must have knocked a bit of equipment – his exposure meter, perhaps – over the parapet on to the ledge just below, and climbed over to get it – and slipped. The police lowered a man down on a rope, and the evidence was very clear.' He paused to sip his port. 'A tragic business. He was one of our most promising young men.'

'And that is the authorized version according to St George and St Denis,' Charles Grail murmured in my ear. 'Do you think Jean Rosemead will be happy with it?'

'Why not?' I said, though I doubted it. I had the feeling Jean's reaction would be very similar to that of the German Minister.

'Why not indeed?' Charles said. 'I suppose no wife wants to believe her husband has committed suicide. And at least he'll be able to have a requiem mass with all the trappings now, won't he?'

'Yes. That'll be nice,' I said, unable to keep the edge from my voice.

'Sorry.' He gave me a wry smile. 'Incidentally, there's to be a Memorial Service in the Embassy Church, three o'clock next Tuesday. Would you – would you ask Jean if she'd like to come?'

'Oh, certainly. I'll even offer to escort her.' And why not volunteer? It would be expected of me anyway.

Suddenly I had a mental picture of Jean in the traditional widow's weeds leaning on my arm as we walked down the aisle. Johnny was galumphing ahead of us and amongst the mourners were the fair-haired Boy and the Japanese girl in the yellow trouser-suit. It was black comedy. But I wasn't amused.

# Chapter 6

The next day I went into the Chancery early and worked through the lunch hour. By the afternoon I was more or less ready for the expedition with the Rosemeads. Nobody seemed to think it unusual that, busy as we were, I should be taking time off. If Jean, like an eighteenth-century Isabelle, expressed:

> '. . . *quelque désir*
> *De faire un tour à Bagatelle*',

then it was accepted that I should accompany her.

Only Charles Grail raised an eyebrow and a query. Julian had worked for him, and he felt a certain guilt about his death. Nevertheless, he found Jean's seemingly farcical journey difficult to take. And, since he knew nothing of Boy and the blackmail attempt, I couldn't explain her real motives; I had to imply that she wanted to retrace Julian's steps for sentimental reasons.

'Of course you must go,' Charles said. 'There's no question. But you must admit it's a little odd and disturbing, even. Mary and I are worried about Jean, you know. She ought not to be left alone at such a time.'

'It's what she wants. And she has got Johnny.'

'Well, if you're sure she's all right and – not likely to do anything stupid . . .'

As I parked the Jag on the Rue Murillo – the little dead-end street was becoming too familiar to me – I asked myself if I was absolutely certain that Jean Rosemead wouldn't 'do anything stupid'. My big, fat, instinctive negative was reassuring. So was the fact that there was no yellow Toyota in sight. I pressed the *entrée* button, said hullo to the policeman and went up to the apartment.

'Come in, Piers. You're early.'

'And you're not ready?'

'Oh yes we are.' She smiled at me. 'We've been waiting for you. Bagatelle's a great treat for us. We've been looking forward to it.'

Johnny came, hurrying, with his queer lop-sided gait, and pumped my hand up and down. 'Hullo. I saw you in the Parc yesterday. You stopped to wave. And Johnny waved.'

'I remember. You were on the balcony. You were wearing a red shirt.'

'Green shirt today. Same as wore with Da. Everything same.'

'I've explained,' Jean said, leading the way to the drawing-room. 'It's a game – a game for you. We're going to do exactly what they did on Sunday. He understands.' She lowered her voice. 'Luckily it's one of his good days.'

She didn't mention that she already had a visitor and I was surprised when, as we came into the room, a man got up from the sofa. He was short, stocky, dark and looked rather like a Breton fisherman. In fact he was a priest. Jean introduced us.

'Father, this is Piers Tyburn, an old friend of Julian's. Father Michelet from St Augustin.'

'Monsieur Piers Tyburn, yes.' His eyes had widened with recognition of my name. 'Julian has spoken to me of you. I was expecting to see you at St Augustin.'

His last sentence puzzled me, but we were speaking English and he was far from fluent.

'I live in Neuilly, Father, some way from your church.'

'Yes.' He frowned, and I got the impression that it was I who had now said something faintly absurd. 'I have been arranging for the funeral service with Madame Rosemead. It will be Friday morning, ten o'clock, at St Augustin. Perhaps you will tell Julian's colleagues – his friends – at the Embassy.'

'Certainly, Father. I will be there myself, of course, and – '

'It is Wednesday.'

'Wednesday? You said Friday.'

'Today is Wednesday, Monsieur Tyburn. The funeral is on Friday.' He looked at me as if I were an extraordinarily stupid pupil. 'But I mustn't delay you, Jean, when you and Johnny want to be off to Bagatelle. *Au'voir, Monsieur Tyburn. À bientôt.*'

'*Au'voir, mon père.*'

I ignored the *à bientôt* and the emphasis he had laid on it. To me Friday was *soon*. I had no desire to see him any sooner – if at all. Should he really want me for some unimaginable reason he could always telephone the Embassy; he knew where to find me.

As the front door shut behind the priest I heard Jean say: 'Change your shoes, Johnny, and fetch your blazer. You won't need a coat. It's warm today. I'll get your wheelchair.' And she came back into the drawing-room. 'I'm glad you met Father Michelet, Piers. He's a good friend of ours – and he's been wonderfully helpful to me.'

'You've known him long?'

'Since we came to Paris. Julian had an introduction to him. Piers, Father Michelet assures me that Julian would never in any circumstances have taken his own life. And he should know. He was Julian's regular confessor. As for those photographs of Boy – '

'You told him about those? Jean, Tom Chriswell asked you not to mention them to anyone.'

'Too bad!' She shrugged. 'Father Michelet hooted with laughter at the idea of Julian being what he called "a puff". He said it was absolute nonsense. Oh, don't you understand? It's not that I didn't know this myself, but it's very – very comforting to have somebody else – somebody who knew Julian well – as positive as I am about it.'

I was thankful that Johnny's return saved me from replying. The priest was obviously more of a diplomat than I was or, in spite of his profession, a better liar. I could guess now why he wanted to have a chat with me; it was something I proposed to avoid.

Having got Johnny into his blazer – a mini-task for a Hercules – we went down in the plush lift to the ground floor. Johnny and the policeman on duty exchanged salutes. There was nobody in the courtyard or in the street – no sign of a yellow Toyota – but the policeman insisted on helping us into the

Jag, perhaps as a relief from his boredom; he had a dull, seemingly unnecessary task. As far as I knew there had been no trouble. I asked Jean.

'None. He's kept away some reporters and a ghoulish English-woman who wanted an interview for her magazine. That's all. I told Monsieur Le Gaillard he was wasting his time, but – '

'Le Gaillard! Did he come and see you? When? What did he want?'

'Nothing really. He turned up this morning and talked for a while. He was very kind. He said he wanted the policeman to stay until after the weekend.'

'Sure. Why not?' I didn't believe Le Gaillard had merely been paying a conventional call on the widow. 'Did he ask you a lot of questions?'

'No, he didn't. In fact, almost none. He talked about what's become the official explanation – that Julian climbed over the parapet to retrieve something he'd dropped. He said he thought it best to seem to accept this story for the moment, but he didn't believe it any more than I did, and he was determined to get at the truth. That's what I want too, Piers, the truth.'

'You don't think that could be a possible explanation?'

Jean laughed scornfully. 'Not in a thousand years. Julian had no head for heights. He wouldn't have dreamt of climbing over any parapet. I can't imagine what he was doing up there at all – except perhaps meeting someone. He certainly wasn't taking pictures. He's only got an old Kodak and that's still in his desk at the apartment. He was never in the least interested in photography.'

I suppressed a sigh. Jean was not unlike Julian. She had the same stubborn streak. Like a terrier with a bone she wouldn't let go. I didn't blame her, but – To relieve my feelings I trod hard on the accelerator and the car surged forward. The sooner we got there . . .

'Here we are,' Jean said. 'Johnny, here we are – at Bagatelle.'

Johnny showed no interest. He continued to stare out of the window as he had done throughout the drive, lost in whatever thoughts he had. I swung the Jag on to the gravel of the forecourt before the Porte d'Honneur – two fine, wrought-iron gates set in an arc of delicate railing with a small lodge between them, all backed by immense trees. I parked, opened the door for Jean, and went round the car to help extricate Johnny.

It wasn't easy. Nothing that required coordination was ever easy for Johnny, but it annoyed me that he didn't try to help. I untangled the seat belt, swung his legs to the ground and made to half lift him out. He shook his head violently.

'What's the matter?'

Turning to answer Jean, I hit my head on the top of the door and swore. Johnny gave me his angelic smile. Somehow he scrambled out of the car and stood in front of me, rubbing his head in imitation.

'Damjaps! Damjaps!' he said, frowning but obviously pleased with himself. 'Damjaps!' He made the silly word sound like swearing and I had to laugh.

Almost immediately his mood changed. He refused to go into the Parc. He wouldn't walk and he wouldn't get in his wheelchair. He wouldn't be cajoled or bribed. Tears rolled down his cheeks and he began to sniffle and then to keen. He sat on the gravel, rocking himself backwards and forwards and burying the heels of his shoes into the ground. He was like a little old man having a tantrum, both pathetic and frightening.

I leant against the Jag, pretending not to be embarrassed, hoping that when this was over we could go home. There was nothing else for me to do. Jean, regardless of her clothes, had sat herself down beside Johnny and was cradling him in her arms. She seemed unaware of me or of where she was or of the large French family that had disgorged from a nearby Renault and was looking at us with curiosity and compassion. Johnny was all that mattered.

Five minutes later we were back in the car, heading not for home but towards the Porte de Sèvres, the other entrance to Bagatelle, on the far side of the Parc. Johnny had taken us literally. Everything was to be exactly 'as it was with Da, Sunday'. The farce was to continue.

I parked on the Route de Sèvres à Neuilly – all the roads in the Bois de Boulogne have these complex names – and this time we had got it right. Johnny was eager to get out of the car. Jean pushed the wheelchair with one hand and took him by the other; automatically he offered his spare hand to me. It was a confiding gesture which made a nonsense of the irritation I had been feeling. In this way we crossed the road and went up the path leading to this far less imposing entrance to the Parc. I bought our tickets at the *pavillon* by the gate, and we went inside.

'This way,' Johnny said, turning to the right, and added something about roses.

'What did he say?'

'He said that he and Da sat in the little house on the hill overlooking the rose garden. He means the Kiosque de l'Impératrice.'

'Oh! And I flattered myself I was beginning to understand him.'

Jean smiled. 'You do amazingly well. It's because you listen to him. You treat him like a human being.'

What could I say to that? Disarmed, I offered to push Johnny's wheelchair but Jean refused. And we walked on, Johnny running clumsily ahead and returning to us like a small child.

It was a clear, bright day with fleecy clouds painted on a blue sky. Bands of tulips marched across the daisy-studded grass. Everywhere growing things were green and thrusting, the indolence of summer still to come. Bagatelle, always well-groomed and elegant, was bursting with vitality. I didn't know how Jean could bear it.

'Jean, can't you be content with your own knowledge – and Father Michelet's assurance – that Julian didn't take his own life?'

'I'm not unrealistic, Piers. I realize I may have to be content with it.'

Purposely brutal, I said: 'You should be thinking about the future – for your own sake and Johnny's.'

'Soon, when I'm convinced nothing more can be done for Julian. But I've not given up hope yet. Monsieur Le Gaillard was very encouraging this morning.'

I stifled the retort I might have made. H.E. had said he intended to tell Le Gaillard about Boy and the attempted blackmail and they must have agreed on the 'official version' of Julian's death. Yet now Le Gaillard was going out of his way to deceive Jean. Why? It suggested to me that, in spite of the assurances H.E. must have given, Le Gaillard suspected that all was not well at the Embassy. H.E. would not be pleased.

'Pretty,' Johnny said, offering us some rose petals he had picked up from the ground. 'Pretty.'

We had reached La Roseraie. The roses, like beautiful young girls, were at the stage of giving much pleasure but promising infinitely more. It would be two or three weeks before they would be *grandes coquettes*. Meanwhile, the voluptuousness of their promise was enough. I wished I could have been walking here with Margot.

Our progress was slow; Johnny insisted on pausing to smell every rose bush with exaggerated care. But at last we climbed up to the Kiosque de l'Impératrice, the little circular gazebo where once Josephine, abandoned by Napoleon and waiting to meet her son, gazed out at the splendid view over the rose garden to the Seine and the distant hills. Doubtless in Josephine's day they had had more comfortable chairs; ours, made of metal, were hard, and after a minute or two I suggested we should go on. Johnny refused.

'Da was watching,' he said. 'You watch.'

'What was he watching?'

'People. Lots of people, Sunday. None today. You pretend.'

'Did he see anybody he knew?'

Johnny nodded furiously. 'We met Mike. Not here, on the grass land. Johnny show you.' He was up and making his ungainly way down the laurel-edged path behind the Kiosque before I could ask him any more questions. He paused only to shout over his shoulder what sounded like 'Mike has four wives'.

I had to be wrong about the last bit. But, in spite of myself, I was excited. This was the first even dimly interesting piece of information that the afternoon had produced.

Jean, lost in her own unhappy thoughts, hadn't grasped what was happening, but she didn't intend to let Johnny out of her sight. She hurried after him. I, however, had to go back to retrieve the wheelchair which had been forgotten in the confusion. As a result, we had passed the Orangerie and were galloping down the Allée d'Honneur before I had a chance to explain to her.

'Mike! Is that what the excitement's about?' To my chagrin she laughed. 'Piers, Mike is a peacock. I think his real name is Léon but Johnny always calls him Mike. He's very tame and Johnny loves him, especially when he spreads his tail for the benefit of his wives.'

A peacock! I was disgusted. But I had to laugh too. Though I had been sure that this was to be an absurd, pointless afternoon whose one purpose was to bring some kind of consolation to Jean, I had dashed after my boy scout's badge at the first encouragement. I had been as pantingly eager as Julian had seemed at the Monument for the Deported. I was a bloody fool!

To console myself I thought again of Margot. She would be at the Embassy now. Lady Paverton was having a preliminary sitting, which meant that Margot would be doing quick sketches and getting to know her subject. It was part of the job that she enjoyed.

Johnny said: 'Here we are! Packet. Da found packet. Damjaps! Damjaps!' He threw back his head and crowed with mirth. 'Johnny clever boy.'

I wasn't to be had a second time. Because my last interpretation of Johnny's garbled speech had turned out to be right, it didn't mean that I had done it again. And, even if I had, there could be an equally simple, if equally esoteric, explanation.

'Here we are!' he repeated. 'Johnny brought you. Clever boy!'

We had, in fact, come to the edge of a lake where ducks glided venturously amongst a profusion of aquatic plants. At the far end an overhang of rock, hollowed so that one could walk beneath, kissed the water. A family, father and mother and three very small girls, were making their way underneath it now, the children squeaking with trepidation. Nearby another couple were admiring the exotic water-lilies.

Johnny was pointing at the rocky overhang. 'Da took me. You come. I show you.' He seized my hand and began to pull.

'All right.' My eyes met Jean's. 'Do you know anything about this?'

'No. But it could be important.'

With Johnny lurching ahead, we went along the path that encircled the lake and, underneath the archway of rock, found ourselves in a tiny chamber, high-roofed – I could just stand upright – but dank and cold. Involuntarily I shivered, struck by the chill of a place never dry and never warmed by sunshine. Yet here, green with moss and besmeared with fungus, was a stone bench, its arms ending in lions' heads, its feet lions' paws. Nobody in his senses would have sat on it.

Johnny did – or rather he knelt. I heard Jean catch back her reproof as he began to search behind the bench. His hand came out, filthy dirty, clutching a handkerchief and a used condom.

'Put it down! At once!' Jean said, her voice sharp.

'Balloon.'

'No. Put it down. And let's get out of here.'

Johnny turned to me. 'Sunday Da found packet.'

Jean seized him by the shoulder and thrust him ahead of her into the sunlight. I let them go on. I didn't expect to find anything, and I didn't, but I wanted to see for myself. Unlike Johnny, who had to kneel, I was tall enough to peer over the bench at the narrow ledge which was part of the rock outcrop. It was covered with dust and mould and an obscure collection of waste that was best left alone. What interested me was the relatively clean, empty space, exactly in the middle. Someone could have cleared it before leaving a packet there; it was as good a post office box as any, provided one had been told where to look.

I emerged into the sunlight, half blinded by its brightness after the gloom of the rock. Johnny, his shirt-sleeves rolled up, was making an effort at hygiene by dabbling his hands and forearms in the lake. Jean was trying to clean his blazer with a small towel she had taken out of her bag. As my eyes adjusted I thought how old she looked, and tired and defeated. And a wave of anger washed over me; Julian had had no right . . .

Julian's son was on his feet. He was a sturdy eight-year-old, his eyes button-bright. He said:

'Whir-r-r! Photos! Damjaps! Damjaps!'

Then, without any warning he sat down, one leg under him, one leg dangling in the water. His head fell on his chest. 'Johnny – tired. Go home.'

'Help me!'

Jean had automatically brought Johnny's wheelchair with her when she left the chamber and it was standing on the path. Between us, with no help from Johnny, we lifted him into it. He seemed to be asleep. Jean adjusted the safety belt, draped his blazer round his shoulders and wiped the spittle from the corner of his mouth. I started to push.

'It was the excitement,' Jean said. 'He suddenly gets unbearably tired so he goes to sleep. It's his escape route. He'll be fine when he wakes.'

'What would you have done if you'd been alone?'

'Waited until someone came who would help, or until he woke, I suppose.' She sounded unsure. 'He hasn't done it for ages. We hoped he had grown out of it. I could manage by myself when he was smaller, of course, and nowadays he usually knows when he's getting tired.'

I glanced sideways at Jean. Weight for weight there wasn't much difference between her and Johnny. As he grew older and bigger she was going to find him more and more difficult to cope with. And if his childish tantrums were translated into adult rages . . . I remembered the baby-sitter whose hand he had bitten. I also remembered that earlier this afternoon I had had the gall to tell Jean she should be thinking about the future. What a future!

I concentrated on pushing Johnny as quickly as I could along the gravel path in the direction of the exit. We were passing the Petit Château with its beautiful formal garden when he began to stir. He shook his head several times and flicked his hand over his face as if he were trying to brush away cobwebs. Then he twisted himself round and looked at me.

'Faster!' he commanded. 'Da went faster. Da put packet in

84

his pocket, me in chair and we're in big hurry.'

'In his pocket?' Jean leaned over him and I slowed in spite of Johnny's urgings. 'Darling, are you sure that Da put the packet in his pocket?'

'Sure.' He nodded violently with the over-emphasis that he gave to every physical movement. 'In pocket.'

'It could have been those photographs of Boy,' Jean said.

'How big was it, Johnny?' I asked.

'Small. For pocket.'

The photographs were a fair size. 'Was it heavy?'

But this was too much for Johnny. 'Photos!' he said, as we went by some enthusiastic photographers filming two black swans. 'Damjaps! Damjaps!'

'What on earth does that mean?' I asked Jean.

'I don't know. I've not heard it before. It's just a new word he's got hold of. Something he's misheard probably, and taken a fancy to. He'll have forgotten it in a few days.'

We passed under a ruined archway into the forecourt. I saw with relief the gates and the *pavillon* beside them. Our expedition to Bagatelle was over – and at least Jean should have got some satisfaction from it; she would be able to tell Le Gaillard about the packet that Julian had picked up. I wondered what the DST would make of it and faced the fact that, because of this mysterious packet, I should have to describe my afternoon to Tom Chriswell. Some things are indescribable.

We went down the path and across the road to where the Jag was waiting for us. Jean stowed away Johnny's wheelchair while I helped Johnny into his seat and struggled with the seat belt.

'Didn't see Mike,' he said regretfully.

'Never mind. We'll see him next time,' I lied, and was suddenly thankful that Jean hadn't heard me.

I looked at my watch and did some quick mental arithmetic – twenty minutes to drive to the Rosemeads' apartment, ten minutes to settle them in and say goodbye. It wouldn't be worth returning to the office. My work was in pretty fair shape and, since I had toiled through the lunch hour, so was my conscience. I thought how pleasant it would be to have a long, leisurely bath and be waiting for Margot when she returned from the Embassy. There was a cocktail party at the Centre des Conférences Internationales, but after that the night was ours.

Jean and Johnny were having an animated conversation. Immersed in my own thoughts, I wasn't paying much attention. Johnny was being insistent: Sunday, Da had taken him home and played music. I was coming up to the Place des Ternes, where only last week I had bought Jean flowers on my first visit to them, when I caught the words: '. . . the sneak thief stole our music, Johnny. You know that, darling. We haven't any now.'

The Place navigated and safe on the Boulevard de Courcelles, I took in what Jean had just said. 'You've had a burglary? What about your policeman?' I asked.

'It wasn't much of a burglary and it was before – before the policeman.'

'But – Not on Monday?'

'Yes. Monday morning. I had to take Johnny to the dentist. We were late and perhaps I was careless about locking the door. Anyway, some sneak thieves got in.'

'Did they take much?'

'No. The radio and the cassette player – that's all. I think they were looking for cash – they seem to have searched in what would be the obvious places – but I never leave any in the house.'

'What did the police say? You did report it?'

There was an appreciable pause before Jean said: 'Piers, a visit to the dentist is always a strain. When we got home, we had lunch and Johnny went to rest. Then the police arrived. Do you understand?'

'I – I understand.'

She hadn't reported it because the police and Mary Grail and the Minister's wife had forestalled her with news of Julian's death. Not that it mattered; the chances of getting back a radio and a cassette player were infinitesimal. And at least the theft had achieved one thing. It had served to explain to Johnny the sudden influx of strangers.

86

Poor Johnny! He was still muttering about his 'music' when I turned into the Rue Murillo and caught myself looking for the yellow Toyota, which of course wasn't there.

Jean said: 'Piers, I'm very grateful to you. This afternoon has been well worthwhile – for me at any rate. I don't understand about the packet but it must be important. Julian never mentioned it to me, which in itself is odd. As soon as I got home last Sunday – I'd been to look at the tapestries in the Musée de Cluny – Julian dashed off to mass at St Augustin, and later he seemed very – distrait, but he didn't explain at all.'

There were a lot of things Julian hadn't explained, I thought ruefully, as I drew up in front of the Rosemeads'. And most of them, if only Jean would accept the fact, were best left alone.

# Chapter 7

Jean didn't invite me to stay for tea or a drink as I had half expected. Perhaps she was worried about Johnny after that sudden collapse of his. Or she may have been exhausted, physically or emotionally, and decided that she had had enough of me. At any rate I was thankful not to have to make excuses.

With a feeling of relief I now realized as customary on leaving the Rosemeads, I got into the Jag, made a U-turn and set off for home. Suspicious after yesterday, I caught myself glancing in the rear-view mirror somewhat more than necessary, but there wasn't a yellow Toyota in sight. I should have been more versatile in my thinking.

He was driving a white Mercedes – a beautiful job.

At a guess white is the most popular colour for cars in Paris and I wouldn't have noticed the Merc so soon if it hadn't been a sexy SL model; much as I love my Jag this was the car I would have chosen to own it, as a good little diplomat, I didn't have to buy British. I had spotted it drawing away from the curb while I was making my U-turn and had followed it when it turned right on to the Rue de Courcelles. Yes, followed it! The clever bastard had taken a calculated risk that had paid off. Presumably, had I gone left, he would have swept around in a quick arc and come after me. As it was he stayed neatly in front, allaying any suspicions I might have had of him. And when we reached the Boulevard de Courcelles he gambled again, with equal success. By now he knew that I wasn't making for the Embassy.

At the Place des Ternes, however, the odds were against him; my choice was wide. Moreover, if he guessed wrong on this occasion the traffic was too dense to permit any fancy driving. He had to let me overtake. Then, stopped by the next traffic lights, when he could have drawn level with the Jag, he chose to tuck himself in behind. And there we sat, in tandem, waiting for the go sign.

If you're interested in performance cars, as I am, you're also mildly interested in the people who drive them, and, having nothing better to do, I tilted my rear-view mirror so that I could see the driver of the Merc. He was a youngish man with a round, flat face, black-haired, Oriental. Paris is full of business men from the Far East and there was nothing to distinguish this one; I had only caught a glimpse yesterday of the driver of the yellow Toyota and couldn't hope to recognize him again. But I recognized the girl beside him, even though she wasn't wearing her yellow trouser-suit. Or I thought I did. It was difficult to be certain.

The lights had changed to green and the chap in the Mercedes had had the nerve to hoot at me. I started with a jerk, which annoyed me, but I was shaken by the probability that for the second time I was being followed from the Rosemeads'. It didn't make sense. I had to be mistaken.

Well, I would find out.

Resisting my instincts, I idled along the Avenue des Ternes, the white Mercedes keeping its distance behind me. I knew what I was going to do. As soon as we reached the Porte des Ternes I intended to turn left as if I were going to my apartment, but instead I would get on to the Périphérique at the Porte Maillot. Then, racing round the ring-road of Paris, I would either lose an innocent Merc or prove myself a better driver than the Jap.

In the event I did neither. At Porte Maillot I joined the Périphérique, merging so fiercely with the mainsteam of traffic that I received several warning hoots. They weren't the last I was to get. I drove fast, jigging from lane to lane, cutting in as closely as I dared. The Jap was doing some precision driving too, and was still on my tail. It wasn't going to be easy to shake him.

The next exit was Porte Dauphine – I was there and past – and, after that, a fair distance ahead, Porte de la Muette. If I came off the Périphérique here I could try to lose him in the one-way streets around the Place de Colombie, a district I knew because of visits to the OECD – the Organization for Economic Cooperation and Development. Alternatively, I could double back to Neuilly through the Bois de Boulogne. But first I decided to make one more attempt to outwit him on the Périphérique.

I eased my speed and got into the centre lane, where I stayed. Around me the traffic roared. We were nearing the Porte de la Muette now, and it was time to make my move. Ahead and to my right a long lorry was flicking its indicator, warning me that it was about to come across. There was an appreciable gap between me and the car ahead, and I scarcely needed to slow to let the lorry in. Behind me, the Jap, judging that I was too late to make the turn, should have relaxed – or so I hoped. I seized my chance.

With frenzied hooting I accelerated. The lorry swerved back into its own lane, the driver doubtless cursing me. But I was past him and flicking my own lights. He would have known I meant business. As I cut in on him, much too sharply, he swung out again and we changed places. It was a nice piece of driving on both our parts and not really dangerous, if you knew what you were doing.

I was on the exit ramp and braking when I heard the crash behind me – the scream of rubber on tarmac, the hollow *whomph* at the point of collision, and the void of noise before the mangling of metal. The sounds were unmistakable. And horrifying. It wasn't my accident, not in the sense that I had caused it. But I was morally responsible.

My thoughts flew to the Japanese, the man whom I had no real reason to dislike and the girl, the rather beautiful girl, with him. They were more guilty than I, but that didn't make it any better. And at least one other vehicle must have been involved – at least one other driver, wholly innocent. Stalled on the exit ramp between a hesitant Cadillac with an Ohio licence plate and a horsebox drawn by a small Renault, I sat in impatient ignorance while my too vivid imagination coloured a multiple accident. I felt slightly sick but there was nothing I could do.

I was glad to get into the Bois and content to follow the

American who, simultaneously driving and reading a map, was weaving a slow, erratic course in front of me. It was pleasant here, the chestnuts in full bloom, their candles shading from white to a deep pink, and after the roar of the Périphérique, very peaceful. I didn't want to hurry. The driver of the Renault, however, had become bored. As we rounded the end of Lac Inférieur, its water dyed green by reflected trees, he drew out to pass and in my rear-view mirror I saw a car coming up behind me very fast. It was a white car, a Mercedes. Evidently I had wasted my pity on the two Japs; whoever had been hurt, it wasn't them.

Hemmed in by the Cadillac and the horsebox – the Renault was making heavy weather of overtaking – I was caught. But anyway I didn't have the heart for more fun and games. If they wanted to follow me home, I thought, let them. With reluctant admiration – the Jap must have been a superlative driver to have got off the Périphérique at Porte de la Muette – I watched the Merc brake hard, and knew that they had spotted me. I couldn't shake them now.

'Damn Japs!' I said aloud, viciously, and in the next instant realized what I had said – or, to be more precise, what Johnny Rosemead had said, over and over. 'Damjaps! Damjaps!' In my excitement I nearly drove into the back of the horsebox.

Since Jean hadn't known what Johnny was corrupting, the probability was that he had picked up the phrase from Julian. But why had Julian sworn at some Japanese? And where and when? And, most important, what significance did it have? As the Renault and its horsebox turned right on the Allée de Longchamp and the American, having at last decided where to go, shot ahead, I ambled along slowly, trying to work it out.

Mare St James jogged my memory. It is a pleasant, domesticated lake on the edge of the Bois, where children sail boats, dogs swim after sticks, boys fish. It has the usual complement of ducks and a few swans. Great trees overshadow the water. Families play *pétanque* – a kind of bowls with steel balls – on the rough ground beside it or sit on benches to watch the scene. Though not elegant like Bagatelle, it is charming and in its own way equally photogenic.

'Damjaps! Photos! Damjaps!'

That was what Julian had said when he had seen someone filming the black swans of Bagatelle. But he had used the same words before, to me, after I had come out of the rocky chamber at the end of the lily pond, and at that particular moment nobody had been taking photographs. It could be some form of association in Johnny's mind or it could be that on Sunday – Suddenly I recalled Julian swearing at a couple of Japs who had blinded us taking photographs inside the Memorial for the Deported. There was, there had to be, some connection . . .

The white Mercedes had closed up on me. The Japs didn't intend to lose me in the narrow streets of Neuilly St James. They were going to follow me home. And then what? It was absurd to feel threatened. This was the Rue de Longchamp on a lovely May afternoon. The schoolkids were streaming out of the *lycée* and tearing up the street on their phut-phutting *quarante-neufs*. Housewives had come out to do their shopping; every second person seemed to be clutching a long loaf. Neuilly had woken up again after its lunchtime snooze. And, as I said, it was absurd to feel threatened.

Ahead of me a Ford drew away from the curb. Now, if I wished, I could leave the Jag on the street and go into the main entrance of my apartment block. It was a temptation. But I have my pride. Hooting at a couple of gossips standing in the middle of the entrance, I swung the car into the driveway, which steeps down to *le parking*.

Nothing followed me.

*Le parking* is an underground place of murk and gloom, with a space between concrete pillars allotted to each apartment. It is a lonely place and has no entrance doors. Anyone who chooses can drive or walk in. Nevertheless, theft and vandalism are practically unheard of and, though I had returned there at all hours of the night, it had never before occurred to me to be nervous. Today was different. After I had backed into my space I found myself sitting in the driver's seat clutching the wheel and waiting for the daylight at the top of the driveway to be blotted out by the descending Merc.

93

Angry at my pusillanimity, I got out of the Jag, slammed the door, and locked it. To hell with them! I was at the entrance to the passage leading to the lift, when I heard the car. I turned and walked back. The car came much too fast down the driveway, swung towards me, blinking its lights, and parked neatly in one of the spaces reserved for guests. It was the popular Parisian white, but it was a Renault. The driver was Margot.

'Hi, Piers! How do you like my automobile? I've rented it for a month. I'm much too American to live without wheels.'

'Hullo, darling.'

She heard the strain in my voice. 'Something wrong?'

'I don't really know. Let's go upstairs and I'll tell you about it.'

'Okay. You can help me with the parcels. I've bought all sorts of stuff. I'm going to cook us a stupendous dinner tonight.'

'Lovely. But how did you find time? Weren't you doing sketches of Lady P this afternoon? I thought you'd still be at the Embassy.'

'I was.'

Clearly something had also gone wrong for Margot, but I didn't ask questions. It would be time enough to swap stories when we got up to the apartment. And there were a couple of other things that had to be done first.

I dumped the shopping on the kitchen table, left Margot to sort it out and went into the sitting-room. Standing well back from the window I looked for the white Mercedes. It was parked almost opposite, where the Ford had been, where I had thought of putting the Jag. I didn't like the idea that it might still be there when Margot and I set off for the party at the Centre des Conférences. Whatever the Japs' business with me might be, I didn't want Margot involved.

Postponing the problem, I telephoned the Embassy and asked for Tom Chriswell. At this point I couldn't face telling him the whole story about the white Merc and its occupants parked outside my apartment, but there was an enquiry I had to set in motion.

'Tom, hullo. This is Piers. Tom – would you do me a favour?'

'What?'

'There was an accident on the Périphérique this afternoon at Porte de la Muette. Could you possibly find out about it? What happened. If anyone was hurt. The usual details. And let me know tomorrow?'

'Why?'

This wasn't very encouraging, but I persisted. 'Because I – I might inadvertently have been the cause of it, by changing lanes to make the exit. I heard the crash behind me as I got on the ramp.'

'Charles Grail told me you'd gone to Bagatelle with Jean Rosemead and her boy.'

'Yes – but that can keep till morning. Tom, please, find out about this accident for me.'

'All right. I'll try.'

I put down the receiver and went back to the window. I had timed it well. The white Mercedes was drawing away from the curb. Presumably the Japs had got whatever they were after, but God knows what it was. I heaved a sigh. Tomorrow I should have to tell Chriswell everything.

'A bad day, my love?' Margot had come into the room.

'Yes. You too?'

'Peculiar and – oh, frustrating.' She tossed back her hair. 'Piers, do we have to go to this dreary party?'

'I do, yes. It's strictly duty. But – ' It hadn't been easy to get an invitation for Margot from the Quai d'Orsay. 'Needless to say, darling, you don't have to come.'

I heard the chill in my voice, and at once regretted it. Catching her by the hand I pulled her to me, held and kissed her. We had both had bloody days. We were both fraught. This was no time to have an argument about my job – one married a man, one didn't marry his job, or did one? To my surprise she kissed me in return, very hard, lips together, sending some message that wasn't sex.

'Lucy Paverton's quite a woman, isn't she?' Margot said.

Doubtfully I grinned at her; I loved her very much. 'Tell me what happened.'

'I'll show you my sketch pad.'

I knew better than to make comments. I let Margot do the talking while I turned over the pages and fragments of Lady P, some oddly familiar, confronted me. I regarded the nose, long, thin but tip-tilted and the straight, elegant authoritative back – both, according to Margot, presenting problems. A profile I thought rather good had an angry line through it. It was followed by a brilliant caricature, which made me laugh aloud.

'Lady P saw this and had you thrown out of the Embassy?'

'I did it while I was waiting. Piers, it really was annoying. This wretched kid turned up – he's at school with Sir Timothy's son – and more or less demanded to speak to Lucy. Alone, if you please! He said it was terribly urgent, absolutely vital, Christ knows what – all in his best Etonian accent. Look!'

Margot flicked over another page of her sketch pad and there was the 'wretched kid'. He was an attractive young man, dark, slim, personable – and Japanese? I felt the muscles of my face grow still.

'And you had to wait while he and Lady P went off to have a private chat?'

'Yes. That was fair enough, I suppose. I didn't mind, though she was gone about forty-five minutes. But the little b had upset her so much that when she did come back she couldn't go on with the sitting. She pleaded a sudden migraine, and I left.'

'Did she say what the boy wanted?' I was doing my best to sound casual.

'Money.'

'Money?' That was a surprise. I don't know what I had expected, but it certainly wasn't that.

'Yes. Lucy said he'd got himself stranded in Paris without a dime. He remembered that the parents of his old school pal lived at the British Embassy, and came along to beg a loan. Frankly, I didn't believe a word of it.'

'Margot!' Of course; this was a perfectly plausible explanation. I had been imagining things, just because the boy was an Oriental. Now I could relax. 'Why on earth should Lady P lie to you?'

'I don't know. I thought perhaps Sir Timothy's son was in some kind of trouble and she didn't want to tell me.'

'Oh no!' I shook my head. 'Definitely not, darling. He's gone on a visit to the States and Canada. His aunt was talking about it the other night at dinner.'

'Okay. But then why was Lucy so upset, Piers? Because she *was* upset. She was white-faced and – and pinched around the mouth.'

I shrugged. 'She probably did have a sudden migraine, as she said. Let's forget her. Margot, are you coming to this party with me, because we'll have to get changed?'

'Okay. But what about your hideous day?'

'I'll tell you on the way to the Avenue Kléber.'

Which I did. I told her about Bagatelle and Jean and Johnny, and the packet that we could assume Julian had picked up on Sunday. But I said nothing about 'Damjaps' or the Périphérique or the white Mercedes. Put into words it would have sounded so melodramatic, and the Rosemeads had already used up my quota of recountable melodrama for the day. Besides I didn't want to worry Margot.

She was full of sympathy – for Jean and Johnny, not for me. 'Isn't there anything we can do for them, Piers, anything at all?'

'We can buy Johnny some "music". That will give them both pleasure,' I said – and had to insist that first we went to the reception.

Later, after we had escaped with indecent haste from what I admit turned out to be one of my more tedious social duties, I again had to insist. We couldn't buy up the shop. Jean might accept a replacement for the cassette player and, stretching a point for Johnny's sake, a few cassettes, but she would not accept a transistor radio as well. I tried to make Margot understand.

'Sure, I realize she wouldn't want to be beholden to just anybody, but you're different, Piers. You were Julian's friend.'

I didn't try to argue any more. Maybe Margot was right. If not, I should have to pretend that I had bought the radio for myself and had included it with the cassette player on the spur of the moment – something like that. And Jean could pretend to believe me.

I said: 'Darling, I don't know about you, but I'm terribly hungry. If we don't get home soon so that you can cook that delectable meal you promised, I'm going to die of starvation.'

Margot laughed. 'Cheer up! It won't take long once I start. But what about delivering Johnny's "music"? Now?'

'No. Tomorrow will do.'

'Okay! To the kitchen!'

I've always believed that a good driver should be no less aware of what's behind him than of what is in front, but this evening I had been checking my rear-view mirror much more than usual. However, there had been no sign of a yellow Toyota or a white Mercedes or any other vehicle sitting on my tail suspiciously long. I turned into the Rue de Longchamp and, nearing home, drove slowly, but I was being over-cautious. There was nobody waiting in a parked car, and only the *concièrge* standing chatting to a neighbour near the entrance to *le parking*.

'*Monsieur Tyburn! Un moment, Monsieur Tyburn.*'

She came hurrying towards me, a tidy but shapeless woman of indeterminate age, with a neat grey chignon, pointed nose, and bright observant eyes. My cousin who owns the apartment once said that she was more intelligent than a bagful of PhDs, and I had no reason to doubt him.

'*Madame, bon soir.*' I shook hands with her through the car window and we exchanged politenesses.

'There was a man, monsieur, who wished to be directed to your apartment. I told him you were not there. I had seen you go out.'

'Did he give his name or say what he wanted?' I wondered if it had been Tom Chriswell.

'No name, monsieur. He said, however, that earlier today he had had the misfortune to scrape the paintwork of your Jaguar when it was in a parking lot. He said the damage had been very slight and he had been in a great hurry, so he had taken your number and later traced you through your Embassy. He wished to make reparation.'

I got out of the car. It hadn't been Chriswell. It hadn't been anyone I knew. And whoever it had been, he hadn't scraped the Jag on a parking lot. Apart from the Chancery courtyard, the only places the car had been left were outside the Rosemeads' on the Rue Murillo and at the entrance to the Parc de Bagatelle.

In fact, as I might have guessed, there wasn't the faintest scratch on the Jag. Madame and I gave it a minute inspection. Margot, who hadn't followed the rapid French, put her head out of the window and asked what was happening.

'Nothing,' I said quickly. 'Nothing. Somebody made a mistake. He must have misread the licence plate,' I added in French.

'Perhaps, monsieur. Perhaps.' The *concièrge* shrugged, too polite to contradict me outright. 'He left you a note, monsieur, which I myself have put under your door. He wished to save me trouble and deliver it himself. Indeed he insisted. But I assured him it was part of my duty to take round parcels and letters.'

She gave me a bland smile. She was telling me as clearly as if she had put it into words that all he had really wanted was to know which was my apartment. And, even though he had apparently failed in his purpose, this suggested unpleasant possibilities.

'*Merci, madame.* I'm very grateful to you.'

'*Je vous en prie, monsieur.*'

I got into the car and when she stood back to let us pass, said as if it were an afterthought: 'What sort of man was he, madame?'

'Persistent, monsieur.' She permitted herself another smile, another shrug. 'If, however, you refer to his appearance, he was a Japanese gentleman. He had a round face . . .'

Her description was detailed and perceptive; the caller had been either the driver of the white Mercedes or his twin brother. I thanked her again and drove slowly down to *le parking*. I was in no hurry to read his note. I didn't anticipate that it would be illuminating.

And, as regards its contents, I was right. Written in French, with an indecipherable signature, it contained an apology for damage to the Jaguar, a promise to make reparation and a

99

request to telephone a given number. Why he had bothered to go into so much detail, I couldn't imagine, unless it were for the benefit of the *concièrge* whom he expected to be curious. The phone number which I couldn't resist dialling, was that of the Hôtel Crillon.

I was also wrong, however. In one respect the note was very interesting. It was written with a felt pen and in beautiful script. Margot said that the script was typical of anyone accustomed to forming ideograms with a pointed brush, but I could have sworn it was similar, if not identical, to the writing on the packet sent to H.E. and on the photographs of Boy they had found behind the painting of Jean in the Rosemeads' flat. Yet Boy, with his long fair hair, was certainly not a Japanese.

Lovely smells were coming from the kitchen. Margot called to me to lay the table and open a bottle of whatever we were going to have. Willingly distracted, I decided to shelve the problem of Julian and the Japs. It could wait till I saw Tom Chriswell in the morning.

# Chapter 8

'Good morning, Piers. Come in. Sit down. Will you have some coffee?'

'I should love some coffee. Thanks. And good morning to you, Tom, though I must say you don't give the impression there's much good about it.'

'I had a rough night.'

'That I might have guessed.'

Tom Chriswell smiled thinly. He looked tired and crumpled. His eyes, red-rimmed, were sunk into the grey flesh; he had shaved, but badly, and had forgotten the bit of cotton wool he had stuck beside the nick at the corner of his mouth; his finger nails were dirty. He was normally an untidy man, but clean. I had never seen him in this state before.

'To be honest, I haven't been to bed at all. Leastways not my own. An old chum turned up unexpectedly and we went on a bender together.' He leered at me. 'Great – at the time.'

'If you like that sort of thing.'

Tom Chriswell was a family man. He had a very young wife and a baby daughter, and was reputed to dote on them both. I didn't believe in his bender. He was lying through his teeth. Nor did I trust his bonhomie, his heartiness, his offer of coffee; they were out of character. Something was wrong, and Tom Chriswell was getting ready to screw me.

'Black or white?'

'White, please.'

His secretary poured and placed beside me a plate of Romary biscuits. I took one, nibbled, tasted the coffee. It was exceedingly strong and I added some milk. Chriswell was drinking his black. He waited for the girl to leave.

'I've been covering up for you,' he said, 'reluctantly, since it was you who dropped me in the dung-heap.'

'I did? How?'

'You told me there had been an accident on the Périphérique near Porte de la Muette yesterday afternoon. You asked me to find out about it. I did. Two cars were involved, both badly damaged. One was driven by a *juge d'instruction*, the other by a middle-aged housewife.'

'Was either of them hurt?'

'Luckily for you, no. Just shock and bruises. But the judge is as mad as a Bedlamite. It was he who drove into the rear of the Citroën so, even though the woman admits she stood her car on its nose without warning, he's the one technically to blame. She says someone cut slap in front of her and she had to jam on the brakes.'

'I plead not guilty, Tom.'

'Do you indeed? Well, I'll accept that. The judge says it was a white Mercedes. But he also says, Piers, that the Merc was playing tag – or whatever the French equivalent is – with a grey Jaguar. And I want to know what the hell you were doing with those Japanese buddies of yours?'

I had been treating Chriswell half dubiously, half facetiously, but now as he bit off the last sentence, everything changed. The mercury in his office must have dropped ten degrees. I became conscious of the chill.

'They followed me from the Rosemeads' apartment. I was trying to lose them.'

'Start from the beginning! You went to Bagatelle, according to Charles Grail, with Jean Rosemead and her batty boy.' He read my expression because he added: 'Her mentally retarded son, if you prefer the euphemism, Piers. Tell me what happened.'

I told him. I kept nothing back. There was no reason why I should. But I didn't like the way he watched me while I talked, keeping his sunken eyes steady on my face. When I finished there was silence, except for the tattoo that his fingers were beating on the desk, two shorts and a long, over and over. He was as nervous as a mother hen.

At last he said: 'Is that the truth?'

'I'm not in the habit of lying.'

'You've a top security clearance, haven't you?'

Startled by the change of subject, I nodded. 'You know I have.'

'You're about to be vetted again.'

'Thanks for warning me.' I leaned forward and helped myself to another Romary biscuit.

'Piers, if there's anything – anything whatsoever that might lay you open to blackmail you'd better tell me. If you don't, you'll regret it.'

For a moment I looked steadily at him. Then I threw back my head and laughed. I wasn't in the least amused but I had to break the tension somehow.

'I have no sexual aberrations, no hidden vices, no debts, no dependants, no undiscovered crimes to my discredit – and I've not sold any secrets lately. My conscience is clear.'

He said: 'I made a mistake about Julian Rosemead. I thought he'd been having it off with a boy-friend and the boy-friend turned nasty and that was all there was to it. I was wrong. Either he was set up for political blackmail or his affair with Boy was discovered and exploited. Now it seems the same people who tried to blackmail Julian are showing an interest in you. Clearly they associate the two of you. And I don't like that, Piers – not one little bit.'

'What did they want from Julian?'

Chriswell gave me a long hard stare. 'I don't know. I wish to God I did. And doubtless, sooner or later – perhaps too late – I will. But whatever's going on I want you out of it, Piers. Do you understand? Out of it. Leave Jean Rosemead alone. Don't go to her apartment again. And if you see or hear anything of those two Japs let me know at once.'

'Very well.' I stood up. If Chriswell thought this was the way to get my cooperation, he was a fool. But he wasn't going to tell me any more. 'Is it all right if I go?'

He nodded and let me get as far as the door before he stopped me. 'Piers – one other thing. You're not to mention this conversation to anybody, anybody whatsoever – and that goes for the popsie you've got living with you.'

'Do you mean Margot Ninian, Tom?'

'Do you keep a harem? Of course I mean Margot Ninian.'

Furious with Chriswell I stormed back to my office. I was prepared to tell him about the Japs – if I saw them again. I would have done that anyway, from a sense of duty. But he could stuff the rest of his instructions.

I dialled Jean Rosemead's home number. She was slow answering and, while I waited, I remembered that I was going to the UK tomorrow for a couple of days. I thought of the weekend ahead with pleasure; my one regret was that Margot wasn't coming with me – instead she was to stay with some American friends in the Dordogne. I had been disappointed at her refusal, but I couldn't really blame her. Next Saturday was my parents' fiftieth wedding anniversary and, inevitably, the occasion for a gathering of the family Tyburn. Not a party for outsiders, as Margot had said, firmly excluding herself.

'Hullo. Who is it?' Jean's voice sounded muffled.

'Hullo, Jean. It's Piers.'

'Yes.'

The monosyllable fell flatly, unwelcoming. I hesitated. Johnny's 'music' had to be delivered sometime today or Margot wouldn't forgive me. But, thumbing my nose at Tom Chriswell, I had dialled without thinking what I was going to say to Jean, and obviously I had chosen a bad moment to do it. As briefly as I could, I said that I had managed to get hold of a cassette player for Johnny and would like to bring it round.

'Would it be convenient if I came about twelve-thirty?'

'Whenever suits you, Piers – if it's after twelve. And thank you.'

She rang off without saying goodbye, leaving me to wish that it had never occurred to me to replace the stolen player. I sighed. Everything was going wrong this morning. Irritably I swung my feet down from my desk and began to work, only to find that it was impossible to concentrate. My mind kept returning to Tom Chriswell; he had disturbed me more than I cared to admit.

'Roll on tomorrow,' I said aloud – and remembered that before I left for the airport I would have to attend Julian's funeral. Softly and fluently, I swore under my breath.

It was precisely twelve o'clock when I left the Embassy. Fifteen minutes later I was in the Rue Murillo. There were four cars and a light van belonging to some interior decorators parked in the road. I inspected each one carefully as I drove past; if Tom Chriswell was achieving nothing else, he was making me neurotic.

The iron gate was open, the policeman inspecting the lawn which was nailed with buttercups and daises. He bent down and uprooted a dandelion with a pocket knife. Caught with a weed in his hand, a stain on his white glove, he grinned at me sheepishly.

'*Bonjour, monsieur*. Madame Rosemead said you were expected. Please to go up.'

The *concièrge* came out into the courtyard, calling to the policeman. I was introduced and she offered me condolences on the death of my friend, Monsieur Rosemead. For a couple of minutes we stood talking in the hall. Then we shook hands again and, as the lift ascended, I saw through the glass and the ironwork the two of them go into the *concièrge*'s apartment, and the door shut. Idly I wondered how much time the bored policeman spent with the *concièrge* when he should have been on duty. Not that it mattered any more; the media had already lost interest in the Rosemeads.

I rang the doorbell. I thought I heard movement in the apartment, a sharp noise, silence. I was probably mistaken. No one answered the door. I played a tune on the bell again and waited. After a minute, when still nobody came, I tried the handle. The latch was up. I went into the hall, put Johnny's 'music' on a chair and hesitantly walked along the passage.

'Jean, are you there? It's Piers.'

There was no answer. Nor was there any sound, of a vacuum cleaner or a waste disposal or any other kitchen gadget that might have prevented her from hearing me. The policeman had said I was expected. The front door had been left open. Yet no one was here. To make sure I shouted as loudly as I could.

'Jean, are you there? Jean! Johnny!'

I subdued a stab of unease when again there was no reply. I told myself that Jean must have run downstairs for a moment to visit her neighbour, the lawyer's wife whom I had met, and taken Johnny with her. Alternatively, since the day was warm and bright, she and Johnny could be sitting on the balcony.

Uncertain, I retreated to the hall. Here the sight of Johnny's 'music' on the chair reminded me of the burglary they had had. At present visitors to the block were meant to go through the double screen of policeman and *concièrge*. Nevertheless it was tempting trouble to leave the front door unlocked. Without clothing my suddenly urgent fears in thought, I retraced my steps along the passage. If Jean and Johnny were not on the balcony I would interrupt the policeman's stolen leisure and demand –

The smell hit me as soon as I opened the door but I was half way into the long, elegant drawing-room before I saw them.

They were lying side by side on the carpet. Jean's arm was around him, his head on her shoulder. Johnny was wearing a scarlet shirt and the blood showed only as a darker patch on his chest, but the wound over Jean's heart was a vivid shock against the white of her blouse. A gun lay by her right hand.

I knelt beside them, a handkerchief over my nose and mouth to stop myself gagging. Johnny must have realized at the very last instant what was happening and from fear or shock or pain his sphincter had failed him; the smell was revolting. I took Jean's wrist. It was cold and clammy and I could find no pulse. She looked as if she weren't there, as if her spirit had fled happily and instantaneously. Johnny, on the contrary, had fought; he hadn't welcomed death.

He was still fighting.

I was on my feet and running as the realization hit me. Johnny was alive. His eyes had opened, regarded me without recognition, closed; and he was breathing.

I tore along the passage, bruising myself as I skidded through the front door. The lift was waiting – I must have been its last occupant – but I couldn't bother with its double gates. The stairs were easier and faster. I all but threw myself down them.

One thumb jabbing at the bell, I banged with the flat of my

other hand on the door of the *concièrge*'s apartment. She opened it so abruptly that I nearly fell into her minute hall. Through an open door I caught sight of the policeman seated at a table covered with a red and white checked cloth. He was ladling soup from a big, flowered tureen on to his plate. Bread, cheese, salad and a bottle of wine were in easy reach. His face was shining with enjoyment.

'*Comment, monsieur? Comment?*'

Angry at the interruption of her meal the *concièrge* barred my way, preventing me from entering her private domain. The policeman, also frowning, continued to ladle soup. And I realized that in my panic I had been speaking English, so that they hadn't understood a word I'd said. Gritting my teeth I began again.

'Madame Rosemead has shot herself and her son. The boy's still alive. Get a doctor – ambulance – help. Hurry!' I shouted at them in French.

They hurried. The policeman thrust back his chair and seized the telephone. He dialled and I waited to make sure he had got through. Then I ran after the *concièrge*. She had rushed past me, obviously intending to go up to the Rosemeads' apartment. When I reached the lift I saw the edge of her skirt and her piano legs ascending above my head. I panted up the stairs after her.

She was fast-moving for such a big woman. She came bustling out of the drawing-room, almost colliding with me in her haste. She was pinching her nose with two fingers in a mime of disgust. But she was more practical than I.

'They are cold,' she said. 'I'll fetch blankets. You go to him, monsieur. You are his friend and he is crying for someone. Try to console him.'

I sat cross-legged beside Johnny and held his hand. He was unconscious but making piteous noises in some nightmare world of his own. Only reality, in which both Jean and Julian had deserted him, could be worse.

'Talk to him, monsieur. Talk to him,' the *concièrge* urged, arriving with the blankets. 'The sound of your voice will reassure him.'

I looked up hopefully, but running footsteps belonged to the policeman. 'Help is coming, monsieur. It'll be here with all speed.' He gave a strangled cry. 'Don't touch, madame!'

He was too late. The *concièrge*, busy tucking in the blankets around Johnny and Jean, had knocked away the gun. 'That will smother some of the stench,' she said firmly.

Johnny groaned, shifted his body a fraction and cried out. His eyelids fluttered, opened. The room was still, the three of us frozen in our unnatural, inadequate positions.

'Ma!' Johnny said. 'Ma!' His head swivelled in my direction. There were tears on his cheeks. 'Da!'

I felt myself gripping his hand. 'It's all right, Johnny. It's me, Piers – Da's friend. You remember. Everything's all right.'

'Da's friend.'

His speech was very slurred. A bubble of spittle appeared at the corner of his mouth, rose-coloured, blood-coloured. It grew and burst. I brushed back the hair from his forehead and wiped his mouth with my handkerchief. Immediately another blood-bubble appeared. A red trickle meandered down his chin. 'Damjaps,' he muttered, and his eyes closed.

'For God's sake go and see where that ambulance is!' I stumbled over the words, incoherent in my anxiety. 'Tell them if they don't get here soon – ' There was no need to finish the sentence.

'Yes, monsieur, yes. *Bien sûr.*'

They left me alone with Johnny and, bending over him, I murmured a mixture of platitudes and endearments in the hope they might give him some comfort. There was nothing else I could do. I thought of looking for the wound, but I could do more harm than good.

He was stirring again now, his face twisted in pain. Suddenly he whimpered like a baby and dug his nails into my hand so that it hurt. He seemed to be having difficulty with his breathing.

'Cold. Johnny cold,' he said. 'Thirsty. Want drink.' And, after a pause: 'Ma, Johnny can't – can't – Gran! Oh Gran!'

For a long minute he was quiet and I thought he had gone. His eyes opened, stared, focussed on me. He gave what would have been his angelic smile, if his face hadn't suddenly distorted in agony and bright, clean blood flowed from his mouth.

'Da – Damjaps – Mike – Bang – Bigbang – Damjaps – Mike – Take care.' And, after an interval. 'Da's friend.'

It was something like that. His grip relaxed and his body went slack. Slowly I stood up. I wondered if he had really been trying to warn Da's friend to take care of the damned Japs. Poor, dear Johnny. I wished he could have seen that peacock on his last visit to Bagatelle.

I looked at Jean, pale as marble. For a moment I thought there was a ripple of animation over her skin but it was a trick of light.

'I'm sorry,' I said aloud.

They all seemed to arrive together, the *Police Secours*, the ambulance, the cameras, the measurements, the questions. What had once been the Rosemeads' drawing-room was suddenly a movie set – the aftermath of a crime or the casualty department of a hospital. None of it was for real.

Monsieur Le Gaillard rescued me. He took me by the elbow and led me along to a room which from the furniture I assumed was Julian's study. He opened a cupboard, well-stocked with liqueurs, and produced a bottle of cognac and two glasses. He poured us drinks, a large one for me, a minute one for himself.

'You need it, *mon vieux*,' he said, 'and, as for me, I am sure Madame Rosemead wouldn't begrudge it.'

On another occasion his carrot-coloured moustache re-flected in a brandy balloon would have made me want to laugh. Even now I had to hide a half-smile. But Monsieur Le Gaillard himself I took seriously; though I must admit I couldn't imagine why he, and presumably the DST, should be interested in the deaths of Jean and Johnny.

'I must leave you for a minute, Monsieur Tyburn. There is something I need to do. On my return we'll have a talk and you can tell me precisely what happened, why you are here, how you found them, everything – yes?'

'Of course, monsieur.'

I couldn't refuse him the facts; he was entitled to those. But I wasn't going to have another cosy chat on what motivated the Rosemeads. It was obvious I hadn't understood about Julian and, as for Jean, she was no more than an acquaintance. I had neither the right nor the wish to pontificate. I was heart-sick with the whole affair.

My eye lit on the telephone and I remembered Tom Chriswell. He would have to be told. After some downright bullying of his secretary I was put through to the great man. Far from being interrupted in conference, he sounded as if he had been sleeping off his hangover, or whatever it was. But I didn't pander to his susceptibilities; I gave him the story straight, and was about to hang up to avoid his recriminations when I heard him say something about Le Gaillard. Hurriedly I clamped the phone back to my ear.

'What was that?'

'I asked you if Monsieur Le Gaillard was there?'

That was what I thought he had said. 'Yes – he's here.' I hadn't even mentioned the DST. Why should Chriswell have assumed – ?

'All right, Piers. I'll be with you as quick as I can. Just take things easy and cooperate with Le Gaillard. Do you understand?'

Understand was the one thing I did not do, but the door was opening. Monsieur Le Gaillard had returned. I murmured a hasty goodbye to Chriswell, replaced the receiver and said:

'I was telephoning my Embassy, monsieur. Tom Chriswell will be along shortly.'

Le Gaillard bowed his head in acknowledgement, helped us both to a second brandy and sat himself down. He had chosen a straight-backed chair, and he sat very upright, knees and feet together, as if he were at attention.

'Now, Monsieur Tyburn, please. From the beginning.'

And when I had finished he asked questions, the obvious things. When had I last seen Jean? Had she seemed particularly depressed? Did I know she had a gun? I did my best to answer factually and avoid all suppositions. It wasn't always easy. Le Gaillard was prepared to accept a series of I-don't-knows about the theft of Johnny's 'music' – he hadn't heard about it before and he seemed to me disproportionately interested – but he pressed me about the gun.

'Don't you think it odd, Monsieur Tyburn, that with a full

bottle of sleeping capsules at her disposal Madame Rosemead chose to shoot herself and her son? Not very kind, was it? Johnny would have known.'

'What do you mean?'

The question was forced out of me. I was aware that Le Gaillard had deliberately altered the tone of his voice and that, like a trout, I was rising to the bait, but I couldn't help myself. God knows why, but he had a genius for complicating the simplest things.

'I mean that Madame Rosemead wasn't very clever. The boy didn't die immediately. As you yourself bear witness, monsieur, it took him some time and not a little pain. And yet she loved him, I am sure, very much.'

'Monsieur Le Gaillard, are you suggesting I actually interrupted Jean, that if I'd been five minutes earlier . . .'

'No, no, monsieur! You mustn't think that.'

When I made no comment he sighed and shrugged. '*Eh bien*, let us hope that the poor lady will be able to tell us herself what she had in mind.'

'Wh – what?' I was utterly shaken. 'Jean – Jean's still alive? But Johnny – ' The full import of what he had said dawned on me. Christ! Sweet Jesus Christ!

'Johnny's dead, yes. He was shot at point blank range through the chest, and there was never any hope for him. Madame Rosemead is seriously ill. They will have to operate to remove the bullet but it has missed her heart. She has perhaps a fifty per cent chance of survival. It's very difficult to shoot oneself through the heart, you know, monsieur.'

'If she does live, what – what will happen to her?'

It was a rhetorical question, but Monsieur Le Gaillard chose to answer it – in his fashion. 'Very little will happen to her, monsieur. She has diplomatic immunity and in the circumstances I am sure that this can be stretched so that things arrange themselves. She will be safe from any criminal proceedings, I assure you.'

This was an aspect of the matter I hadn't even begun to consider and I am sure Le Gaillard knew it. He swirled the remains of his brandy around in its balloon, drank it and, leaning towards me, said earnestly:

'As for the rest, we must trust to the good God. Meanwhile I beg of you, Monsieur Tyburn, don't blame yourself in any way for what has happened. It is improbable that you could have done anything to alter events. This was not your war, monsieur. It was Monsieur Rosemead's war. Remember that.'

# Truce

I loosened the seat belt, ordered a (quarter bottle) of champagne ^SPLIT
and relaxed. The roar of the jet engines sounded like a benison.
There had been a time when I thought that I wasn't going to
make this flight but here I was in the shining bright sky above
the cloud-layer, the fields of France hidden beneath me. Next
stop, London. I was looking forward to a pleasant, peaceful
weekend, unwinding with the rest of the Tyburns – an ordinary,
family weekend. It was what I needed. The last eight days,
since I had dined with the Rosemeads, had been unspeakable;
and that in spite of Margot. Today had been a fitting anticlimax.

It had begun badly. After a short, fretful night the alarm
woke me at six; Margot had wanted to make an early start for
the Dordogne, while the traffic was light. After I kissed her
goodbye I was tempted and I went back to bed, forgot to reset
the alarm, overslept and was late for the office. I had achieved
almost nothing when it was time to go to Julian's funeral.

Funerals aren't meant to be cheerful affairs, I know, but this
one had been sad beyond measure. In default of Jean, who was
still clinging to life, H.E. and Lady Paverton were the chief
mourners. The rest consisted of a handful of Brits, some
representatives from other embassies, one or two official-
looking characters and Monsieur Le Gaillard. There were no
relatives, not even a distant cousin, and no personal friends if
you discount the lawyer and his wife, Jean's English girl-friend
– and myself. And I was doing my best to be as inconspicuous
as possible.

Father Michelet's sharp eyes must have noted my presence
in his church, but I had no intention of speaking to him; once
he had suggested an actual meeting it would be impossible to

refuse and I had already decided that a *post mortem* on Julian's behaviour would serve no purpose. In the event he seemed to avoid me too – perhaps he had changed his mind – so that problem was solved but, perversely, I wasn't happy about it. As I said, it had been an altogether frustrating day.

Nevertheless I had made it to Airport Charlie, and caught my plane. Now I was going to enjoy myself. After all, it wasn't every weekend that one's parents celebrated such an anniversary. Determined to forget the Rosemeads and the office and everything connected with them for the next couple of days, I settled myself comfortably in my seat, drank my champagne and concentrated on a copy of *Le Canard Enchainé* – the French equivalent of *Private Eye* or *New Yorker Magazine* – which had some very unkind things to say about the Anglo-French meetings to be held in Paris next week. I was laughing at one of Vazque de Sola's cartoons depicting an 'entente most discordiale' when we landed at Heathrow.

I was met by my youngest sister and her husband, who is an up-and-coming architect, tucked into the back of their Rover with the crib containing my latest nephew and driven down to the Kent-Sussex border. It was good to be home. My parents live in a large, rambling house, but for this occasion they had commandeered the village inn as well. Including those who came just for the Saturday, we were quite a gathering.

Like most large families we are a close-knit lot, but we don't live in each other's pockets. Nor do we always see eye to eye; for instance the brother next to me, who is a Junior Minister, has become something of a prune and disapproves of my doctor sister who is separated from her husband. However, there's not the slightest doubt that if any one of us were in a difficulty, the others would rally around – a fact I had always taken for granted until this business of the Rosemeads.

Needless to say I couldn't forget them completely. All sorts of little things reminded me. A nephew was Johnny's age and everything that Johnny should have been. A brother-in-law had a deep voice, not unlike Julian's; I hadn't noticed it before. Then there were items in the newspapers, on radio and television, and the questions that the family asked, though no one pressed me unduly.

But this was a very special weekend – its highlight, the celebratory dinner on Saturday night, a magnificent affair – and like everyone else I was enjoying myself. Luckily Margot didn't telephone until it was almost over.

I had been told only that there was a call for me from France and I had assumed that it was from the Embassy. Margot's voice, faint and tinny, then suddenly clear, surprised me.

'Piers? Are you there? Hullo!'

'Hullo, darling. Yes, it's me – Piers. Are you all right?'

'I've been trying to get you for hours, but your telephone system's impossible. Why can't you Europeans make phones that work?' She sounded tetchy.

'That's what's known as "a good question". I've often asked it myself.' I hesitated. 'Darling, I don't imagine you phoned just to say you were missing me. Is something the matter?'

'I – I don't know. Probably not. Probably I've got it wrong. But you described everything so vividly. I had a clear visual picture. It was the same about the painting and when we were playing tennis this afternoon I suddenly saw – '

'Margot! Darling, you're not making much sense.'

'Sorry!'

The telephone made an explosive noise in my ear and I heard a Frenchman trying to explain to his wife why he would have to stay over in London until Monday; she was taking it badly. Behind them someone, possibly Margot, continued to talk. I swore at the Frenchman, in English.

And Margot said, loud and clear: 'Piers, don't shout and don't cuss me either. It's not my fault your bloody phones don't function.'

I wanted to laugh but I was afraid that, if I did, Margot might cut us off. Instead I apologized. I didn't explain about the Frenchman and his wife; that was too difficult.

'Darling, I'm sorry about the telephone but I can't help it. Please will you start again, from the beginning?'

'Okay. I'll try. I wish you were here. It would be much easier to make sketches.'

117

I murmured encouragement, mentally urging her to get on with it. It wasn't like Margot to be so indecisive or so diffident. Something must be badly wrong.

'Piers, I told you we were playing tennis this afternoon. At one point I was watching. There was a young girl, the daughter of another houseguest, and she was serving. She could have been the model for that painting of Jean Rosemead you – you described to me in such detail. The line of the body, the arms, everything was the same. She was left-handed too.' Margot paused as if she expected me to say something. When I didn't, she added fiercely: 'Think, Piers, think!'

I thought but nothing came to me. The telephone crackled ominously. Any moment we might be cut off and I would be left with an insoluble puzzle – and a puzzle that had to be important or Margot wouldn't have taken the trouble to call me.

'Darling Margot, I'm not feeling very bright. Please tell me what this is all about.'

'No. I don't want to do that.'

'Why the hell not?'

'I don't want to put ideas – pictures – into your head.'

I took a deep breath. 'Margot, we're not getting anywhere.'

'No. Sorry. Piers, think about Thursday when you went to the Rosemeads. Visualize Jean and Johnny lying on the floor. You remember how you described them to me. My love, I've never told you, but when you've had a lot to drink or you're a bit fraught, you gesticulate – more than most Anglo-Saxons. It must be your French mother. And you made me see it all, the whole scene. You sat beside Johnny, held his hand, wiped his mouth. Jean was on the other side of him. She had one arm around him, and the gun – the gun, Piers!'

'Christ! Dear Christ!'

Why hadn't I noticed it at once? Why hadn't it hit me? Of course, Jean was left-handed. And the gun had been by her right hand, until the *concièrge* knocked it away.

'Piers! Are you still there?'

'Yes. Yes. I'm here.' My mind was reeling with the implications of what I had just learnt. 'Margot, you've been absolutely brilliant. This could be terribly important, as I know you've guessed. Look, I'll be back in Paris tomorrow night as planned, and I'll get in touch with the authorities at once. Meanwhile, darling, please don't worry about it. Enjoy the rest of the weekend. I'll see you Monday.'

'Okay. But, Piers – '

At this point the telephone brought our conversation to an end with expletive violence. I found myself simultaneously rubbing my ear and shouting into the mouthpiece: 'Goodbye, darling. I love you. Thank you. Till Monday.' I put down the receiver. My hand was shaking so much that I made the whole instrument rattle.

Naturally, as a result of this telephone call, I had to stand some amused comment from the family about Margot's apparent devotion. It was a strain to parry the teasing. I hoped nobody would notice how on edge I was but this was a fond hope.

When I kissed my mother goodnight, she said: 'Piers, *mon chéri*, is it your friend's wife – what does she call herself? – Jean Rosemead, that you're worried about? Because you mustn't be. If she lives, you must ask her to come here to stay. We'll be happy to have her until she's well again and wants to make other plans.'

And after I had gone to bed my second brother, Philip, the priest, with whom I was sharing a room, said: 'Would you like to talk, Piers, or would you rather not?'

He didn't have to be more specific. Philip and I have always been close. Yet if he had asked me the same question the previous night I would have said 'no'; all I had wanted then was to forget the Rosemeads. Margot, however, had made that quite impossible. Now I could think of nothing else and I was aware of a desperate need to sort things out in my own mind before I got back to Paris. Philip could help.

'It's very complicated.'

'No matter. We've hours of time – if it's what you want.'

'Yes, it's what I want. But it's difficult.'

In the event, once I had begun, I didn't find it difficult. I told Philip the whole story without any reservations and with far more detail than I had given Chriswell or even Margot.

And suddenly, while we were talking, something occurred to me.

'Philip, I've just thought. After Julian picked up this packet in the Parc de Bagatelle last Sunday – assuming that's what he did – he went home. As soon as Jean came in he told her he was going to St Augustin. In fact he came to my apartment. When I didn't answer the bell, maybe he did go to Father Michelet. They were good friends. Julian could have shown it to him, told him what was going on and led Father Michelet to suppose that I would be coming to visit him – though I can't think why.'

'That's an idea, Piers. Father Michelet may even have the packet. Julian could have given it to him for safe-keeping. You know – I wouldn't be surprised if it turned out to be a tape cassette.'

'What?'

'A cassette! Doesn't it strike you as odd that Julian should have collected this thing, driven home as fast as he could, and then played "music"? It would be logical, however, if Johnny's "music" were in the form of words – conceivably a blackmail demand. Johnny wouldn't have understood the words, would he?'

'No – o. I doubt it.'

If I seemed to hesitate it was because I was thinking of something else, not because I doubted that Philip was right. I was thinking of the so-called sneak thieves who had stolen Johnny's 'music'. They could have been looking for a particular cassette. I wondered if they had come back on Thursday and shot Jean and Johnny. Somebody had. Someone had been prepared to murder them. And if them, why not Julian? My mind reeled.

Philip was already ahead of me. He said: 'You know, I don't believe that Julian was being blackmailed. I think he told you the truth. The only evidence against him is those photographs of Boy. Could they have been faked, Piers?'

I shook my head. 'No. I'm sure they're genuine. But he could have been doped before they were taken, I suppose. Then it would have been easy to send some prints to H.E. The others, the ones that were taped to the back of Jean's portrait, could have been put there by whoever stole Johnny's "music".'

'Yes. But if these photographs were bogus, why should a man like Julian kill himself? Wouldn't he have gone to your security people? Personally I think it's the same pattern as with Jean and Johnny. Someone killed Julian and tried to make his death look like suicide. Yet it seems that all he did was get in the way of a blackmail attempt. Piers, there must be more behind this. There must.'

After that Philip was silent for so long I thought he had gone to sleep. I lay in bed and tried to decide if I should by-pass Chriswell and go straight to H.E. when I got back to Paris, or if I should first see Father Michelet at St Augustin. All the time I was thrusting to the back of my mind memories of the Japanese, the couple taking photographs at the Memorial for the Deported, another couple in the museum of the Arc de Triomphe, the girl in the yellow trouser-suit, the driver of the Mercedes, Johnny's 'Damjaps'. I don't admit to being scared, but there was a nasty empty feeling in the pit of my stomach.

And Philip said: 'What Le Gaillard called "Rosemead's war" is over, Piers. I only hope and pray that "Tyburn's war" isn't going to start.'

It wasn't exactly an encouraging remark.

# Tyburn's War

# Chapter 1

Sunday was slow to pass. I was now as impatient to be back in Paris as on Friday I had been glad to leave. Inevitably in the circumstances I arrived early at the airport and then, being perverse, resented having to hang about.

The evening was hot and sultry, unseasonably so for May, the sky fierce with thunder clouds. In the departure lounge at Heathrow the tired, dispirited, irritable travellers were tense, waiting for the storm that didn't come. A woman sitting near me complained that the coffee was undrinkable, and quarrelled noisily with her husband when he refused to return it to the bar. A baby began to cry. Several flights had already been delayed and obviously, though no announcement had yet been made, mine was going to be late too. At this point we should have been boarding, but no arrow glowed red beside Paris Charles de Gaulle on the notice board.

Restlessly I picked up the newspaper that someone had left on the seat beside me. It turned out to be one of the more lurid Sundays. I was about to discard it with a cursory glance when a picture caught my eye. The headline – 'He Died in My Arms' – was so large that I hadn't noticed it, and anyway I wouldn't have made the connection. But the face staring at me from the page of this rag was my own, and that I couldn't fail to notice.

The photograph was an old one and didn't flatter me. I looked about twenty, slightly drunk and vacant, and the text of the accompanying story did little to rectify such an impression. The facts were not inaccurate; if Johnny hadn't actually died in my arms, he had died holding my hand. But the style was mawkish – for example, 'the dying boy was able to whisper his last message to the British diplomat in his mother tongue' – and absurd dialogue had been put into my mouth. The whole thing made me cringe.

I balled the paper and thrust it into a rubbish bin as my flight was announced. Striding along one of Heathrow's corridors – interminable if one has anything much to carry – I worked off my anger. It wasn't fair to blame the press. The fiction they had created was no more fantastic than the truth.

The plane was only half full and we boarded quickly. Suddenly everyone seemed in a hurry. Perhaps the pilot wanted to get airborne before the storm broke. At any rate we were barely strapped in when we began to taxi and, having reached the runway, we took off without any delay. We were about thirty minutes late.

It wasn't a pleasant flight. We bumped around the edge of a thunderhead and, after circling Charles de Gaulle for five minutes, had to be talked down. Even on the ground it wasn't comfortable. The plane was engulfed in wind and sheeting rain as we crawled to our terminal in Satellite 6.

No one was more glad to arrive than the woman beside me. She had been gripping the arms of her seat throughout the flight. Now she took time to collect herself and her various parcels; she had bought up half London. Like a fool I had chosen a window seat so I had to wait while she dropped and picked up one thing after another. Eventually, however, I got off the plane, to be greeted by an Air France hostess standing by the entrance to the satellite lounge holding a slate with my name on it.

'Monsieur Tyburn, you are wanted on the telephone.'

She led me round a bank of orange seats to a desk and pointed to the instrument. There was a volley of thunder as I thanked her and picked up the receiver. I said hullo into the mouthpiece.

'Piers, is that you?'

'Margot! Where are you?'

'Right here, at Airport Charlie.'

'But you weren't going to be in Paris till tomorrow. Has – has something else happened?'

'No. It was just that I felt restless and decided to drive up today. Incidentally, I haven't been to the apartment. If I was to meet your flight I had to come straight out to the airport. But I assumed you hadn't got the Jag.'

'No. I left it in the garage Friday morning. I went to the office by taxi and a staff car took me out to Charles de Gaulle.'

'Great. Collect me from the *Point de Recontre* then, and let's have a drink before we set off.'

'Darling, I'll be with you in five minutes.'

Thunder crashed again as I replaced the receiver. Water was pouring down the glass walls of the lounge so that it was impossible to see outside. The lights flickered. If they failed, since the various satellites are connected to the main building by tunnels with moving walkways, I was in for a long, dark walk.

I picked up my briefcase, which was the only baggage I had, and waved to the Air France hostess to show that I had finished my call. My fellow-passengers had already disappeared ahead of me. I hurried after them. Another load was departing to Tokyo at the other side of the lounge.

I reached the top of the moving tracks, which were still moving though the lights were dimmer than they should have been. I got on, tucking my briefcase between my feet for I was about to be carried down what seemed like a forty-five degree incline into the tunnel, and relaxed.

Once on the level, where I could simultaneously walk and be carried, I picked up my briefcase again. With Margot waiting for me I needed to make the best possible speed. As I straightened myself I felt the wide, metal slats shiver beneath my feet. Someone was running behind me, a dangerous thing to do on such a steep and fast-moving slope. Curious, I glanced over my shoulder to see who the rash character might be.

As I turned he stopped running. Then with long strides he advanced towards me. He was a young man, neat, compact, medium height, in a dark business suit. Hundreds such as he fly backwards and forwards across the Channel daily. All that distinguished this one was his left hand, which was heavily bandaged. But he was a Japanese.

For a moment I stared at him, mesmerized. My guts knotted in fear. I thought his mouth widened in a thin-lipped smile as he returned my stare. He was within a yard of me and I still hadn't moved. He knew I was afraid.

By now we must have been in the middle of the tunnel and out of sight of anyone not on level ground. He looked around, presumably to make sure we were unobserved; if one of the guards who police the airport or even a harmless tourist had suddenly appeared I suppose he would have played the innocent traveller. But it wasn't necessary. I sensed that we were alone. He raised his arm and, as we were carried past a globe advertising Chanel perfumes, I thought light glinted on something in his right hand. It could have been a knife.

I acted instinctively.

In the fleeting moments while all this was happening I had become conscious of the briefcase hanging heavy against my side. It was a rather superior briefcase, a Samsonite executive with metal corners, a birthday present from my father. With all my strength I hurled it in the face of the Japanese.

He dodged. He was quick but not quick enough. Over-confident, he hadn't expected an attack and his footing was unsure on the moving track. The briefcase caught him on the side of the temple and he fell backwards, hitting his head hard on the metal slats. He lay there, blood beginning to seep from the wound I had inflicted on him by a fluke.

Under my feet I felt the shift of the track as it began the steep ascent out of the tunnel. In a minute I and the unconscious Japanese would come gliding out into the full view of the guards whose duty it was to check passengers going out to the satellite for guns, knives, hand-grenades or other weapons. How was I to account for the Jap? I foresaw endless explanations, embarrassment, trouble. But there was no means of saving myself.

The storm intervened. The lights, which had been feeble for some while, were suddenly extinguished. At the same moment the moving walkway jerked to a halt, throwing me off balance. The storm had bought me time, though not much.

Excited voices came from the far end of the tunnel where people had started down the steep incline. They might wait or, if they were in a hurry, decide to grope through the darkness.

128

And the emergency power supply would come on almost immediately. I had time, but how much?

Frantically I felt for the Jap's body, seized him under the shoulders and lifted him over the guard rail. I let him drop in the space between the track on which I stood and the one that should have been moving in the opposite direction. If the lights had gone on at this point I should have been fairly caught, but I wanted to give the impression that he had become confused and, intending to climb into the outer non-moving pathway near the tunnel wall where it might have been safer to walk in the dark, had fallen into the narrow passage between the tracks. I hoped this might account for his injuries.

Then, after some fumbling around on the metal floor, I found my briefcase, retrieved it and felt my way up the incline. As I emerged from the tunnel three things happened. The lights came on again, the moving track gave a great forward jerk and there was a distant cry behind me. Perhaps the Jap had been seen or, what would be better for me since it would lend verisimilitude to the 'accident' I had staged, perhaps someone had fallen as the track restarted.

I had no compunction about the Japanese. He wasn't dead – he had been breathing heavily when I lifted him – and he would be found very soon. Moreover, I hadn't the slightest doubt that he had intended to kill me. But I did have a sense of guilt. It required an effort not to hurry from the scene of my crime and I had to force myself to have a jolly about the storm with the chap who stamped my passport – especially when I noticed the smear of blood on my trouser-leg. I was glad to reach the *Point de Rencontre* and Margot.

I kissed Margot perfunctorily. 'Let's get out of here, darling.'

'What about the drink you promised me?'

'When we get home.'

'Piers, are you all right?'

It was a question we were continually asking each other these days, as if we were a couple of elderly hypochondriacs. I tried to laugh, but the sound didn't come out right. However, it stopped Margot from arguing. She tucked her hand into the crook of my arm and said:

'Okay. Let's go. The Renault's parked outside Gate 32 which is strictly forbidden, but a charming policeman swore he'd keep his eye on it for me so I guess there's no need to worry.'

And at that I managed a real laugh.

The Renault was where she had left it, the 'charming policeman' standing guard. The look he gave me was understandably jaundiced but he helped tuck Margot into the car and, rewarded by a smile and a glimpse of long thighs, saluted smartly as we drove off.

After last night's talk with my brother Philip I had a lot to tell Margot but for the moment I didn't feel much like it. This was one of those occasions when I wished I smoked; a cigarette or a small cigar could have been infinitely soothing. Instead I pictured a double whisky, one ice cube and a good squirt of soda. As soon as we got home, I promised myself. Meanwhile I brooded.

In spite of the rain Margot drove fast and, since there was little traffic, we were on the Périphérique before I told her about the Japanese. To my chagrin she was sceptical.

'Are you sure he intended to kill you, Piers?'

'He was damn well going to stick a knife in me and one assumes that would have done the trick. What's more, if you hadn't phoned me from the *Point de Rencontre* he'd probably have succeeded. It was the fact that I was alone and, of course, suspicious that saved me. If the other passengers on my flight had been bunched on the track with me he could easily have pushed past, knifed me and been on his way before anyone realized I'd been killed and not merely taken ill.'

'Ye – es.' She still sounded doubtful. 'I won't ask why these people – whoever they are – should want you dead. Obviously it's something to do with the Rosemeads. My God, if they could shoot Jean and that poor boy! But what I don't understand, Piers, is how they traced you to that particular flight.'

It was one of the questions I had been considering while we were on the Autoroute; and I had come up with a reasonable explanation. I tried it out on Margot.

'Once they had cottoned on to the fact that I was away for

the weekend – and they could have done that easily enough – a check on *le parking* at Rue de Longchamps would have shown I hadn't gone by car. And from that it wouldn't have been difficult to guess at and confirm a Sunday night booking from London, would it?'

'Okay! Okay!' she said fiercely. 'Damn them to everlasting hell! I didn't want to believe it but now I must, and Piers, my love, I – I'm scared for you. What are we going to do?'

I had given that some thought too. 'First thing tomorrow you're going to ask Lady Paverton if you can stay at the Embassy. You'll be safe there.'

'I'll do no such thing. She wouldn't have me anyway, not with your PM and Foreign Secretary arriving on Wednesday.'

'Then you had better go to my cousins at Versailles. I'm sure they'd love to have you and – '

'No, Piers!'

I let it pass. What with lack of sleep and nervous strain I was in no mood for argument. Besides we were on the Rue de Longchamp, almost home, and I thought again of the whisky I had promised myself.

Margot swung the Renault on to the steep driveway that descends to *le parking*. She parked the car in its visitor's slot and we got out her weekend bag and my briefcase. I went to check on the Jaguar. It had been sitting here since Friday but had come to no harm. Margot was waiting for me by the lift, holding the door open. As we got in, she said casually:

'What happened to the knife?'

I nearly said: 'What knife?' My mind was on Father Michelet. I had decided that if Philip was right and Julian had given him a cassette, I ought to hear what was on it before I went to the Chancery and bearded H.E. But it was too late to telephone tonight; I would go along to St Augustin as early as possible in the morning.

'Margot, I don't know. The Jap must have dropped the knife when I hit him. Why do you ask?'

'You told me you had arranged things to look like an accident. Presumably the Jap will support that. He won't want to be investigated, will he? But it's going to look a mite odd if there's a knife lying near him.'

'Too bad!'

It was another complication but there was nothing I could do about it, nothing I could have done. Even if I had remembered the knife I had had no time to search for it in the darkness of the tunnel. Let the police worry. Let the Jap explain.

We got out of the lift with our bags. Margot pressed the *minuterie* to give us light and I fitted my key into the top lock; it didn't turn. Stepping back I checked that this was indeed the door of my apartment and we hadn't inadvertently come to the wrong floor. I tried the bottom lock in which, had it been secure, my key should have turned twice. The latch slipped back at the first twist. The door sighed open.

I hesitated. My *femme de ménage* was a most punctillious woman. It was extremely unlikely that she had forgotten to lock the door when she left on Friday. Since then nobody should have gone into the apartment. But someone had. Someone could still be there. I felt my stomach contract.

'What is it, Piers?'

'Wait here.'

Gently I swung the door open until it lay flush with the wall. There was nobody hiding behind it, nobody in the hall closet. I glanced in the kitchen. Then systematically I went through the passage with its hanging cupboards, the two bedrooms, the bathroom and lavatory, the big living-room with its dining area. There was nobody in the apartment and everything seemed in order. Embarrassed that I had been so melodramatic, I called to Margot.

She came, licking her first finger, as if she were trying it for taste. 'Sugar!' she said.

'It's not like her,' I said. 'but my *femme de ménage* must have forgotten to lock – What did you say about sugar?'

'Is it like her to spill sugar and not sweep it up properly?'

'No, not a bit.'

'Someone has.'

We went into the kitchen together. I was wearing rubber soles and mightn't have been aware of the sugar if I hadn't heard it grit under the leather of Margot's shoes. I got out the glass jar labelled *sucre*. It was a big jar and, when full, would have held a couple of kilos. It told us nothing.

'Oh, to hell with everything!' I said, wishing that I hadn't suddenly remembered the Rosemeads' sneak thieves. 'Let's have a drink.'

I strode into the dining area, to the sideboard where I keep the liquor. And, for the first time, the scarlet multiflora begonia which hadn't been there on Friday morning when I went to the office, impinged on my consciousness. Both a note and a florist's envelope were propped against the pot.

The note was from my *femme de menage*. The plant had been delivered soon after she arrived. She had protested that I was away for the weekend but the boy didn't care. She had given it a good watering and hoped it would be all right.

I opened the envelope. The florist was one of the most reputable in Neuilly. I extracted the card. It had the florist's name and a spray of flowers in the top left-hand corner. It was unsigned.

'Someone sent you a present, Piers?'

'The Japs, I rather think.'

'The Japs? But why?' She looked at the begonia as if it might explode.

'They knew my name. They knew I lived in this block, but not which apartment. They didn't get much change from the *concièrge* with their story about scraping my Jag on Wednesday, so they thought this up. They bought a plant, perhaps waited till the *concièrge* had gone to the shops and then tried an apartment – any apartment. Someone would have told them, sooner or later, where Monsieur Tyburn of the British Embassy lived.'

'Then why bother to deliver the plant?'

'To confirm the information. Or, by chance, they might have tried the woman opposite. She would have been curious enough to watch what happened.'

'And now they know. So what will they do next?'

'I rather think –' I said slowly – 'in fact, I'm sure that they've already done.'

While we had been talking I had opened the doors of the sideboard. Squatting on my heels I surveyed the array of whisky, gin, brandy, sherry. Since space is limited I arrange my liquor methodically and I would have laid fifty to one that it was not as I had left it. I passed a bottle of whisky and a bottle of gin to Margot.

'The place has been searched, darling.'

When we looked for it there was other evidence. Some books were out of order, some papers disarranged and a mattress not square on its box-spring, the bed too hurriedly re-made. The search had been very thorough – witness the jar of sugar – and careful; if the improperly locked door hadn't alerted me I could easily have missed it. Yet this didn't jibe with the blatant attack I had just managed to parry.

I drank the first whisky straight and poured myself another. Margot had kicked off her shoes and, curled up on the sofa, was brooding over her gin and tonic. I went and sat beside her.

'At least they didn't find it,' Margot said. 'I'm assuming they were looking for the packet Julian collected at Bagatelle.'

'One of my brothers thinks it was a cassette,' I said, and told her the rest of Philip's theory.

She shivered and I put my arm around her. 'Piers, I never saw the photographs of Boy. Is it possible he was a Japanese in a blond wig?'

'No. He was a strictly Nordic type. Either he sympathizes with their objective, whatever that may be, or they have some hold on him.'

'But what is their objective?' Margot demanded, stung to irritation. 'You can't just dismiss it with a "whatever that may be". Piers, I know governments do the most appalling things, like causing riots and fostering civil wars and arranging assassinations. Or at least they turn blind eyes while their intelligence services do the jobs for them. But I find it very difficult to believe that the Japanese are prepared to take the risk of committing such – such casual murders in France.'

When I didn't answer at once she kicked me gently with her stockinged foot. 'What do you think? Tell me! It's too late for secrets now, my love. And pour me another gin, please. When we've both finished I'll make us an omelette or something. You've not eaten, have you?'

I shook my head. I wasn't hungry, but I got up to pour Margot her drink. Before I sat down again I drew the curtains, taking the opportunity to make sure that the windows were securely fastened. I would check them all before we went to bed; I had already bolted the front door. The storm would give me a good excuse. It was circling around, the thunder growling in the distance, the dark sky over the Bois de Boulogne slit by lightning, the rain heavy.

'Margot, have you heard of the Japanese *Rengo Sekigun*, the Red Army?'

'You mean the fanatics who massacred those passengers at that Israeli airport?' She stared at me, her green eyes wide with disbelief of what I was implying. 'I've a friend in New York whose brother was killed at – at Lod, wasn't it? But here, in Paris – '

'Those are the people. They're also the ones who seized the French Embassy in The Hague and the Japanese Embassy in Kuwait. They've hijacked a Jumbo jet and blown up an oil tank in Singapore, but mainly they go in for soft targets – hostage and hijack raids against diplomats and embassies. Incidentally Paris is said to be one of their operational bases.'

'They're nothing at all to do with the Japanese Government?'

'Nothing whatsoever. The Red Army's a totally anarchic terrorist organization. It's prepared to attack anything in any country that it opposes ideologically. And its members are as ready to die as to kill if they can push the revolution forward. Which makes it a most godawful menace.'

'And scary, Piers – horribly, horribly scary.'

'Which is why you're getting out of here tomorrow, darling,' I tried again.

'But what about you? You're the one in danger. Piers, once you've explained everything to the Ambassador, why can't you ask him for leave? He couldn't possibly refuse under the circumstances. Then we could drive down to the Dordogne together. Why not, Piers? Why not?'

I pulled her into my arms and kissed her to stop her talking.

She didn't need me to tell her why not. She knew that if I ran I would always hate myself; Julian hadn't run. I held Margot close and rocked her gently.

'I love you, Piers,' she murmured.

It was the first time she had actually said the words and I drew in my breath. The temptation to take advantage of the moment and again ask her to marry me was enormous. But I put it from me. My private life would have to wait until Tyburn's war was won. Instead, I slapped her on the bottom.

'Come on, darling,' I said. 'I'm dying of starvation and hours ago you promised me an omelette.'

# Chapter 2

After last night's storm the morning was bright and iridescent. I leant out of the kitchen window and took great draughts of air into my lungs. Everything was fresh and clean, washed by the rain. It was seven o'clock. Less than twelve hours ago somebody had tried to kill me, not because I had done him or his chums any personal harm but because inadvertently I had become some kind of nuisance to them. It's not a pleasant thought that someone's prepared to swat you like a fly.

I shut the window and finished my coffee. In the bedroom Margot was still asleep. I collected my clothes and went into the bathroom, where I showered, shaved and dressed. I hesitated about waking her; she looked so beautiful. She was lying on her back, her hair spread over the pillow, one arm outflung as if reaching for me, one breast uncovered. I felt a surge of lust and love, and bent to kiss her nipple. Her eyes opened.

'Good morning, darling.'

'Piers!'

She made to pull me down on her but I resisted gently. 'I'm just going to St Augustin. I want you to bolt the door after me.'

A shadow passed across her face as she awoke fully and remembered. She got out of bed, slipped on a gown and followed me to the front door. She put her arms around my neck.

'Take care, my love. Please take care.'

'Not to worry, darling. You have some breakfast – I've made the coffee – and get dressed. I shouldn't be more than an hour, and as soon as I get back we can decide what to do, depending on what Father Michelet has to say.'

I kissed her on the mouth and waited outside the front door

until I heard the bolt slide to. I didn't believe she was in any danger, but I was taking no chances. If anything happened to Margot . . .

The lift carried me down to the basement. I walked along the passage and opened the door that leads to *le parking*. It was dark and quiet and smelt of petrol. I switched on the overhead lights, but they are so weak and widely spaced that the gloom was scarcely relieved. I turned on my torch; it's a big heavy flashlight, encased in rubber, that I'd bought in New York, and could easily double as a weapon. The powerful beam shone along the row of stationary cars. There was no one about. Gripping the torch firmly I made my way towards the Jag.

Then I heard the noise. Immediately I stopped and stood with my back against the wall, swinging the beam from side to side. The noise continued. It was a slithering, scraping sound as if someone was dragging a sack of potatoes along the cement floor. The obvious explanation was that the *concièrge* was pulling the daily bins of rubbish up the driveway to the road, where they would later be emptied by the Neuilly sanitation department. But, if it were the *concièrge*, why hadn't she turned on the lights?

'*C'est vous, madame?*' I called.

My voice echoed in the cavern of *le parking*. I was thankful that it sounded steady, under control. My nerves were rasping.

Nobody answered me. The noise had stopped. Deliberately I walked to the Jaguar and shone the light on it. It looked as it had done last night, dusty after a weekend of disuse. I smeared my thumb along the paint work, leaving a solitary snail's trail in the dirt; the car hadn't been touched. I went around it, kicking the tyres. I told myself I was becoming too suspicious.

I slid behind the wheel, started the engine and edged out of my parking slot. I had turned the Jag towards the exit when I heard footsteps pounding in the opposite direction. I braked and peered out of the rear window, but I couldn't see anyone. Whoever had been in *le parking* had fled, not caring who heard him. He hadn't waited for me to go so that he could come up the driveway on to the Rue de Longchamp. He had fled to the back of the underground garage, where the only way out was through the garden and over a high wall. But perhaps he hadn't known that.

He could have been a casual thief, hoping to find some loot in an unlocked car. He could have been an early camper in the Bois de Boulogne who had sought more solid shelter from last night's storm. He was clearly nothing to do with the *concièrge*, for the garbage was already neatly stacked at the top of the driveway. Nor was there any reason to suppose that he was anything to do with me, that he was another damned Jap. I had best forget him.

Turning on to the Avenue de Neuilly I glanced at my watch. It was twenty to eight. I was later than I had intended. Paris wakes up earlier than London or even New York, and it was the morning rush hour. There was a lot of traffic. However, I was lucky; everything was bowling along at high speed, there were no hold-ups and nearly all the lights were with me. I reached Place St Augustin in fifteen minutes and realized, as I was looking for somewhere to park near the church, that for the first time since Monday of last week I had driven round the Arc de Triomphe without giving a thought to Julian Rosemead. I felt ashamed of myself.

The Church of St Augustin is on the north side of Place St Augustin. It is mid-nineteenth century and the most interesting thing about it is its shape, dictated by the triangular site. The porch, overlooking the Place, is at the apex of the triangle, where Boulevard Malesherbes and Avenue César-Caire meet, and from there the church widens back to the chancel which is capped with a vast dome.

I had been here twice before, once when I had arrived too early for a party at the Cercle Militaire – a rather luxurious club for service officers which is also situated on the Place – and once, last Friday, when I had come to Julian's funeral. Now I parked the Jag at the end of César-Caire, put a franc in the meter, crossed the road and climbed the steps to the porch. I was not alone. Two elderly women, a man on crutches and a very young and pregnant girl accompanied me into the church. Clearly there was an eight o'clock mass.

As I dipped my fingers in the holy water stoup and crossed

myself the priest came in. It wasn't Father Michelet. I stood at the back of the nave and savoured the familiar smell of stale incense. I was at home. And, since I couldn't believe that any of the meagre congregation wished me harm and I was sure that no one had followed me here, I felt safe – at least for the moment.

I walked up the aisle and knocked on the vestry door. It was opened by a youngish man in black trousers and a grey alpaca coat. He looked at me enquiringly.

'I'd like to speak to Father Michelet, please.'

He shook his head and my heart sank. Father Michelet could be almost anywhere, hearing confession in a hospital or prison, giving extreme unction at a death bed, saying mass at a church in the suburbs. But I had assumed that he would be here at St Augustin, and available. In fact, he was, though it must have taken me three or four minutes to persuade this black-trousered, grey-coated dragon to disturb the good priest's breakfast with a message.

Once the message was delivered, however, I had no more difficulty. The dragon, though still grumbling about people who had no consideration for their priests, led me through a second door in the vestry, along a passage and into what appeared to be a common room.

'Your visitor, Father.'

Father Michelet was seated at a table on which were the remains of several breakfasts. He got up and shook hands with me.

'Good morning, Monsieur Tyburn. I'm very pleased to see you. I knew you would come, in your own good time.'

I was glad he spoke in French; at our last meeting his poor English must have been for Jean's benefit.

'I've only just realized the necessity, Father.'

'*Vraiment?*' He raised his thick eyebrows. Off duty, in a pair of dark trousers and a roll-neck sweater, he looked more than ever like a Breton fisherman. He waved at the dirty crockery. 'Have you eaten, Monsieur Tyburn, or will you join me?'

'I'd love some coffee, if I may. And please call me Piers.'

'Thank you, Piers.' He found a clean cup and poured coffee

for me. 'Let us sit over here. It will be more comfortable.'

He led the way to armchairs on either side of an empty grate. It was a cheerless room with dark, heavy furniture, cluttered and untidy, and was made more depressing by wall-paper patterned with purple birds perched on strands of purple convolvulus with dull green leaves. I wondered how the priests endured it.

'You know why I am here, Father?'

'Julian Rosemead said that either you or he would come to collect the packet. That was the Sunday before he died, Monsieur – Piers. So I've been waiting for you.'

I sighed with relief; Philip had been right. Father Michelet did have the packet. Tentatively I sipped the coffee and found it very good. Things were looking up.

'Did he tell you what was in it, Father?'

'Yes. Evidence that a senior person at your Embassy was being blackmailed. Do you want to know what else he told me?'

'Please.'

Father Michelet's story was substantially what I already knew or guessed. It added some details, and confirmed the rest. Julian had been ninety per cent sure who was being blackmailed before he collected the packet from the Parc de Bagatelle, and afterwards he had been in no doubt at all.

'Julian didn't name the unhappy man, Piers, and I didn't ask who it was, so I hope his identity will be obvious to you too. But he did tell me that the people who were doing the blackmailing called themselves the Sons of Orion.'

'The Sons of Orion? He didn't say anything about the – the *Rengo Sekigun*, the Japanese Red Army?'

'No–o, but one doesn't necessarily preclude the other, does it? Monsieur Le Gaillard, whom I know you've met – '

'Le Gaillard! He's been to see you. What did you tell him, Father?'

'Not very much. He knew there was or had been a packet, but I was able to say I hadn't got it and had no idea where it was.'

'What?'

'Julian was insistent that, if he didn't come for it himself, I was to give the packet to you and nobody but you. So, in case there were any awkward enquiries, I asked one of my fellow-priests to keep it for me. He will have put it somewhere – somewhere safe. I'll get it for you in a minute.'

Father Michelet smiled at his own cleverness, and I grinned in return. Silently I gave thanks for his subterfuge and for the fact that Julian had impressed the priest with the necessity for guile. I wanted to hear that cassette before anyone else had a chance.

'Monsieur Le Gaillard said that the Sons of Orion might well be part of a terrorist organization. He mentioned the Red Army, which is Japanese but has infiltrated France, Europe, the Middle East. You see, Piers, I spun Monsieur Le Gaillard a yarn about Julian being unwittingly involved in something too big for him – a facet of the truth, you might call it.'

'Which he accepted, Father?'

The priest shrugged. 'He pretended to. I was very vague. I hid behind the sanctity of the confessional and the occasional language barrier between Julian and myself. Nevertheless, Monsieur Le Gaillard knew I was telling him all I could. You understand, Piers, I had to warn him about the Sons of Orion. Others may be in danger from them. Jean – '

'I understand, Father. How is Jean? I meant to ask you before. I've been away for the weekend.'

'The operation was a success. The bullet just failed to graze her heart. Perhaps you knew that?'

I nodded. 'Is she conscious yet?'

'Yes, but the doctors won't allow her to be questioned. She's still extremely ill, extremely ill.'

I told him then about the gun being by Jean's right hand though she was left-handed. He wasn't surprised, but he was pleased because it was concrete evidence for the police. And leaving me to help myself to more coffee, he went off to get the cassette. I let curiosity gnaw at me. Soon now it would be satisfied; I should know who was being blackmailed and possibly why. Suppressing an unexpected frisson of fear, I licked my lips, which were suddenly dry.

Father Michelet returned, his hands empty, and for a

dreadful moment I thought the packet was lost or stolen; but he produced it from his trouser pocket. It was small, as Johnny had said, wrapped in brown paper and heavily Scotch-taped so that it wouldn't be easy to open. It was the right size, shape and weight to be a cassette.

'Thank you, Father, very much.'

'I hope – ' he hesitated. 'I hope it doesn't bring you the misfortune that I suspect it brought the Rosemeads.'

'I intend to see that it doesn't, Father.'

'I've given it to you because that's what I promised Julian I would do. I would much prefer to have given it to Monsieur Le Gaillard or your Monsieur Chriswell, whose business – '

'Chriswell! Tom Chriswell! Did he come here, asking you about the packet?'

'He did indeed. I told him exactly what I had told Monsieur Le Gaillard – after I had satisfied myself that he was who he said he was. Your friend Monsieur West was a different matter.'

'Monsieur West? Father – I don't know anyone called West. Who is he?'

'He was my third visitor to enquire after the packet and supposedly a First Secretary at the British Embassy. He said that you and he had planned to play a practical joke on Julian which involved a tape cassette, that Julian's death had fortuitously intervened and made the joke in bad taste. If, as he surmised, Julian had given it to me, please could he have it back. Naturally, I denied all knowledge of any cassette. Julian never said what form the evidence took. And I think he believed me.'

'He can't have been a Japanese, not if he claimed to be at the Embassy.'

'No, he wasn't. I would say from his speech that he was German, though his French accent was almost as good as yours. Later, when I talked to Monsieur Le Gaillard and he showed me a photograph, I was able to identify him as a young man called Boy.'

'I see. Father, I'm very grateful. If it hadn't been for you . . .'

But he brushed aside my thanks and urged me to be careful. It was an unnecessary warning. Now I had the packet I felt horribly vulnerable, the more so as everyone else seemed to be at least a couple of moves ahead of me. Le Gaillard and Chriswell were presumably on my side, but I had no illusions about the Sons of Orion.

I said goodbye to Father Michelet at the door of the vestry and hurried through the church. The priest had almost finished saying his mass. It did occur to me to kneel for the last blessing, but I wanted to get back to Margot, and my cassette player.

Emerging from the interior gloom of St Augustin into the daylight of the Place I paused for a moment at the top of the steps to let my eyes adjust. Automatically I glanced at my watch. It was twenty minutes to nine. I should have been on my way to the Chancery.

The Jaguar was parked across the street between a Renault and a yellow van with a blue stripe, the insignia of the French *P et T – Postes et Télécommunications*. My mind registered the fact that they had left me precious little room to get out. Then, as I started down the steps, there was a great thud of sound, a gush of orange flame and the Jaguar seemed to disintegrate.

Something hit me. I realized afterwards that it must have been the shock wave from the explosion that had caught me off balance. Bits of metal were flying through the air but none of them were near me. I found myself falling. I grasped blindly at the steps which battered and bruised me as I slithered down them like an uncontrolled toboggan.

I landed on the pavement in a heap of tangled limbs. My eyes were tightly shut. I didn't want to open them. I was conscious of my own breathing, fast and harsh. My nose hurt, was bleeding. Somewhere, someone was screaming.

Reluctantly I opened my eyes and stared at the place where my Jaguar had been. There was a mess of metal, smoke and flame. That was all. On either side of it the Renault and the *P et T* van were twisted beyond recognition. And close to them a man lay on his back, staring sightless at the sky.

I propped myself up on one elbow and tried to control my breathing. I felt sick. People were running and shouting. Whistles were blowing, cars hooting, klaxons blaring. And the thin screaming continued. Someone bent over me.

'Piers! Piers! Are you all right?'

I looked up into a long, narrow face, creased with anxiety. It wasn't Father Michelet, whom I might have expected to see, and I had to make a positive effort to adjust my mind.

'Hullo, Alain.'

Alain Joubert helped me to my feet and half supported me while I tried to stem the blood from my nose with his hand-kerchief. He was a kind man, and very concerned for me. I didn't know him well but he was a distant cousin on my mother's side and had made me welcome to Paris. He was a Commandant in the French Army.

'Let's get out of here. There's nothing we can do to help and the Place is beginning to swarm with police. No point in us getting involved.'

I didn't tell him that I was already involved, that it was my car which had been blown up, that if I had been three or four minutes earlier – say the time it had taken to persuade the dragon to let me see Father Michelet – I would have been blown up with it. He was looking at me curiously, no doubt wondering why I was so shaken. I was young and healthy. A fall down some steps, even though caused by an explosion, a few bruises and a nose-bleed shouldn't have gutted me to this extent. I had to pull myself together.

'Come along, Piers. Let's go across to the Cercle. You need to wash up, and a cognac wouldn't do you any harm.'

'Thanks, Alain, I'd be grateful. What are you doing here anyway?'

'I've a free day today and I was going to the Cercle.'

Holding the handkerchief to my face, I went with him across Place St Augustin; glass scrunched under our feet. Later the police would have to be told that the Jaguar, what remained of it, was mine, but I didn't want to be delayed by a lot of questions now. Nor, at this point, did I want my proximity to St Augustin and Father Michelet to be brought to Le Gaillard's attention.

And Alain was right; there was nothing useful we could do. Already too many sight-seers had gathered and were getting in the way of the arriving police, ambulances, firemen, riot squads and God knows what other officials. The French are swift and efficient in dealing with such emergencies.

I was still dazed and it was a relief to pass into the gilded world of the club which, with its fine marble staircase, crimson carpets and curtains and splendid chandeliers, implied opulence, privilege, security. It was surprisingly busy for this time of the morning. I caught the odd scrap of conversation as Alain led me across the vestibule.

'. . . done a lot of damage. If you want to blow up a car you don't need all that amount of *plastique*. Half these bombers are amateurs.'

'. . . been lucky at the Cercle. Not a window broken. Blast's a funny thing.'

'. . . and Jeanne's safe too. What would we have done if she'd had her head blown off?'

'It's no joking matter. There's too much violence in Paris. Nobody's safe any more.'

'No. That unfortunate Japanese . . .'

Alain said something about washing my bloody nose and I didn't manage to catch the end of the sentence. I wasn't even sure that I had heard the beginning of it correctly. I had understood the reference to Jeanne – there was a statue of Jeanne d'Arc in the middle of Place St Augustin – but not the reference to the Japanese. 'Unfortunate' was not the adjective I would have applied to that Son of Orion who had been creeping around *le parking* below my apartment block earlier this morning, fixing a bomb underneath the Jag.

As I dipped my face into the wide marble wash-basin, dyeing the water pink with my blood, I thought colourful thoughts of him. I remembered the slithering noise under the cars, the courageous way I had gripped my torch, my call to the *concièrge*, my fear when there was no answer. I remembered my careful inspection of the Jaguar and the reassurance I had felt because the dust on it was undisturbed. I remembered the pounding feet as I drove out of the garage, feet pounding in the wrong direction, away from the exit, anywhere to put distance between us; because he knew that at any moment the Jag, with me in it, could explode.

I swore vehemently and Alain laughed. 'Good. Better be

angry than afraid, eh?'

I twisted my mouth into the semblance of a smile and realized that my bruised face was stiffening. It was going to hurt like hell in an hour or two and I would look like a punch-drunk boxer. Why, I asked myself, hadn't I had the wit to protect it as I fell down the church steps? Then I thought of that uncontrollable screaming. Others had been hurt far more than I, perhaps maimed or killed. And in no sense was it their war.

Alain almost echoed this thought while we drank our coffee and brandy. 'Everyone's at risk these days. If an innocent person's not safe on a Monday morning in Place St Augustin or catching a plane at Charles de Gaulle, where is he safe?'

'Charles de Gaulle?'

'Haven't you seen a paper? *Le Figaro* made a big thing of it. A wretched Japanese business man, who was on his way to Tokyo, was found in the tunnel that joins one of the satellites to the main terminal. He'd been attacked during the storm yesterday evening, concussed, had his head cut open and left for dead – all for no apparent reason.'

I buried my face in the coffee cup so that Alain shouldn't read my expression, which must have mixed disbelief, amusement and scorn. I wondered why the Jap hadn't pleaded an accident during the temporary power cut. Then I remembered the knife.

'What happened? Was he – knifed?'

'No. Evidently the assailant, whom the Jap described as tall and Spanish-looking, smashed him in the face with something heavy – and that was the last thing he knew until he reached the hospital. But no weapon was found. The tunnel was thoroughly searched.'

I was mildly surprised; the Jap had stuck very close to the truth. And I remembered that, as I had left the satellite, passengers had begun to board a Tokyo flight; he could have been booked on it. If my own flight hadn't been late and Margot hadn't delayed me by telephoning from the *Point de Rencontre* he could have killed me, returned to the satellite and had plenty of time to catch his plane to Japan. As it was, time

147

had been short, I had been lucky and he had failed.

'. . . perfectly respectable business man,' Alain was saying.

'What? This Japanese?'

'Yes. Don't sound so suspicious, Piers. They're an old established Paris firm. Grandpa started by importing silks from Japan more than fifty years ago and he's still the titular head of the business. In fact, Pa runs it with the help of his two sons. It was the elder son who got clobbered.'

For a fraction of a second I was back in the tunnel. I saw again the Oriental face, the pleased smile, the raised arm and the glint of a knife. What had happened to the knife? Suddenly doubt caught at me. I had never actually seen a knife. Could I have been mistaken? Could I have been deceived – perhaps by light shining on a watch, worn on the right wrist because the left hand was bandaged? But the Jap had been hurrying away from his plane to Tokyo, not towards it.

Alain said: 'It was very bad luck. If the poor chap hadn't forgotten a parcel at one of the duty-free shops and gone back to get it just as his plane was boarding, none of this would have – ' He stopped abruptly. I suppose I must have been looking sick. 'Piers, are you all right? Would you like another cognac?'

'No thanks, Alain, really. I'm not used to brandy at this hour of the morning. And anyway I must be going. Could you possibly get me a taxi? I – I haven't got a car.'

# Chapter 3

I had insisted on a taxi. Alain had offered to drive me to the Embassy or, when I said I must change my blood-spotted shirt, to my apartment, but I had refused. His concern was beginning to grit on me. I wanted to be by myself.

It was a relief when the taxi threaded its way into the traffic. I sat back in a corner and stretched my legs diagonally across the floor. The taxi-driver's terrier, who had been regarding me suspiciously from the front seat next to his master, relaxed too. I stared out of the window. Place St Augustin seemed to have returned to normal except for one roped-off section where the Jaguar had been parked and from which I averted my eyes. I tried to make my mind a blank.

I didn't have much success. Resigned, I leant forward intending to ask the driver if he would stop at the nearest newspaper kiosk but instead, seeing that he had a copy of *Le Figaro* beside him, asked if I might borrow it. Simultaneously I stretched my hand towards it. The terrier growled deep in his throat and bared sharp, white teeth. I jerked my hand away.

'Careful, monsieur! Careful,' the driver said. He patted the dog's head and then passed me the newspaper. 'You startled him, monsieur.'

'I'm sorry. Does he often bite your passengers?'

The man gave a deep belly-laugh. 'Not often, monsieur. But in my business you need a bit of protection, especially at night, and he's company too. I wouldn't be without him. A lot of Paris cab-drivers have dogs, you know.'

I grunted – I didn't want to talk – and buried myself behind *Le Figaro*. The story of the Japanese at Charles de Gaulle was given the place of honour on the front page. Alain had already told me the salient facts, but the newspaper added considerably more detail. I skimmed through the particulars about the growth of the family business; I wasn't really interested that it encompassed a flourishing interior decorating firm, though this reminded me momentarily of something I couldn't quite place. What was important was that there was no doubt about the *bona-fides* of the Japanese whom I had assaulted. He was, while still in his twenties, a well-known and esteemed member of the Paris business community. And absolutely nothing in the newspaper account suggested any reason why he could have wanted to harm me.

Hopefully I studied the photograph of two Japanese printed beside the story. It was a good photograph and, in spite of his dark glasses, I recognized the taller of the two who was now, thanks to me, in hospital. I had to admit however that I had never seen his brother before; I would have been happy to identify him as the flat-faced driver of the Toyota and the Mercedes. I sighed. There seemed no doubt that I had made an appalling mistake. And yet, after what had happened this morning . . .

'Here we are, monsieur.'

'Thanks. If your dog won't object, may I give you back your paper?'

'Ah, monsieur!' He roared with laughter again. 'He wouldn't hurt you. Taxi dogs are well-trained. They have to be. They're very fierce, but they don't bite except on command.'

'That's nice to know.'

Wondering how on earth I could make such silly, irrelevant conversation at the present time, I paid the fare and added a generous tip. I didn't hurry over it. I was taking the opportunity to look around me, at the parked cars and the pedestrians. The Rue de Longchamp appeared to be its usual bustling Monday morning self. Everything was in order.

I went through the iron gate and, as it clanged shut behind me, glanced up at the face of the apartment building. Margot must have been watching for me. She had come out on to the balcony and was waving. I waved back. By some casual coincidence she was wearing a scarlet shirt and the memory of Johnny hailing me across the Parc de Monceau and literally jumping with joy when I responded made me choke. I broke into a run. I didn't wait for the lift but dashed up the stairs. She had the front door open. We stood in the hall, clinging to each other, pressing our bodies together. Margot was the first to break away.

'Piers, where the hell have you been?'

Then she saw my battered face. She kicked shut the door and drew me into the living-room.

'Tell me!' It was an order.

'Yes. But where's the *femme de ménage*? It's after nine. Hasn't she come?'

'She's gone to do the shopping.'

'Good. Let's play the cassette before she gets back. Margot, Philip was right. Father Michelet did have the packet, and it does seem to be a blackmail threat.'

'Damn the packet! What's happened to you? And why did you come home in a taxi? Where's the Jag?'

I told her, as undramatically as possible, while I fetched scissors and struggled with the Scotch tape. Her eyes grew wide, with a compound of horror and incredulity. Though the day was warm and she stood in a patch of sunshine she hugged herself, her arms wound around her body as if she were cold.

'But why, Piers? Why should the Sons of Orion want to kill you so desperately? It won't help them get their cassette back, will it?'

'I've no idea, darling. But if they'd kill the Rosemeads because of it, why not me?'

Margot was suddenly thoughtful. 'Perhaps Julian was being bloody-minded and wouldn't tell them what he'd done with it, in spite of their threats to throw him off the Arc de Triomphe. Perhaps he struggled and they couldn't stop him falling. And we don't know what happened at Jean's. Anyway, Piers, they've never even asked you about it. They search your apartment – and then decide to kill you!'

I made a gesture of impatience. I had got the packet open and the cassette lay in the palm of my hand. I slipped it into the player. I wet my lips and swallowed saliva; my mouth was dry with excitement. I was only half listening to Margot.

'Piers, don't you understand what I'm trying to say? We should have realized last night, but there was so much else to think about. These – these Sons of Orion seem to want you dead, *regardless* of the cassette.'

I had been smoothing out the wrapping paper. Julian had secured the package at St Augustin after he had failed to get hold of me on Sunday afternoon; it was conceivable that he had included a note. But there was nothing, no message. He had left the packet with Father Michelet for safe-keeping and had expected to tell me about it on Monday. He had been concerned only for the packet, not for himself.

'Darling, does it matter what their reason is?' There was an edge on my words.

'No. I suppose not,' she said flatly.

'Margot, I'm sorry.' I pulled her to me and kissed her. 'We'll think about it later, shall we? But first things first. Let's hear what's on the tape.'

'Okay.' She gave me a wide, forgiving smile.

I returned my attention to the player. I had an intense feeling of urgency. Yet I pressed the 'Playback' button with reluctance. This was rather like eavesdropping, or reading someone's letters; it couldn't be pleasant.

For a full minute there was no sound except the gentlest hiss. The tape was blank. Then a voice spoke.

'Dad, this is Paul – your son, Paul. That's a stupid thing to say, isn't it, as if there could be any other Paul for you except me? But I'm nervous, scared. Dad, please listen carefully. It's terribly important you understand and do what I ask because – because God knows what will happen to me if you don't. Dad, I've been kidnapped.'

I don't know what I had expected. I suppose a threat to reveal some crime or folly or unmentionable sin. I certainly hadn't expected anything like this young English voice – a voice that, in spite of every effort to keep steady, had wobbled more than once. It was a pleasant, cultivated, normally self-possessed voice that I connected with things like summer holidays and one's first car and girls and sport and happiness, and not with any form of horror.

'The people who've got me are called the Sons of Orion. They say they're part of *Rengo Sekigun,* the Japanese Red Army. I've never heard of them, but I'm sure you have. They're a ghastly terrorist outfit – '

There was the sound of a vicious blow, a choking intake of breath and then only the hiss of the blank tape. Beside me Margot gasped and squeezed my hand tight. The room was very still. We waited for the boy's voice to resume, or for someone else to speak. Instead the telephone rang. We were so concentrated that the interruption seemed remote, and my reaction was slow. I had to force myself to get up from the sofa, turn off the player, pick up the receiver.

'Piers, this is Charles Grail. Where are you?'

'I – I'm at home.'

'Really. May I ask why you're not in the office?'

Charles spoke with asperity. To have received a stupid answer to his stupid question would ordinarily have made him laugh, but for once he was acid and prepared to pull rank. I gathered my wits together and lied glibly.

'Terribly sorry, Charles. I was just going to phone you. I don't think I can make it this morning. I had an accident, fell down some steps. There's nothing broken, but I'm a bit battered.'

'Bad luck! What did the doctor say?'

Charles sounded neither sympathetic nor credulous. Margot was hissing something about the Pavertons in my ear and urging me to hang up. I shook my head at her and regretted it; my face hurt.

'Charles, I don't need a doctor and I'll be in after lunch. Is that all right?'

'As far as I'm concerned, yes. But the police want to see you, urgently.'

'The police?'

'Something about an assault at Charles de Gaulle airport last night. They're interviewing passengers who were at Satellite – six, I think it was – between certain hours. I've a number here for you to phone.'

'Thanks.' I didn't bother to write it down; the police would have to wait, but I wasn't happy that they had got on to me so quickly. I wondered how long it would take them to trace the ruins of the Jaguar to me too. I was feeling beset. Even Margot –

'For God's sake, get rid of him,' she said.

'What was that?' Charles asked sharply. 'Piers – are you in trouble of some sort?'

I gave a great big, soundless laugh. 'I'm fine, Charles. I'll see you later. Goodbye for now.'

As I replaced the receiver in its cradle Margot pressed the button of the cassette player. I began to ask what she had been saying while I was on the phone, but she shushed me. And the taped voice recommenced, as if nothing had happened.

'I'm afraid this must be a shock to you, Dad, when you thought I was having a good time in Canada. I was in the departure lounge at Heathrow when I got a message to say you'd had a heart attack – I'm glad that was a lie – and I was to go to Paris at once. A car would take me to the other terminal, where a Paris flight was boarding. I remember getting into the car – and I woke up here.'

I found myself gazing at the player like a man hypnotized by a snake. Although I had never seen Paul, I could visualize him. I knew quite a lot about him, mostly from what his aunt, Mrs Wintersham, had told me at the Pavertons' dinner party. She had said that he had his mother's good looks and his father's brains, he had just won a scholarship to Oxford, and before he went up he was spending some months in Canada and the States. I didn't remember her calling him Paul, but –

'Margot,' I said urgently, 'what were you saying before, about the Pavertons?'

'Sir Timothy's son's named Paul. Lucy's spoken of him and there's a signed photograph in her private sitting-room. It must be him, Piers. It must. You told me he was supposed to be in Canada.'

'And there was that Japanese who insisted on seeing Lady P when you were sketching her, the one who upset her so much. I'd forgotten about him. Oh God!'

I stood up and walked round the room. I couldn't bear to sit still. Sir Timothy Paverton's son, his only child and, according to Mrs Wintersham, the apple of his eye, was in the hands of the *Rengo Sekigun*. That was bad enough. But what appalled me even more was the inference that the British Ambassador to France was wide open to blackmail. The kidnappers would believe they could demand and get almost anything in exchange for Paul. And what were they demanding?

'. . . not treating me badly. I've a bright, sunny room with a fine view of the country. Sorry. I'm not allowed to tell you more than that. This place is like my prep school, lots of rules that must be obeyed, but I'm too old for prep school. Cor, Dad, I want to be free of rules! This place is for the birds!'

He had been talking fast, but now there was a pause. It seemed to give added emphasis to what he had just said. When he continued he sounded calmer, less near to breaking point and less affecting.

'Now, please listen very carefully because these are orders, Dad. First you are not to tell anyone except Ma what's happened. If anyone gets to know – police, intelligence, the FCO, anyone at all – I shall be killed. Luckily I'm meant to be in North America, and nobody's going to miss me and ask awkward questions.

'Next, you're to wait. To wait and do nothing will be hard, but it will only be for a matter of days. Then you'll get instructions. I'm to tell you they'll seem strange, but you're to follow them to the letter. And Ma has got to help you. You won't like it. Neither of you will like it. Letting yourself be coerced like this is contrary to everything you believe in, I know, but it's either doing what they say or it'll be the – the end of me. And I don't want to die.

'I know I can depend on you, Dad. I always have. You're that sort of person, thank God.' His voice sounded hoarse, and he cleared his throat. 'I think that's all. Please, please do exactly what I ask. My love to you and Ma and goodbye.'

I let the tape run in case there was a postscript, but there was nothing more. A great deal was now clear. No wonder the Sons of Orion had been prepared to kill to safeguard their operation. If any of H.E.'s colleagues knew and told the authorities their hold over their potential prize would be gone.

No wonder Julian had wanted my help in putting the story about 'a senior colleague' direct to London.

The telephone rang again. I turned off the player, slipped out the cassette and put it in my trouser pocket. I would have liked to play it again. There were bits of it that had sounded off-key or affected, but then I didn't know Paul Paverton. Obviously he was under a great strain and couldn't say what he wanted. He was bound to seem stilted, stuffed even; it couldn't be easy to plead for one's life in these circumstances. Anyway there was no time to replay the cassette now.

'Piers, aren't you going to answer the phone?'

'No, I don't think so. There are too many people it might be that I don't want to talk to at the moment. In fact, it would probably be best to get out of the apartment. Let's collect the makings of a picnic and go into the Bois.'

'A picnic in the Bois? Today? Piers, are you crazy?'

'Why not? Assuming they know I'm still alive the Japs won't have had a chance to devise another way of killing me yet. And it's the last place the French authorities or Tom Chriswell are likely to look for me.'

'Okay, my love, if it's really what you want.'

We went into the kitchen. I was hungry; I had had nothing so far this morning except coffee and brandy. But the refrigerator was almost empty and I was about to abandon the idea of a picnic when the *femme de ménage* returned. She and Margot collected fresh bread, pâté, cheese, tomatoes, lettuce and fruit while I provided a bottle of wine. In other circumstances I could have enjoyed this. As it was I didn't feel like Nero fiddling, however insouciant my behaviour may have seemed to Margot. I felt more like a young fox whose instincts were urging him to go to earth. What's more, those instincts were right.

We had just finished packing the picnic bag when a clang of the iron gate made me automatically look out of the kitchen window. Monsieur Le Gaillard was striding towards the entrance of the apartment block. No one could mistake that military bearing surmounted by its carrot top and matching moustache. He was the last person I wanted to see. I would have preferred Chriswell.

The *concièrge* must have been outside. Her words, opportunely delaying Le Gaillard, floated up to us through the open window.

'Monsieur, can I help you?'

'Let's go,' I said to Margot. And to the *femme de ménage*, 'Madame, if I'm not at my office, you don't know where I am. You don't expect me home to lunch. You don't know what I'm doing.'

'And that, Monsieur Tyburn, will be the truth,' she said dryly.

The telephone began to ring again and Margot and I fled. We were fortunate in that the lift was at our floor. Feeling a fool I bent my knees as we got in so as to disguise my height. If Le Gaillard was waiting in the entrance hall he would see shadows through the frosted glass of the lift door and I didn't want him running down to the basement after us.

In the event, it was an unnecessary precaution. We reached the basement without seeing a sign of him and went through to *le parking*. I blessed Margot's American need for wheels. Her rented Renault, sitting in its visitor's slot, was indistinguishable from hundreds of others in Paris and promised us safe transport.

'You drive, darling. Don't waste time at the top of the driveway, but don't draw attention to yourself either. Le Gaillard will have a car with at least one man in it, and they'll be keeping their eyes open.'

I got into the back of the Renault and made myself as small as possible, thinking that if we were stopped I would pretend I had dropped a five franc piece on the floor. I should have had more faith in Margot. With beautiful judgement she swung the car on to the Rue de Longchamp in front of a slow-moving delivery van. Nobody paid any attention to us. We turned right, and right again into the Avenue de Madrid, and then straight on to the Bois.

When I was sure we weren't being followed, Margot stopped and I moved to the seat beside her. The roads through the Bois can be very confusing and I had no idea where we were. Choosing a secondary track at random we left the car and walked along a rough path. It was hot and heavy under the trees and I began to sweat; I wasn't dressed for this sort of expedition. But the track led unexpectedly into another which circumscribed a lake. By chance we had found a pleasant place where we could sit on the grass and have our lunch at the water's edge.

Apart from the need to deal with the food and drink we scarcely spoke. Margot ate sparingly but I was ravenous and consumed whatever she put in front of me, though I wouldn't have noticed if it had been inedible. My mind was churning.

'Why are you smiling, Piers?'

'Was I?'

'Yes – a savage kind of smile.'

'I was wondering what the hell I ought to do next.' I stood up and pulled Margot to her feet. 'Let's walk for a while, shall we? I'll tell you the alternatives.'

We hid the picnic basket under a bush to be retrieved on the way back and set off round the lake. It was very peaceful. I remembered Paul Paverton saying: 'I don't want to die.' I didn't want to die either.

'If I had any sense I'd drive out to Charles de Gaulle, catch the next flight to London and go straight to the FCO. I know the right people and, given this cassette, they'd listen. Then, duty done, you and I could go on leave together.' I sighed. 'It isn't as simple as that, really. For one thing I hate the idea of accusing H.E.'

'Accusing? Good God, it's not the poor man's fault!'

'That's not the point, Margot – or not the whole point. The rules are quite clear. If anyone in the FCO, for any reason, becomes a potential victim of blackmail, it's his duty to inform his superiors immediately. The more senior the man the greater the responsibility. The crucial question is: has H.E. gone to the authorities or not? If he has, there's no problem and I should get the cassette to him as soon as possible. But he may have decided that his son's life is worth more than whatever the Sons of Orion are demanding. And, in that case, it's my duty to stop him.'

Margot looked at me coldly. 'What else might you do, apart from running off to London?'

'I could go to Tom Chriswell. He's responsible for security at the Embassy. But I don't like him and, perhaps because of that, I don't altogether trust him. Then there's Charles Grail, who's my immediate boss and the obvious choice, except somehow it doesn't seem fair to involve him. Also, though I like and trust him I'm not sure of his judgement. He's a very – kind man. I think he might let H.E. persuade him, for Paul's sake, to take no action.'

'And would that be bad?'

'Margot, it just isn't practical.'

We had taken another path which led us past a small Resistance memorial near an oak tree. In front of the tree stood an elderly man wearing a black beret. As we came up he blew his nose violently on a spotted handkerchief, crossed himself and shuffled away. Margot read aloud from the plaque attached to the oak:

> '*Passant*
> *Respecte ce chêne.*
> *Il porte les traces de balles*
> *qui ont tué nos martyrs.*
> *Ici ont été fusillées*
> *35 martyrs de la Résistance*
> *le 16 août 1944.*'

She rubbed her hand over the bark of the tree, feeling the bullet wounds. 'Maybe one of the men the Germans shot was the son of that old man. Maybe he could have saved his son, but he didn't; he preferred to keep to the rules.'

'Darling,' I said gently, 'you're being fanciful, which isn't like you, but I take your point. And you don't have to plead for Sir Timothy. The sensible thing to do' – I didn't add: and the safest – 'would be to go straight to London, but I won't do it behind his back. Let's get along to the Embassy. I'll tell H.E. all I know, play him the tape, and at least hear what he says. I can't do more than that.'

Margot gave me a dazzling smile, which was my reward. Its effect was only spoilt by my immediate intuition that I was likely to regret my decision.

# Chapter 4

H.E. sat at his desk, seemingly imperturbable, and gave me a benign but practised smile. It was the far edge of lunchtime and the aroma of his post-prandial cigar lingered about him. He looked at my battered face, expressed concern and waited.

I was tongue-tied. Looking at him closely I could see the cracks in his carapace, the red-rimmed eyes, the tired set of his mouth in repose. I felt a rush of pity for him, but words didn't come. Patiently his hands formed their usual pyramid and he raised his eyebrows at me.

'You wanted to see me about Julian Rosemead. You said it was of the utmost urgency, Piers.'

'Yes, sir.'

Having asked for the interview, I had gone in the deep end without considering in advance just what I should say. I made an effort to marshal my thoughts. H.E. was prepared to help me.

'The memorial service we planned for Julian at St Michael's tomorrow has been postponed. In the circumstances, with his son dead and his wife in hospital, it seemed advisable.'

'Sir – about Julian. I don't think there's any doubt he was murdered – by some people who call themselves the Sons of Orion.'

'That makes our decision to postpone the service seem even wiser,' H.E. said calmly. 'Do you have any proof of this – er – killing?'

'Of the actual murder, no, sir.'

'Piers – are they trying to blackmail you now?'

The question took me by surprise, though I remembered that Chriswell had hinted at such a possibility. It also acted as a kind of catalyst. If H.E. was going to be devious, I should be no match for him and we would get at cross-purposes. The only thing was to be blunt.

'No, they're not trying to blackmail me. But I've found out, as Julian did, that they have a hold over you, sir. I know they've kidnapped Paul.'

What happened next was totally unexpected. H.E. brought the flat of his hand down on the desk with a loud slap, not unlike a pistol shot. The telephones joggled in their rests, a pen bounced out of its tray, paper clips spilled across the blotting-pad. H.E. swore. His vocabulary was wide and erudite.

When he had got the worst of it out of his system, he glared at me and said: 'Why the hell didn't you do what you were told? Why didn't you keep out of it? Chriswell warned you, days ago. So did Le Gaillard.' He shook his head sadly, his anger evaporating. 'God knows what damage you've done.'

Stung by his outburst, I said coldly: 'Julian involved me in the beginning, and since then I've not had much choice; things have just happened to me. It wasn't till this morning that I discovered you were the "senior colleague" Julian said was being blackmailed. And it wasn't till this morning that I discovered why. So I came to you. I – I hoped you'd explain – '

'Explain? Ah – you mean it occurred to you that I might not have informed the authorities. Let me set your mind at rest. I have.'

Feeling myself flush, I damned his astuteness. 'Yes, sir. I'm sorry. Obviously you have, if Chriswell and Le Gaillard know about it.'

'Don't apologize, Piers. It was the hardest decision I've made in my life. But you can't give in to blackmail. A short-term good may result sometimes, but in the long run only harm can come of it. Paul agreed with me. We talked about it several times, though I must admit we cast me as the hostage. And, God! How I wish I were! But Paul wouldn't expect me to think differently because it's ~~him~~. He's a – a clear-sighted young man.'

H.E. paused. I bit my tongue. There were a hundred questions I wanted to ask, but this wasn't the right moment. I thought of the cassette in my pocket and hoped it wasn't going to disappoint him. He was proud of his son. Mostly, however, I was relieved; he had told London and my part in the affair was virtually over.

'Well, now you know what I feel about the matter, Piers, we'd better get down to business.' He pressed the switch on his intercom. 'Celia, I want to see Tom Chriswell in my office at once, and Monsieur Le Gaillard – at his convenience, naturally. All my afternoon appointments to be cancelled.'

'Monsieur Le Gaillard is due at three-thirty, Sir Timothy.'

'He is? Good. I'd forgotten. Let that stand but cancel the rest.'

H.E. cut her off when she was half way through her 'Very good, Sir Timothy', pushed back his chair and stood up. 'I think we both need a drink, Piers. Brandy?'

Apart from the one outburst that, in retrospect, seemed to have been a deliberate release of his feelings rather than an actual loss of temper, H.E. had kept his cool. Now, as we sat sipping brandy and listening to the cassette I had produced, he looked as if he were concentrating on the tape of some important speech he hadn't been able to attend in person. Watching him I marvelled at his self-control.

A shadow passed across his face when Paul was struck. Once he nodded his head as if something had been confirmed and once, unless it was my imagination, he made a fractional gesture with his brandy balloon, offering a silent toast. Other wise he showed no emotion. To me the whole scene was unreal.

As the tape came to an end Celia's voice on the intercom announced Tom Chriswell. There wasn't time for H.E. to comment. Motioning me to let Tom in, he took the two balloons and put them away, unwashed, in the cabinet.

Tom Chriswell came in, red-faced and untidy as usual. He gave me a startled, suspicious glance and then ignored me. He addressed himself to H.E.

'Sorry I've taken so long to get here, sir. I've been at the hospital. Jean Rosemead had a good night and they thought I might be able to question her this morning, but she's still sleeping and they wouldn't wake her.'

'I should hope not. I don't know why you want to question

her, anyway.'

'It's important to confirm what did happen, sir. Le Gaillard's convinced she didn't shoot the boy or herself, but the ballistic experts won't – '

'She didn't shoot herself,' I said. 'Jean was left-handed, but when I found her the gun was by her right hand.'

There was a momentary silence. Chriswell cut off an obscenity that the Ambassador would have despised. His Excellency gave me what my father would have described as an old-fashioned look. And I made a gallant effort to appear unaware of their reactions.

'Perhaps if we all cooperated, pooled our information, we might – just might make a little more progress,' H.E. said pleasantly. 'However, first I must talk to London.'

He pulled the red telephone towards him and lifted the receiver. Almost at once he spoke. 'Is he there? . . . Hullo, Dick, any news? . . . No . . . No. Quite . . . We've got another cassette. It's much the same but not identical. Probably recorded earlier . . . Of course I'll let you have it, but meanwhile there's something you can get your teeth into. After a reference to his prep school Paul says: "Cor, Dad, this place is for the birds". That's absolutely clear. From his room he must be able to see or hear the cawing of rooks. What? . . . No, I haven't the faintest idea how many rookeries there are in the home counties . . . That's your job, Dick, not mine. You find the right one . . . All right. Goodbye – and thanks.'

My opinion of Paul Paverton had been growing as I listened. He was ingenious and he had guts. I took back the uncomplimentary thoughts I had had of him. But I didn't give much for his chances. Nor did I look forward to impressing his father with the fact that the Sons of Orion attached little importance to human life – if H.E. hadn't already guessed.

'Now,' H.E. said, appearing to relax, 'let's try to get the story straight from the beginning and let's not mind repeating ourselves. Piers, you start. Tom, you pick holes in everything. We'll put it all on tape and get Le Gaillard working on it later.'

I took a deep breath and began. 'The Friday before last I went with Julian to the Memorial for the Deported . . .'

I tried to make my account as straightforward and factual as I could, but so much of it was hearsay. I was constantly saying: 'Julian told me . . .' When I got to the conversation that Julian claimed to have overheard on the phone – the threat to a member of the Embassy and the orders to meet at the Memorial – I was glad to look at H.E. for confirmation.

'That fits,' he said. 'I received that call on Tuesday, supposedly from a friend of Paul's. He said Paul was in trouble and I must meet him at the Memorial to discuss it. I didn't believe him; the whole thing sounded phoney. Only twenty-four hours earlier Alice Wintersham, my sister-in-law, had telephoned to say she'd seen Paul off at Heathrow, and he was in very good form. And I'd spoken to Paul myself over the weekend. I told the chap to come to the Chancery and hung up on him, expecting that to be the last of it.'

'Didn't he mention the Parc de Bagatelle, sir?'

'No.' H.E. was definite.

'And you haven't mentioned any of this until now, Piers. Why?' Chriswell demanded.

We had hit the first of the snags. I had to explain that I'd not considered it important, not once H.E. had told me that Julian himself was being blackmailed. I had accepted H.E.'s version, Chriswell's version. In fact, Chriswell was still inclined to believe that the Sons of Orion had set Julian up to play some definite part in whatever they were planning. But in the face of Father Michelet's evidence and mine, the cassette found at Bagatelle and the theft of Johnny's 'music', he had to agree. Julian, by accident and then from a sense of duty, had involved himself – and me.

How Julian had learnt of the packet hidden by the lily pond at Bagatelle remained a mystery. We could only assume that instructions had been sent to H.E. on the Friday, after he had set off for London, and that Julian, who had been acting as his Private Secretary, had intercepted them.

And other things could only be guessed at, such as what had happened to Julian before he was thrown off the Arc de Triomphe. But maybe some questions were better left unanswered or blurred. At least Jean would be happy that Julian's

165

death no longer carried any stigma.

'Poor boy!' H.E. said. 'Poor wretched boy! Such a dreadful way to die.'

'Can't think why they didn't push him under a bus or in front of a Métro train,' Chriswell said. 'Less trouble, but of course it wouldn't have brought us so much bad publicity.'

It went on and on, until at last we had beaten out a comprehensive chain of events that satisfied H.E. and Chriswell. I myself learnt next to nothing, except for confirmation that the Japanese youth who had interrupted Margot's sketching session with Lady Paverton had indeed brought a cassette from Paul. According to Chriswell it was at this point that 'all hell broke loose, security-wise' and I remembered, not without malice, the lies he had told me the following morning about his hangover.

'Sir,' I said finally. 'I realize the authorities in the UK are trying to find your son, but what's happening in Paris?'

'Yes. They're making enquiries – with the utmost discretion. In the meantime, on orders from London and with the full support of the French, I'm doing precisely what the Sons of Orion tell me. So far they've asked for architect's drawings of the Residence, number of staff, security arrangements and a detailed schedule, lists of guests, everything concerning the banquet the PM is giving here on Thursday night for the President of France.' H.E.'s lips twisted into a sardonic smile. 'It's believed that I'm destined for a more important role eventually, but that's all they've asked of me to date.'

'The DST warned us something like this might happen. They're cooperating fully, but we're bringing some Special Branch men over too,' Chriswell said grimly. 'We plan to move in at the very last minute, so that we learn as much as possible about the Sons of Orion and net as many of the buggers as we can.'

'Quite,' H.E. said, expressionless.

Today was Monday. 'The very last minute' couldn't be more than seventy-two hours away. They wouldn't dare leave it any later, not when the French President, the British Prime Minister and Foreign Secretary and God knows what other

VIPs would be at risk. Apart from anything else, if some monstrous calamity befell them on what was technically British soil the political repercussions would be appalling. Paul Paverton didn't have much time left.

H.E. pushed back his chair. 'Piers, I'm going to take you through to the Residence. You can have tea – it'll probably be coffee – with my wife and Miss Ninian. They're having the first sitting for the portrait this afternoon, I believe. We'll want to see you later, of course.' He stood up. 'Tom, will you entertain Le Gaillard when he comes? Play him the cassette Piers brought us. It's not quite the same as the one we have and he'll like to hear it.'

H.E. led me along a passage, past a guard, through a door he had to unlock, and into the Residence. I had never been in this part of the house before. There were more passages, stairs and another door. H.E. stopped.

'Piers, how much does Miss Ninian know about this business?'

I hesitated. 'Practically everything, sir.'

He grunted. 'A pity!'

We went into the bright, sparsely furnished room that had become Margot's temporary studio. She was standing at an easel in a yellow smock and flat yellow sandals, working hard. Reflected in a long mirror I could see what appeared to be a lightning portrait of Lady Paverton. Tomorrow, I knew, Margot would paint it out – she maintained that this practice helped to give the final portrait depth – but at the moment she was lavishing her skill on it. She looked up, frowning at our interruption.

Lady Paverton, on the contrary, appeared pleased by it. She was, I thought, not looking her best. Exquisitely packaged as always, she seemed to lack the vitality that was perhaps her greatest attraction.

'How very nice,' she said. 'Have you come to tea?'

'Certainly not,' H.E. said, smiling to remove any sting from his words. 'I've work to do, my dear. But I want you to take care of Piers until I need him again.'

'That will be a pleasure and a good excuse for a rest. Margot's been making me work hard too. I had no idea that having one's portrait painted was – '

'Lucy!'

With one word H.E. shattered the social scene that his wife had created. Margot, already tense, gestured wildly with the brush and a spatter of ultramarine, the colour of Lady P's blouse, patterned the protective dust-sheet under the easel and reached to the parquet floor. She stared at the marks guiltily and then began to clean them up with a turpentine rag. Lady Paverton hadn't moved.

'Everybody, please do relax,' H.E. said somewhat testily. 'Lucy, my dear, Piers knows about Paul and he's told Miss Ninian. He's been most helpful and I think we may be making some progress.'

He gave a few encouraging details. He didn't mention the Japanese who might need to be compensated for my attack on him; I was in favour and Tom Chriswell could deal with the Jap. But he did mention my car, ignoring his wife's exclamation of distress and directing his remarks at Margot with a purpose. He wanted to be rid of her.

'Miss Ninian, I can't order you but I do beseech you to leave Paris – just till the beginning of next week. I don't believe you're in any personal danger but you might get caught up in something – and if you did Lady Paverton and I would feel responsible.'

Margot began to clean her brushes. 'I'm sorry, Sir Timothy, but if Piers has to stay in Paris I stay in Paris. I'm an American citizen and you don't have to feel responsible for me.'

'My dear young lady, it's for your own sake – '

'Margot, please!'

'No. I refuse to be intimidated.'

H.E. gave me a quizzical glance. I don't think he was sure if Margot was referring to himself or to me or to the Sons of Orion. Then he shrugged; he didn't have time to argue. Le Gaillard would be waiting.

There was a tap on the door, and Lady Paverton's social secretary came in with coffee and biscuits. Smiling, she said:

'I'll fetch some more cups.'

'Not for me, thanks. I'm just off.'

'There's a letter for you, Lady Paverton. Not personal. It's from some interior decorators – *Murasaki et Fils*.'

'What do they want? To do the Residence over, I suppose.'

I had been watching Margot and not really listening but the words *Murasaki et Fils* impinged on my consciousness like an alarm clock. I didn't wait to explain. I dashed after H.E. He had been moving at top Ambassadorial speed – not quite a canter, but covering the ground in a dignified fashion – and I didn't catch up with him until he was at the door of the Chancery.

'Sir, Lady Paverton's just received a letter from – from *Murasaki et Fils* – an unsolicited letter.'

He followed my train of thought immediately. 'It can't be a coincidence.'

'No, it can't, sir. I knew when someone said the Jap I'd laid out was an interior decorator that it ought to mean something to me. Now I've remembered. I saw their van, a white van with neat black lettering, parked on the Rue Murillo, Thursday – just before I found Jean and Johnny.'

'Well done, Piers.' H.E. was as excited as I was. 'This could be a real break. Let's go and see what they have to say.'

The letter was not very informative. Supposedly in reply to a request from Lady Paverton it assured her that Monsieur Murasaki and his esteemed daughter-in-law – he didn't mention his esteemed son in hospital – would call at the Residence on Wednesday at ten-thirty to take measurements, show Her Excellency samples of material and give her the benefit of their long and valuable experience. It ended with flowery expressions of devotion to Her Excellency's service and no hint of any sort of threat.

And, when I was later summoned back to H.E.'s office, I found the reaction of both Le Gaillard and Chriswell deflating. They pointed out that the evidence was still only circum-stantial. The Sons of Orion might have written in Lady Paverton's name to Monsieur Murasaki with the intention of using his business in some way; the van in the Rue Murillo could have an innocent explanation; and I could be mistaken about what had happened in the tunnel at Charles de Gaulle. It wasn't possible, at any rate for the moment, to take any action against the Murasakis. Naturally enquiries would continue.

Forestalling the venomous remarks on the tip of my tongue, H.E. said acidly: 'Well, we shall have to hope you come up with something soon, Monsieur Le Gaillard.'

Le Gaillard stroked his moustache; he didn't like the implied rebuke. '*Bien sûr*, Sir Timothy. I assure you I have every intention of doing whatever is possible. Meanwhile I think we should keep an open mind.'

H.E. nodded. 'Provided we don't forget that there may have been two attempts to kill Piers in the last twenty-four hours.' He turned to me. 'And now, Piers . . .'

I was aware of a subtle change in the atmosphere. There was nothing to be learnt from H.E.'s apparent benevolence. I glanced at La Gaillard, who was studying his nails, dissociating himself from whatever was about to be said or done by *les Anglais*, and then at Chriswell. Tom Chriswell was not detached. He was watching me, his mouth curved in a cynical smile, his small eyes glittering with amusement.

'You understand the present position as well as anyone,' H.E. continued. 'As to what's likely to happen, it's the general consensus that the terrorists will make their attack on Thursday, most probably at the banquet. The dining-room would be difficult to hold for any length of time, but half a dozen of them could hold it for long enough to seize a small group of VIPs. They could then take them to a place easier to defend, perhaps a guest suite – a bathroom's always useful on these occasions – and demand the release of some so-called political prisoners, money, whatever their objectives may be.'

'We don't believe they want to remove any hostages from the Residence, except possibly as part of an escape plan. It would present too many problems,' Chriswell said as H.E. paused. 'One interesting thing is how they plan to get themselves into the Residence. They must know security'll be as tight as a drum. Even the PM's mother won't be able to get into the place without the right papers. So, presumably, this is where they're going to demand help from Sir Timothy.'

H.E. coughed. 'Piers, there's no question now of this attempt succeeding, but the longer I seem to cooperate the greater our opportunity to obtain information about the activities of the *Rengo Sekigun* and to lay hands on some of them. It may – and I stress the "may" – also give Paul more of a chance. However, there's such a thing as diminishing returns. We've already had too much death and injury without striking a blow ourselves – unless we're allowed to count young Murasaki.' He gave me a sudden half-smile, which included Le Gaillard. 'If you're to go on fighting, Piers, the decision must be yours.'

'I – I don't quite understand, sir.'

'You're the joker in the pack, old boy.'

'Tom, please!' H.E. didn't bother to hide his distaste, but Chriswell only grinned. 'One is somewhat chary of airports at this moment, but a car could be provided for you and Miss Ninian. By tomorrow morning you could be almost anywhere, out of the country, completely safe. Alternatively, you can decide to stay here – and this could be very advantageous to us. Tom will explain. It was his idea.'

'We don't want you dead, which would serve no purpose,' Chriswell said harshly. 'But we want you to stay, to build up Sir Timothy's image as a collaborator, to give us more time before these bug – I mean terrorists – suspect they've had it. They're due to contact Sir Timothy at six o'clock. He could spin them a yarn. You remembered something Julian had said to you, found the cassette under the shelf in a confessional at St Augustin – that will cover the priest – and accused H.E. of selling secrets. He managed to persuade you that the black-mailers only want money and the police are looking for his son and you're happy to leave it at that.'

Chriswell hesitated, giving me a ruminative look before he continued: 'Once the terrorists are convinced you've handed over the cassette to Sir Timothy and to no one else, and you're no longer a menace to them, they're not going to kill you. What do you say, Piers? Do you go or stay? Don't you see, if you go now, suddenly, and the terrorists know of it, they could regard it as evidence that Sir Timothy's been to the authorities.

They could kill Paul. What's more, they could change their plans, and we'd have less chance of a coup.'

I swallowed. There was only one answer and, whatever their personal feelings, the three of them knew it. Not even H.E. asked me to reconsider. Chriswell nodded his head in self-satisfaction. Le Gaillard, making a solitary contribution to the discussion, said:

'It should be all right, Monsieur Tyburn, but certain precautions must be taken.'

# Chapter 5

I didn't sleep well. I spent most of the night in that twilight zone between sleeping and waking. But every now and then I came fully awake, with a heart-stopping jolt. Sitting up in bed, I listened. If I heard the DST man, whom Le Gaillard had ordered to stay with us overnight, padding about the apartment, I wondered what had disturbed him. If there was silence I wondered where he was. Either way my imagination was too vivid for comfort.

In theory I was no longer in any danger. The Sons of Orion, as far as one could judge, had accepted the story that H.E. had spun them. Their reaction had been to reiterate their threats to Paul. They said that if I as much as started a suspicion of their hold over H.E., however accidentally, Paul would die a horrible death. H.E. didn't have to pretend to believe them.

Oddly enough all this made him more anxious about my own safety. Chriswell thought I should behave as usual and take no precautions, except perhaps for avoiding the Métro and being careful when crossing the road; he was against anything that might alert the terrorists. Le Gaillard, on the other hand, wanted my apartment searched for booby traps and listening devices, and two men on duty, one in the apartment itself and the other, as long as we were using the car Margot had rented, at night in the garage. The decision was H.E.'s and he came down heavily in favour of Le Gaillard.

I should have felt completely safe. In fact, as I kept rousing myself from the nightmare of dream to the nightmare of reality, my heart banged against my ribs, sweat stood on my brow and my teeth gritted together. I was ashamed of my feebleness but I couldn't help it. I was thankful when morning came.

Things began to improve. The DST man went out to buy us *croissants* – he wouldn't let me go to the baker's myself – and later on our drive to the Embassy was uneventful. Margot was spending the day at the Residence. There was plenty of work for her to do on the portrait before Lady Paverton's next sitting, and it was good to know I didn't have to worry about her. As for myself, in spite of a piled in-tray and a couple of nasty memoranda whose writers complained that I was always inaccessible, I had never thought my office so desirable. I hoped it was going to be a quiet, normal workday – apart from Johnny's funeral.

It began rather well. The people who had been inconvenienced or delayed by my absence, such as Charles Grail, forgot the unpleasant things they had intended to say as soon as they saw my face. The results of my slide down the steps of St Augustin had become much more apparent today. One eye was black, there was a purple bruise along my cheekbone, and my nose and lips were thick. It had been difficult to shave and impossible to kiss Margot but, except for some stiffness, the pain was negligible and a small price to pay for the sympathy I received. What's more, if I didn't feel positively happy, I felt confident again and free of nightmares. By lunchtime, even after Johnny's pathetic funeral, I was prepared to admit that it was being a fair day.

In the middle of the afternoon Chriswell telephoned. Would I come along to his office? He wanted to see me and so did Le Gaillard, who would be there in half an hour. I sighed. I didn't want to see either of them. I would have much preferred to get on with the minute I was drafting for Charles. I didn't even feel stirrings of curiosity until Chriswell, waving me to a chair, said:

'I've been talking to Jean Rosemead.'

'How is she?'

'Low. She couldn't stop crying. They'd just told her about her boy. Funny. You'd think she'd be grateful he's dead, wouldn't you?'

'No.'

'Why not? She's alive, and without him she's got a future.

She wants to see you, incidentally.'

'She does? When?'

'Tomorrow, but I'm not sure it's a good thing, security-wise.'

'If she wants to see me, I'll go.'

'You'll do what you're bloody well told, Piers.'

Monsieur Le Gaillard saved us from further bickering. By the time he had shaken hands with both of us, and settled himself comfortably in Chriswell's best visitor's chair, the temperature had sunk to normal. Chriswell, now speaking his execrable French, continued to talk about Jean.

'. . . two of them. They had stocking masks over their heads so she won't be able to identify them. They forced her into the drawing-room and said she could start by telling them where the cassette was. She didn't know what they were getting at and could think only of Johnny. Johnny came in just as one of the guys smacked her across the face, and the little idiot went for him.

'He took the guy by surprise. After all, nobody in his senses charges straight at a gun. And, of course, he got shot. Jean's sure it was an accident and she's almost certainly right. They wouldn't have bothered to wear masks otherwise. The gun would have been for show. They didn't expect to use it. But, once they had, they'd nothing to lose. Jean knew then that they'd kill her – even if she could answer their questions, and mostly she couldn't.

'Anyway, they hadn't got very far with their questioning before you arrived, Piers. They'd knocked her down and she was lying there, half stunned, when the doorbell went. You know, that may well have saved her life. She doesn't remember what happened next, but obviously they arranged her "suicide" in such a hell of a hurry they botched the job.' Chriswell grinned at me. 'I imagine they were hiding behind the curtains when you went in, old boy, and they'd have escaped after you dashed downstairs.'

I was fascinated by the story, but it only confirmed what we had more or less guessed, and I couldn't understand why Le Gaillard was so obviously pleased with it. He was preening his moustache with all the satisfaction of a cat attending to its toilet. Annoyingly, however, he was in no hurry to share his pleasure.

'What about you, monsieur?' Chriswell prompted. 'Do you have any interesting news for us?'

'Perhaps.' Le Gaillard gave his Gallic shrug. 'Monsieur Murasaki, who was recovering well from the injuries Monsieur Tyburn inflicted on him, has had a relapse. Delayed shock, the doctor says. A pity, when he was about to go home. It's now expected that won't be possible until – after Thursday.'

'You mean you've caught him out over something?'

'Monsieur Tyburn, we've checked and rechecked his account of what happened on Sunday evening and no flaw can be found in it. It appears beyond doubt that you made an unprovoked attack on him.'

Disappointed and irritable, I pushed back my chair and stood up. 'Then why have you arranged for him to be kept in hospital, Monsieur Le Gaillard? Because that's what you have done, isn't it? I don't understand.'

'You don't have to,' Chriswell said. 'Sit down, Piers!'

I sat, but half-arsed on the edge of the desk. Otherwise I ignored Chriswell. I concentrated on Le Gaillard.

'Monsieur Tyburn, *je vous en prie.*' He made a deprecatory gesture. 'As a last hope I decided to go and see the Director of the hospital. Alas, he said no, there was nothing unusual about this patient. But I pressed him – he's an old friend of mine – and he admitted that Monsieur Murasaki had been inordinately angry when he regained consciousness because a nurse had replaced the dirty bandage on his hand. Later he apologized to her and tried to make light of the incident, but for her own protection she had already reported it.

'He had a bad week, our Monsieur Murasaki. We know what happened to him on Sunday evening. And on the previous Thursday he had been bitten, it seems, by one of those dogs that often sit beside Paris taxi-drivers to protect them.'

'Bitten! By a taxi dog?' Chriswell guffawed; the idea evidently struck him as hilarious.

I had no inclination to laugh. The taxi ride from the Cercle

Militaire yesterday morning was too vivid in my mind. Although I had startled the terrier, almost inviting attack, the dog hadn't even nipped me. But Murasaki had been so badly bitten that three days afterwards his hand was still heavily bandaged. I didn't believe it, unless . . .

'What – what did you do, Monsieur Le Gaillard?' My voice was hoarse.

'I arranged a little accident. Monsieur Murasaki was honoured to receive a visit from the Director, but not pleased when my friend managed to knock a glass of fruit juice over his poor hand. Of course, he couldn't be angry. He had made so much fuss the last time the bandages were changed. And the Director, who insisted on repairing the damage he had done, had a good chance to examine the wound. It was a very nasty bite indeed.'

'But not a dog bite?'

'No, Monsieur Tyburn, not a dog bite.'

'For Christ's sake! What was it then?'

'Johnny!' I said positively. 'Murasaki must have been one of the thugs in the Rosemeads' apartment. When he hit Jean Johnny went for him. Johnny was strong and big for his age and – and sometimes uncontrolled. He would have kicked and bitten anyone who hurt his mother.'

'I remembered you told me, Monsieur Tyburn, that the first time you went to dinner with the Rosemeads Johnny bit the girl who was supposed to be looking after him . . .'

I stopped listening. Chriswell said something about the boy being dangerous and, when Le Gaillard denied it, he laughed and likened Johnny to a taxi dog. I heard the words, but their meaning washed over me. I was thinking of Johnny doing his over-simple jigsaw puzzle on the bedroom floor, waving to me from the balcony as I walked across the Parc de Monceau, having that embarrassing tantrum and searching for Mike the peacock at Bagatelle, holding tightly to my hand while the life ran out of him. 'Take care, Da's friend!' It had been a brief friendship. But I hated the man who was responsible for Johnny's death.

'What have you done with him?' I had interrupted their

conversation and had to explain. 'This Murasaki.'

'He felt unwell during the night. When his brother came to take him home this morning he was sleeping very heavily. The brother returns tomorrow.' Le Gaillard shrugged. 'I'm not sure about him.'

'And the rest of this reputable old-established firm?'

'Monsieur Tyburn, I'm not sure about any of them. I would have said that *Murasaki et Fils* were – above reproach. I still believe old Monsieur Murasaki himself may be innocent. But – who knows?'

I went back to my office. I was delighted at what Le Gaillard had done. For the rest of the afternoon I gave an impression of working but I didn't achieve much. Thoughts of *Murasaki et Fils* obtruded themselves in the most unlikely places.

Shortly before five Lady Paverton's social secretary brought Margot across from the Residence. Margot hadn't been in my office before and she wanted to examine everything. I was slightly embarrassed when Charles Grail walked in as she was questioning me about one of the organization charts I had pinned up on the wall. I needn't have worried.

Charles waved away my explanations. 'I've just had Mary on the telephone and she suggested that if you had no plans for the evening the two of you might like to have a few drinks and a scratch meal with us.'

'There's nothing we'd like better,' I said and meant it.

I had been wondering what we were going to do with ourselves. The presence of the DST man made the apartment somewhat less than cosy. Paris itself wasn't inviting when anyone, Japanese or not, might be the enemy; I would see every raised hand, even if it held a wine glass, preparing to deliver a karate chop. And, though I had considered taking Margot to visit my cousins in Versailles, the potential of the dark drive home put me off. I had become timid.

The Grails' invitation was the perfect solution. They lived in the 16th *arrondisement*, in a very superior block of apartments, where visitors' cars were parked in a courtyard inside a guarded gate. Privacy and protection were both ensured. I would be as safe as at the Embassy and thus able to relax and enjoy myself.

We could have a good evening.

I must have been over-profuse with my thanks for Charles gave me a quizzical look. 'My dear boy, we're delighted. I'll give you a ring just before I leave the office, then you can follow me home.'

Stopping on the way to buy some flowers for Mary we arrived a little later than Charles. But we found him chatting to his *concièrge* while he waited for us. He commented on the hired Renault.

'A change from your beautiful Jaguar, Piers. Incidentally is it a complete write-off or can the garage do anything?'

'It's an utter wreck, Charles.'

I don't like lying, especially to friends, but I had to give Charles some reason for the eagerness of the French police to interview me, and I had told him I had had a car accident. Unfortunately he had repeated the story to Mary, so now I had to repeat my lies – plus some extra ones to account for my battered face.

However, once we got off the subject of the dangerous life I seemed to lead, the evening was everything I had hoped for, pleasant, relaxing, undemanding. I would have been happy to extend it to the small hours, but not long after dinner I caught Charles smothering a yawn. It wasn't fair to stay. He had been working very hard recently and he could clearly do with an early night.

We left soon after ten.

'I suppose we ought to go straight home,' Margot said, 'but I'd love a brandy, wouldn't you, Piers?'

'I would indeed. We'll go to Colette's.'

Why not? I couldn't believe the Sons of Orion had been watching us ever since we left the Embassy and were following us now. Besides, even if they were, it would only be to check on the normalcy of my behaviour. They had agreed I was no longer important to them.

The whisky and wine I had drunk weren't making me rash – I wouldn't have taken Margot to some Montmartre nightclub – but they were putting some needed stuffing into me. Anyway, the risk was negligible. What could be safer than Colette's?

It was a beautiful night, very warm for May. Though some of the cafés lining the Champs Elysées were shut, most of them had a scattering of people still sitting outside. Colette's was no exception. And we were lucky. I had thought the car might be a problem, but we were able to park it within sight. What's more, there was a table at the rear of the pavement where we could sit with our backs to the restaurant. I ordered two cognacs.

'Nice,' Margot murmured. 'Very nice.'

We sat, drinking our brandies and watching the scene, which was almost as bright as day. Traffic roared along the Avenue. Passers-by, chatting in a variety of languages, looked at us with mild curiosity, which we returned in kind. A sudden breeze rustled through the ornamental shrubs that formed a demarcation between the drinkers and the strollers, and rattled the awning above our heads.

As if at some signal two limousines drew up directly outside Colette's. Like twins their respective chauffeurs slid from their seats, opened the rear doors of their cars and stood to attention. A party of ten, escorted by the *maître d'* and a flurry of waiters, emerged from the restaurant and walked in leisurely fashion along the path to the limousines. There were two black Africans, majestic in their native robes, two whites in dinner jackets, probably Americans, four extremely beautiful and elegantly-dressed girls, also white, and two hulking black bodyguards in European lounge suits. They got into the cars without any fuss – everyone knew his or her place – and were driven away.

'Who were they, Piers?'

'At a guess a Trade Mission, pretty important, being shown the town by some local representatives.'

'Lovely robes they were wearing.'

'And lovely brown, liquid eyes, that stripped you down, I noticed.'

Margot laughed, mocking me. 'Don't tell me you were jealous?' Then sharply she added: 'Piers, what is it?'

'Nothing, darling.'

But I motioned towards the pavement. A woman was bending over a child who lolled, drooling at the mouth, in one of those canvas and aluminium wheelchairs. She seemed to be tucking a rug round his legs. I couldn't see too clearly. They were standing in a patch of shadow.

'It reminds you of Johnny?'

'Yes.'

'My love, you did all you could for him. Don't let it nag you.' Margot put her hand on my thigh. 'Shall we go home or shall we have another brandy?'

'Home.'

'Okay. But I must have a pee first.'

Margot disappeared into the interior of the restaurant. I called the waiter, paid the bill, got my change. It had been a good evening, not sensational but very pleasant. I yawned. I was tired.

The woman with the child was coming back again. I watched with pity as she retraced her steps. She was slight of build and pushed the wheelchair with difficulty, her shoulders bent, her head down. As she came level with the path that led between the two blocks of tables and chairs to the entrance to the restaurant, she paused. For an instant I thought she was going to turn in, perhaps to beg from group to group. But suddenly she straightened her shoulders, lifted her head and looked directly at me.

Several things happened simultaneously. They happened fast, though I had the impression that they unrolled in some unnatural form of slow motion. A waiter bustled out of the restaurant and down the path, as if to tell the woman with the wheelchair to go away. The child, who seemed to be clutching something to his chest, tossed aside the rug covering his legs and raised his right arm; it was the same threatening attitude as Murasaki's in the tunnel at Charles de Gaulle.

The boy threw whatever he was holding – not a knife but a black, pear-shaped object. He aimed it straight at me. It was a good shot, but fractionally misjudged. I think he was distracted by the sudden appearance of the waiter. In any case the object hit the tray the waiter was carrying and was deflected, away from me and towards the tables on the other side of the path.

I flung myself to the ground, seeking what protection there

was from the base of the glass-fronted building, and pulling the table at which we had been sitting down on top of me. Everything seemed to be collapsing. I remember thinking that Margot should be safe inside the restaurant and praying that she was still in the cloakroom. Then I felt a dull blow on the side of the head, and blacked out.

The whole film had taken the time between two sips of brandy . . .

I groped my way back to reality. I hadn't been out more than a few seconds. The big wind had subsided but somewhere nearby Japanese lanterns were tinkling, tinkling. I tried to move and winced as sharpness cut into my flesh. I opened my eyes but the dark remained opaque. I couldn't see. I was blind.

I fought my rising panic, biting my lip until I tasted blood. Something was pressing down on me, smothering me, a rough sort of blanket – which, of course, was why I couldn't see. I felt it harsh against my skin, canvas – the awning in front of Colette's. Memory returned in a rush. And now I was aware of horror around me.

There was crying, screaming, groaning, dreadful animal noises – and a great shattering of glass as a window belatedly fell out. With extreme caution, my eyes tight shut, I managed to push away some of the stuff from my face and, slitting open my eyelids, looked upwards. Thank God, there was nothing wrong with my sight.

Not that I could see much. I was wedged tightly against the bottom of the building between a wooden tub containing plants and a table that had acted as a metal shield against the blast. And on top of this were folds and folds of awning. I struggled with it as if it were a monster. Indeed, it was a monster since it was covered with glass. It was this, raining down, that had reminded me, half-conscious, of Japanese lanterns tinkling in a breeze. Now every time I moved, however little, splinters of glass pricked me, sliced me, embedded themselves in me, but I went on struggling. I had to get free, to get to Margot.

Concentrating on my own problem, I was not unaware that help had arrived. Amid the cries of pain were other sounds, encouraging, practical sounds. There was the wail of an ambulance, police whistles, and close to me a voice with a Boston accent said:

'Let me look. I won't hurt you. I'm a doctor.'

And another voice, high with fear, said: 'Help me. Please help me. I can't move this bloody thing and he's under here somewhere. He must be.'

It was Margot. Purged with relief that she was relatively unharmed, I called to her, warning her to be careful of the glass, and heard the hysteria in her response. It wasn't until afterwards that I realized how badly she had already lacerated her hands trying to reach me.

Seconds later the weight that had been pinning me down was pulled aside and I was helped to stand. Apart from bruises and a multiplicity of small cuts I was whole. It was more than could be said of some of the poor devils lying around. The front of Colette's was a shambles, especially on the other side of the entrance where the waiter had chanced to redirect the bomb. Dead and dying and injured – many fewer, thank God, than there would have been if the place had been anything like full – lay in a tangle of what had once been a café. And everywhere was glass; it was responsible for most of the injuries.

'Piers, let's go. Let's get out of here. They don't need us to help.'

I nodded. I couldn't trust myself to speak. I had just seen a hand, a woman's hand with rings on the fingers. It lay by itself, severed at the wrist. Choking down bile I leaned on Margot, pulling her to me so that she shouldn't see the ghastly thing. Together we stumbled into the restaurant.

'What about the automobile?'

'No. Let's leave it.'

The Renault was probably undamaged, but it would be hemmed in by police cars, fire trucks, ambulances. Anyhow it didn't seem right that we should simply get in and drive away. We went through the restaurant where some of the less injured were sitting or lying on the banquettes, through the kitchens and along a laneway into a quiet back street. Nobody spoke to us or looked at us twice.

I took off my jacket, took the things out of the pockets and shook it. Glass tinkled into the gutter. I turned out my trouser pockets. I loosened my tie and flapped my shirt. I inspected my shoes. That was the best I could do for the moment. I could still feel a thousand pinpricks of glass. Margot, leaning against a plane tree, suddenly vomited, and I did the same.

Then we walked on, our arms around each other, uncertainly, like drunks, until at last we picked up a taxi that took us to the Rue de Longchamp.

# Chapter 6

The DST man was admirably efficient. He gave us one look and went into action. He hadn't any doubt about his priorities. Throwing short, sharp questions at me he got clear what had happened and assured himself that we were in no immediate danger. Then he picked up the telephone.

I was too concerned about Margot to listen to what he was saying. Some form of delayed shock had hit her while we were in the taxi and she had begun to shake. Now she sat, slumped in an armchair, quivering. Fat tears rolled down her cheeks and when I made to leave her for a minute she clung to me.

'Stay with me, Piers. Please, stay!'

'Darling, I'll only be a second.'

I kissed her and freed myself. As I dashed into the bedroom the DST man shouted at me not to switch on any lights unless the shutters were closed. I pulled the cover off the bed and seized the duvet as the best thing available to keep Margot warm. Tripping over it in my haste, I ran back and started tucking it around her. She cried out when I accidentally touched one of her poor, lacerated hands.

The DST man covered the receiver. 'Put on the kettle, monsieur. Make hot sweet tea for mademoiselle – and for yourself.'

'She needs a doctor. Ask them to send one.'

'I've already done so. He's on his way.'

The doorbell rang – three short, well-defined rings – as I was coaxing Margot to sip the tea, which she disliked and didn't want to drink. The DST man brought in the new arrivals. Le Gaillard was his usual imperturbable self; he might have anticipated just this situation. The doctor, whom I had last seen at the Rosemeads' apartment shaking his head over Jean and Johnny, looked as if he had been roused from a deep sleep and resented the fact.

To my annoyance they were both extremely formal, shaking my hand, bowing to Margot, making polite conversation – wasting time when the doctor could have been attending to his patient. But my annoyance evaporated rapidly when I saw the result of their treatment. Margot was making a visible effort to respond. She finished her tea and began to think of her appearance.

'I must be a frightful sight. Piers, my purse. Where – where is it?'

I frowned. I couldn't recall seeing Margot's purse since she had gone to the cloakroom at Colette's. Either she had left it there when the bomb exploded or she had put it down in her attempts to pull the awning off me.

'Darling, you don't need it.'

'You mean it's lost? But it's got all my things – passport, keys, travellers' cheques, make-up. Did I leave it in the taxi?'

'No. It's probably at Colette's.'

'Mademoiselle, you mustn't worry,' the doctor intervened. 'It will be found for you. Monsieur Le Gaillard will arrange everything. Now, please, may I look at your hands?'

The doctor opened his black bag and became very professional. Le Gaillard drew me away. He also had work to do.

'Monsieur Tyburn, you are convinced that the bomb at Colette's was intended for you?'

I must have looked my surprise, but I didn't put it into words. Le Gaillard never asked pointless questions. Instead, I explained precisely what had happened – or as precisely as I could considering that my head was throbbing and I was feeling inordinately tired.

'If it hadn't been deflected by the waiter could the bomb have gone straight through the doors into the restaurant, monsieur?'

'Possibly.'

'You've heard of President Kanudin, of course?'

'Yes, I – Good Lord! We saw him – and his entourage. That was Kanudin?'

'Yes. He dined at Colette's and left shortly before the

explosion. It could have been an assassination attempt. Kanudin's said to be popular but rulers of his kind are always vulnerable. And it would make more sense than the Sons of Orion trying to kill you at this particular moment, wouldn't it, Monsieur Tyburn?'

'I suppose so, but – ' I stopped. I was sure there were cogent reasons against a Kanudin theory, but I couldn't think of them. My mind wasn't functioning very well. 'I still believe they meant it for me.'

Le Gaillard smiled slightly. 'Oddly enough, so do I, Monsieur Tyburn. But the man – he wasn't a boy and he and his companion were both Japanese – said they were hired to assassinate Kanudin.'

'You've caught them?'

'There was a gun battle and they were shot. The woman was killed instantly. The man has been taken to the prison hospital.' Le Gaillard gave his little shrug. 'However, monsieur, we mustn't waste any more time. I hope to take advantage of the situation, and I propose to move you and Mademoiselle Ninian immediately to the safety of your Embassy.'

'The Embassy? You mean the Residence? But – '

'If you stay openly in Paris much longer you will be dead, I am sure. If you go away, the Sons of Orion will suspect Sir Timothy, and our hopes of a counter-coup against the *Rengo Sekigun* will be nullified. But if it appears that you were killed tonight at Colette's – it's a piece of luck mademoiselle left her purse there – then, Monsieur Tyburn, you will be out of danger and no harm will be done to our plans.' He permitted himself to pat me gently on the shoulder. 'It's only for a day or two, monsieur.'

I could think of several reasons why I didn't want to 'die', even for a day or two, not least the shock it would be for my parents, but somehow I couldn't bring myself to argue with Le Gaillard. Besides, the doctor was making signals; he would want Margot put to bed as soon as possible.

'Pack a few things, monsieur. Not a razor or anything like that. It's important we don't suggest you've been back here. Please hurry.'

In the bedroom I wiped the sweat off my forehead. I found myself considering each article I packed with exaggerated care. Margot's belongings, of course, were more difficult than mine, and I was wondering whether she would prefer to have her sketch pad or an extra skirt when Le Gaillard came in and vetoed both. He also checked everything else I had put in.

'Come along, Monsieur Tyburn. The sooner we leave the better.'

Margot gave me a loving smile when I returned to the living-room, but she was almost asleep on her feet. The doctor and the DST man had to support her into the lift. Le Gaillard carried the bags and with a bit of effort I managed to fit myself in. We went down to the basement.

In the garage was a large Renault, indistinguishable from any private car, in which Le Gaillard and the doctor had arrived. Beside it stood the other DST man and Le Gaillard's driver, a young attractive woman. Margot was helped into the back where, sitting between me and Le Gaillard, she promptly let her head fall on his shoulder and went to sleep. The doctor got in the front.

Against my will my own head was nodding, and before we turned into the Avenue Charles de Gaulle my heavy eyelids drooped and I was asleep too. From time to time I surfaced enough to be conscious of a murmur of conversation but I didn't come fully awake until we had passed through the gates of the Residence. The Renault stopped. And, as the car door was opened, the cold of the early morning air hit me like a physical blow. I began to shiver uncontrollably.

I managed to get out of the car by myself but I was glad of Le Gaillard's arm to steer me into the building. Chriswell was there to greet us. I gritted my teeth, trying to make my body behave normally, but I need not have bothered. Chriswell wasn't interested in my person. It was something else that interested him, as I soon realized. He could barely wait for us to reach the room that had been set aside as a temporary security centre before beginning to question me.

The doctor protested. He said I wasn't fit. He said he hadn't yet examined me but I was certainly suffering from shock and possible concussion and he refused to be responsible. He did his best for me, but we were in the Residence now and I knew he couldn't win. Le Gaillard knew it too and didn't waste his breath.

To put an end to the argument I said: 'I'm all right, thank you, doctor. What about Margot?'

'More than anything mademoiselle needs a good night's sleep. In the morning she will be well again – she's strong and healthy and only her hands will need attention.'

'My assistant, who drove us here, is also a trained nurse,' Le Gaillard said. 'She's putting mademoiselle to bed at this moment, and she'll stay with her all night. You need not worry for her, Monsieur Tyburn.'

'Thanks.'

I had managed to subdue my shivering at last and, though I would have liked to know which room Margot was in, I was content enough. It couldn't take long to tell Chriswell what had happened and once he had satisfied his curiosity I hoped that I, like Margot, could sleep and sleep and sleep. Just the thought of it made me yawn prodigiously.

I should have known better. Unfortunately my brain was functioning minus a cog or two and it took me some while to realize that neither Chriswell nor Le Gaillard cared a damn about how I'd nearly been killed. What was important to them was why. And if Chriswell's questioning had been severe before it was mild to what he did to me now. He put me through a squeezer until every drop of juice had been extracted.

The result was a big round nothing.

'I do not understand it!' Chriswell said, after a string of oaths which Le Gaillard obviously found offensive. 'Why should they want Tyburn dead? Why should they think he's a danger to them? It's not because of that cassette. It's surely not because they don't trust H.E. to make him toe the line. There must be another reason. Tyburn must know something he hasn't told us – unless of course it was a fantastic chance and the bomb was meant for that bloody President.'

A telephone rang. Chriswell picked up the receiver, listened, grunted and passed it to Le Gaillard. Le Gaillard listened, making little humming noises at intervals, and returned the receiver to Chriswell, who replaced it. To me they both seemed larger than life, figures that grew big, black-outlined, and then receded. I was feeling very odd.

'. . . so that's a possibility we can rule out,' Le Gaillard said. 'President Kanudin was not the intended victim. The Sons of Orion wouldn't undertake his assassination and this operation against the British Embassy at the same time. And in spite of his denials there's no doubt that the bomber was one of the Sons. His unconscious gave him away all right.'

'What?'

'For Christ's sake, Piers! Haven't you been listening?'

Le Gaillard frowned at me, puzzled. 'Monsieur, I was explaining. When the bomber lapsed into unconsciousness he talked of becoming a star on Orion's Belt. Nobody fully understands the *Rengo Sekigun* and their motivation, but it's part of their mystique that when they die they are assumed into the heavens.'

'So we're back where we were. You, Piers, know something that could ruin these buggers' plans for Thursday night. My God, right now it's tomorrow night! And whatever we may guess we still know damn all about their intentions. Come on. Let's start again. Julian Rosemead unexpectedly invited you to dinner – '

'No.'

'What do you mean – no?'

Chriswell leaned across his desk. His face was huge and seemed to be growing bigger. I opened my mouth to cry out, to ask Le Gaillard for help. Then Chriswell resumed his normal size. I wiped a hand across my forehead; it was damp with sweat.

I said, with great care because my tongue was large and dry and somehow unmanageable: 'Last week the Sons of Orion had plenty of opportunity to kill me, but clearly they didn't want to. Between Friday and Sunday they changed their mind or something changed it for them. I haven't the faintest idea what.'

'Let's start with the weekend, then. Friday – what happened

on Friday?'

Chriswell had decided to alter his size again. He was growing big once more, and hurriedly I turned to Le Gaillard. This was a mistake. Seated on my side of the desk, he was nearer to me and loomed, closer and more menacing. Besides, my movement had upset the balance of the room. The walls began to tilt. The floor was coming up, was going to hit me.

My voice said: 'How should I know? Friday I went to the UK to spend the weekend with my family.'

And as I fell into space the room collapsed about me.

I forced my way back to reality through folds and folds of canvas that were threatening to smother me; the awning from Colette's was engulfing my bed. Because I was in bed, in a strange room I had never seen before, and it was morning. Daylight was shining brightly through the thin curtains.

Gradually my mind cleared and I raised myself on my elbows to look about me. I was in a sort of attic, furnished with what must have been cast-offs from some child's nursery. But it wasn't my own past; I felt no nostalgia. I knew that I was in an infrequently-used room in a corner of the Residence and that today was Wednesday, the day the Prime Minister and Foreign Secretary would arrive in Paris. In the circumstances I could scarcely resent relegation to such quarters. I was lucky to be given house-room.

From my surroundings I turned my attention to myself. I had already seen my over-night bag standing beside a dilapidated old rocking-horse. Now I realized I was wearing pyjamas. Before putting me to bed someone had undressed me. I had also been cleaned of glass splinters, had my small cuts treated and a dressing fixed to the back of my head. I touched it tentatively. It felt very tender; so did my face. But otherwise I wasn't in bad shape.

There was a tap at the door and it opened slowly. Of all the visitors I might have expected Lady Paverton was the last. But there she stood, immaculately groomed and wearing a beautifully-tailored silk suit. She could have been dressed for a formal luncheon. In fact she was ready to go to Charles de

Gaulle to welcome the PM and His Nibs when they flew in at noon. Before that, however, she had a couple of distinctly unusual duties to perform.

'Good morning, Piers. How are you?'

'Good morning, Lady Paverton. I'm almost as good as new, thank you – and hungry.'

She laughed. I slid out of bed and took the tray that a security man had carried for her. Then I wondered what to do with it; there wasn't a bedside table. I bent to put it on the floor, and was at once conscious of the gaping front of my pyjama trousers. Lady Paverton produced a wooden chair.

'It's the longest time since I've been in this part of the Residence, but I think the bathroom's along there on your left, Piers, if you want to wash,' she said. 'But please be quick.'

Blessing her for her thoughtfulness, I hurried as much as I could. Annoyingly, even this amount of exertion made me sweat and forced me to accept that I was decidedly fragile. I went back to the bedroom hoping nobody would expect much of me during the day ahead.

'I'm sorry to harry you, Piers, but I've a very tight schedule. You eat breakfast while I talk.'

I sat on the edge of the bed and did as I was told. It was an excellent breakfast, fresh orange juice, bacon and eggs, *croissants* and a gallon of best Brazilian coffee. Lady Paverton leaned on the window ledge. She was taut but not edgy.

'It's ten of nine now. If you can be ready by about twenty after we'll go to the hospital. You mustn't be seen – '

'The hospital? Margot. Oh God, she's not – '

'No, no, no!' Lady P sounded both impatient and amused. 'Margot's fine. Still fast asleep, bless her. I'm talking about Jean Rosemead. You knew she asked to see you. It seems an unnecessary risk, I know, since you're supposed to be dead, and the doctor doesn't think you're well enough, but Tom Chriswell and Monsieur Le Gaillard believe that a chat with Jean might call to mind whatever it is you're supposed to have forgotten.'

I suppressed a groan. It was depressing that Chriswell and Le Gaillard were concentrating so hard on me; it had to mean they were making no progress in other directions. The whole affair would probably end in a stalemate, the Sons of Orion frustrated but precious little else achieved.

'We have to be back by half after ten when the *Murasaki et Fils* representatives arrive. Tom Chriswell wants you to get a look at them in case you recognize them and I have to be here to show them around.' Lady Paverton sighed. 'It's been decided that unless we've found out exactly what the Sons of Orion are planning, we'll have to call off the PM's banquet first thing tomorrow. And that will be a disaster. It'll give the whole game away. They'll know we've been deceiving them all along.'

'Is – is there any news of Paul?'

'Nothing definite. The British believe they know which house he's being kept in. They'll act when they get word from this end. But it's no use kidding ourselves. It'll be a miracle if Paul comes out of this alive.'

'Miracles do happen, Lady Paverton.'

'That's what my husband says, but I don't have his faith or courage.' Abruptly she pushed herself away from the window-sill and glanced at her watch. 'Someone'll come and collect you in fifteen minutes. Okay, Piers?'

It was a rush but I made it. The breakfast had been a big help and Lady Paverton's stoic calm was oddly bracing. A security man, whom I remembered from last night, took me downstairs and bundled me into the Rolls. Folding my length into as small a space as possible I sat on the floor, while he draped a rug over me. Then the car drew away from the side door and parked, I guessed, in front of the main entrance to the Residence. I didn't have to guess about the elegant pair of legs that tucked themselves beside me. Lady Paverton was about to pay a duty call.

Half way to the hospital I was allowed to remove the rug, which was a relief; being smothered by the awning outside Colette's had made me somewhat claustrophobic. But I had to stay on the floor. Even in a Rolls this isn't the most comfortable way to travel. By the time we arrived I was feeling slightly sick, and when I got out of the car my steps were unsteady. I was grateful for the pressure of Lady P's hand on my elbow, hastening me into the building.

Once in Jean's room, however, all concern for myself vanished. Jean lay back against the pillows, her bloodless face shadowed with grey, her hair dank from old sweat, her hands on the coverlet like discarded bits of paper. She was wearing an operating gown, which can have done nothing for her morale, and I wondered that nobody had thought to send her a night-dress. We were alone, except for a nurse in the corner – a DST woman who also acted as a guard.

Jean must have sensed my presence because her blue-veined lids trembled and her eyes opened, slowly, as if it were an effort. For a moment they were blank. Then, recognizing me, she smiled. I bent and kissed her.

'Piers!'

Her voice was scarcely audible. I pulled a chair close to the bed so that she didn't have to strain to make herself heard, and sat down. I took her hand – the skin was dry and brittle – and she let it lie passively in mine.

'Jean, dear, I won't ask how you are. The doctors say you're going to get well, and that's all that matters.'

Her mouth twisted. 'Julian's dead – and Johnny.'

She didn't elaborate. And what could I say? No one had told me what was expected of this meeting – except that it might dredge some vital but forgotten fact from my memory – and such advice as I had received had been contradictory. The doctor who had met us and had discreetly escorted Lady Paverton away, had said I mustn't tire Jean or let her talk much. The nurse had seemed to think that Jean needed to talk, to get the horror of what had happened out of her system. I decided to compromise.

'Jean, I won't be allowed to stay long because of tiring you. Is there anything you need at the moment, anything I can do for you?'

'No – thank you. I just want to know the truth, why Julian and Johnny were killed – what for, Piers. You understand, don't you? Nobody will tell me what's been going on.'

I told her, very briefly – about the Sons of Orion, the attempt to blackmail H.E., the significance of the cassette and the threatened coup at the PM's banquet tomorrow night. She didn't ask for details. She knew now all that she needed to know.

'. . . Julian died bravely and honourably. The authorities appreciate that, Jean. You can be proud of him, as I'm sure you're proud of Johnny. Johnny died trying to protect you, didn't he?'

'Yes. One of the men had hit me and he was going to hit me again. He threatened Johnny with his gun but Johnny went for him all the same. My poor fool of a son,' she blinked away her tears. 'He didn't understand about guns.'

The nurse coughed gently. I had forgotten she was there. When I glanced in her direction she pointed to her watch and held up her hand, fingers spread. I had five minutes left.

'I'm glad you were with Johnny when he died,' Jean said. 'He liked you, Piers. You were "Da's friend". Was he very – afraid?'

'No, I don't think so,' I lied. 'Most of the time he was unconscious. He wanted you, of course, and Julian. He kept on asking for you both, especially you.' I smiled at her and pushed back my chair. 'Jean, I must go – '

'Not yet. Tell me everything about – Johnny.'

I swallowed a sigh. I wasn't sure if she really wanted to know or if she just wanted me to stay. Either way I was caught.

'There isn't much to tell. Although it seemed ages before the doctor came, in fact it was only a very short while. Johnny died very quickly, and without too much pain.'

'Go on.'

I thought bitterly of the lurid newspaper account of Johnny dying in my arms that I had read at Heathrow. The reality was less melodramatic, but much less pleasant.

'I sat beside him and held his hand. He was asking for you and Julian, as I said, and his Gran. And at one point, I remember, he talked about Mike. Perhaps he thought he was at Bagatelle.'

'Perhaps. He – he loved that peacock.'

'He was confused, Jean, rambling. He didn't know what was happening to him. But he recognized me. The – the last thing he said was: "Take care, Da's friend." '

'But you didn't heed him, did you? Your face is all bruised.'

'I fell down the steps in front of St Augustin . . .'

The nurse interrupted us. 'Madame, it's time that monsieur left. You're tired. You must rest.'

Jean didn't protest. Her eyes were closing and her cheeks blue-shadowed; she looked exhausted. I placed the hand I had been holding back on the coverlet and she let it lie there. I kissed her goodbye.

'You'll come again, Piers?' It was the merest whisper. 'And bring Margot?'

'I promise. And as soon as you can travel, you're going to England to stay with my parents. It was Mother's invitation and I accepted for you.'

Her eyes widened in amazement. 'But – I can't. It would be an – an imposition.'

I shook my head. 'Nonsense. Julian and I were old friends. Of course you must stay with the family.'

I spoke with complete sincerity and it wasn't until I was once more sitting at Lady Paverton's feet in the Rolls that I appreciated the sardonic amusement with which my 'old friend' Julian would have greeted my remarks. The joke was on me, and it left a sour taste.

# Chapter 7

And now it was Thursday, though still very early. I tossed and turned in my uncomfortable bed. I thought about yesterday. It was impossible to sleep.

Returning to the Residence, I had been made to hide in an alcove on the ground floor, like some Polonius behind a curtain, and wait until Lady Paverton came past with the representatives of *Murasaki et Fils*. It was a waste of time. I had never seen either of them before.

The elderly man was Monsieur Murasaki himself. I heard him apologizing in French for the absence of his sons; one was recovering, he said, from a vicious attack at Charles de Gaulle airport and, most unfortunately, the other had been unable to come. While I guessed at what number two might be doing, Monsieur Murasaki hastened to assure Lady Paverton that there was no problem; his daughter-in-law, the wife of his son in hospital, was unrivalled in expertise as an interior decorator and was also fluent in English, a language she and his sons were accustomed to speak amongst themselves.

I looked at the daughter-in-law. She was ignoring the compliments being paid to her; presumably she was busy making a mental film of everything in sight. She was a little older than the girl in the yellow trouser-suit, but not less attractive – except for the small neat smirk stitched on her small neat mouth. I took an instant dislike to her.

When Lady P and her party had gone by, one of the security chaps rescued me from the alcove and brought me upstairs to Margot, who had been given a room similar to mine, though somewhat better furnished. Margot was happy to see me, of course, but she was still sedated and, after lunch, wanted only to sleep. I stretched myself out on the chaise-longue. I was tired, but on edge. I yearned to know what was going on.

Dinner came and went. The doctor paid us a call. Margot and I hadn't been totally forgotten, but it seemed we were no longer of any interest. At ten I kissed her goodnight – she was again half asleep – and went to my own room. A while later, as I was getting into bed after what had turned out to be a very frustrating day, Le Gaillard arrived. He sat on my hard wooden chair and told me what had happened.

The Murasaki woman, as soon as she was alone with Lady P, had given her the terrorists' instructions. They had been precise and explicit. With the enforced help of H.E. and Lady Paverton the Sons of Orion would infiltrate the Residence. Then, at the banquet, they would seize the President of France and the British and French Prime Ministers, and hold them as hostages until specific prisoners were released, a huge ransom paid and arrangements for their own get-away ensured. The pattern was classical – it was what the British Security Service and the French DST had suspected from the beginning – but its success would have constituted a real achievement. As it was, thanks to H.E.'s courage and integrity, the plan had always been doomed to failure.

I thought of our counter-measures, that Le Gaillard had told me about. Some of the Sons of Orion would probably escape the DST net and Paul Paverton's chances were slim, but if everything went well for us the *Rengo Sekigun* would be dealt a decisive blow as far as its European operations were concerned. If everything went well . . .

I plumped up my pillow and made another effort to get comfortable in the over-short bed. In a very few hours the Sons of Orion would be going into action. So would the DST and the British. My heartbeat quickened. It was impossible to sleep . . .

At eight o'clock the security man arrived with breakfast. He was a pleasant chap and accepted his nursemaid duties as part of his job. He even drew the curtains to let in the early morning sunshine.

Without conscious thought, I said: 'Would you tell Tom

Chriswell that I must speak to him?'

'I will, but he's pretty busy, sir. Could I perhaps give him a message?'

'Tell him I can't stay here all day not knowing what's going on. I hope he can use me in some way. There must be something I can do. I don't mind what.'

'I'll give him the message. I'll find you in Miss Ninian's room, shall I?'

I nodded and began my breakfast. Time was running short. A large cabinet and a chest were due to be delivered to the Residence by *Murasaki et Fils* at nine-thirty. They would get past the security checks unsearched, on Lady Paverton's say-so, and were to be placed as directed and left untouched. In fact, they contained the terrorists and their weapons. Later, the actual coup would be facilitated by certain orders that H.E. had been directed to give.

It was a simple plan, as Le Gaillard had said, but whoever had devised it would be confident of its success. The Sons of Orion had had their troubles – with Julian and the cassette and with me – but those were behind them now. The Pavertons were cooperating nicely. The Murasaki woman must have thought she had every reason to smirk.

Chriswell and Le Gaillard were equally confident, though they were still puzzled as to why the Sons of Orion wanted me dead and why, at this stage of the affair, Madame Murasaki should have troubled to lie about it. Yesterday she had gone out of her way to deny any responsibility for my 'death'. She had assured Lady Paverton that the bomb at Colette's was the work of some unknown Japanese mercenaries paid to assassinate President Kanudin, and nothing to do with the Sons of Orion. That she had bothered to tell such a lie compounded the mystery.

I hurried to get dressed, and went along to Margot. She was sitting up in bed, reading the *Herald Tribune*. Her hands were bandaged but otherwise she looked quite recovered – and more beautiful and desirable than ever.

She passed me the newspaper. 'It's horrible, Piers. Worse – worse than I realized. They must have needed your death really badly.'

I glanced at the article with the photograph of President Kanudin, resplendent in his national costume. The number of people killed and maimed was horrendous. Several of them had been important or even distinguished, a French politician, an Italian actress, a party of high-powered American businessmen – and the talented young portrait painter, Margot Ninian. Only the celebrities were mentioned by name; I was referred to simply as 'a British diplomat'. Some of the bodies had not yet been identified.

'Darling – ' I began, and stopped.

It was all horror. And there weren't any words. I sat on the bed, took Margot in my arms and looked surreptitiously at my watch; it was ten minutes to nine. The security man was far more embarrassed than I when he interrupted us.

'Sir, Mr Chriswell said you can come.'

'Thank you.'

He took me along to Chriswell's temporary security centre, where the number of telephones seemed to have doubled overnight. The air was thick with cigarette smoke and suppressed excitement. Chriswell himself looked as ghastly as he had the morning after the supposed binge with his old chum. Anxiety hit me.

'Has something gone wrong, Tom?'

'Not as far as I know. At this moment *Murasaki et Fils* are moving the furniture into the Residence. Each piece is being put precisely where that Murasaki bitch said it should go. We'll move it later.'

'How much later?'

'When the VIPs have gone to the Elysée Palace and the Jap delivery men have left. Then we'll see what we've caught.'

'Meanwhile we just wait?'

'We do, yes – because we're responsible for the Residence. But Le Gaillard and his DST chaps are rounding up anyone faintly connected with the Sons of Orion and the poor old Brits are trying to rescue Paul Paverton. So there's no dearth of action elsewhere.'

Chriswell left his vantage place at the window overlooking

the courtyard and went back to his desk. He opened a drawer and took out a gun. He held it out to me.

'Do you know how to use one of these?'

'Yes, but I don't guarantee to hit my target.'

'When in doubt, aim at the stomach. You can scarcely miss the bugger that way.'

He went back to the window and, making sure the safety-catch was on, I slid the gun into my trouser pocket. As a boy I had potted the odd rabbit and I had a rudimentary knowledge of firearms, but I couldn't conceive of myself killing anyone. Or could I? I thought of Johnny Rosemead.

After a while Chriswell said: 'There they go, our political masters. Christ, what a life! Never knowing whether you're going to be assassinated or kidnapped or have rotten eggs thrown at you.' He laughed abruptly, seeing nothing ironic in his remark.

We were half way to the door when the telephone rang. The operator held up his hand. He listened with a dead-pan expression, which made it impossible for us to anticipate 'good' or 'bad'. We waited.

'Ta,' he said at last, and put down the receiver. He grinned at us, exposing very pink gums. 'They've got young Paverton, sir – alive, though in poor physical shape. His captors cleared out over the weekend. They left him tied to a bed without food or water. But the doc says there's no need to worry. The boy's come through amazingly well and there shouldn't be any lasting effects.'

'Well, I'm damned! Who'd have believed it? But – like father, like son,' Chriswell murmured to himself; and to the operator: 'That's splendid. Try to catch Sir Timothy before he goes into the conference, will you? If not, see he gets a message. And make sure Lady Paverton's informed. Understand?' He turned to me. 'Let's hope it's a good omen.'

'Of course it is,' I said. My spirits soared. Lady P had been wrong; miracles still happened. 'It's the best news for days.'

Chriswell grunted. 'We can't expect a hundred per cent success. If Le Gaillard and the DST take in the three Murasakis and their lieutenants and we don't have too much difficulty with the bunch of devils we've got here, we'll be lucky. In fact, we'll chalk up one hell of a victory. It'll be something to celebrate tonight, Piers.'

By the look of him I thought he was more likely to be fast asleep than celebrating, but I didn't say so. We had arrived in the dining-room where the staff should already have been laying the long tables for the PM's banquet. Instead there was a most extraordinary scene. Men in their shirt-sleeves were heaving and sweating to get a red-lacquered cabinet on to a low trolley, in order to trundle it from the room. Another man watched them, his gun drawn, his eyes unwavering even when Chriswell spoke to him.

'You've shifted the other thing?'

'Yes. It wasn't so heavy. This is the worst.'

'Will it go through the door?'

'Should do. We measured. If not, we'll have to turn it lengthways. Maybe that would be a good idea anyhow. Shake the contents – before taking.'

Chriswell laughed but the man with the gun didn't twitch a muscle. Probably he was kind to animals and small children, but he scared me. I was glad he was on our side.

'Come on, Piers,' Chriswell said. 'I'll show you the scene.'

The scene was in an ante-room, little more than a large passageway. The occasional furniture that normally stood about in it had been removed. Pictures had been taken from the walls – you could see the dirty marks on the paper – and the two windows boarded on the inside. The chandelier had been replaced by a row of floodlights.

Parallel with one wall lay a black-lacquered chest guarded by another unblinking man. It was a modern piece and had almost certainly been made for the occasion, but it was beautifully proportioned and great care had been taken with the carving and ornamentation. The handles, shaped like serpents, were especially attractive. I wouldn't have minded owning it myself.

I had barely time to take in the other objects in the room, a sort of metal screen, some bales of hay and what looked like a couple of old mattresses, when the trolley bearing the large cabinet appeared from the dining-room. In spite of the efforts of the men surrounding it, the trolley moved slowly and unevenly, its wheels sticking in the pile of the carpet. As it came through the door the cabinet swayed and for an awful moment I thought it was going to fall. But they managed to steady it – not, however, before there was a sharp, stifled cry from inside.

Chriswell nodded his head with satisfaction. 'Hurry it up if you can. This place will have to be back to normal for tonight, and it'll need a clean after we've finished.'

They did their best but it took several minutes before the cabinet was standing beside the chest. It was, I now realized, an even finer piece than the other, and more elaborately decorated. The doors were of particular interest. They seemed to join in a fall of stars, presumably intended to represent Orion's Belt. Chriswell was fascinated by it too.

'We'll start with that one,' he said.

But we weren't ready to start yet. The gap between the wall and the two pieces of furniture was first filled with bundles of hay. More hay and mattresses were propped on either side of the cabinet. The metal screen was moved behind the row of lights, which were turned on so that both cabinet and chest were floodlit. The men who had been acting as furniture movers now dressed themselves in helmets and flak-jackets and produced shields. I was amazed at the precautions.

'Courtesy of the DST,' Chriswell said of the equipment and, seeing my expression, added: 'You diplomats don't know what it's all about, do you?'

'I'm learning,' I said dryly.

'Maybe you are at that.' He was suddenly sober. 'Look, chum, I don't anticipate trouble but you never know with these fanatics. Life means nothing to them. They could decide to blow us all sky-high. So, if you want out, just get. But if you want to stay, remember you asked for it.'

'I'll stay. What shall I do?'

Chriswell positioned his troops. I must admit I thought he made rather heavy weather of it. He assigned a man to either door of the room, and a third between the windows. The two original guards he placed behind the screen with me.

'They're crack shots, Piers. No need for you to be nervous,' he said. 'But keep your head down and watch through the slits.'

Obeying orders, I discovered I had an excellent view. And, though my pulse rate was high, I wasn't unduly nervous. I took the gun that Chriswell had given me from my pocket and released the safety-catch. It gave me added confidence, albeit spurious. I glanced at my watch; the time was twenty minutes past eleven.

In the Elysée Palace the Anglo-French talks had begun. At the end of the morning there would be champagne to celebrate the new *entente cordiale*, photographs and a press conference – all televised. After lunch there would be more talks and tonight the Prime Minister would entertain at the British Embassy. The VIPs were going to have a full day. I wondered if H.E. knew yet that his son was safe and if, when he heard the news, he spared a thought for what was happening here at his Residence.

Without any signal that I saw, Chriswell, wearing a helmet and flak-jacket, suddenly strode across the room and hit the door of the cabinet with the flat of his hand. He had large, beefy hands and the blow was delivered with as much force as he could muster. The effect on those inside the cabinet must have been shocking.

'Listen! And do what you're told!' Chriswell said, very loudly and clearly, in English. 'I shall say: one, two, three, out! And out you come, hands on top of heads, no weapons. Try any tricks and you're dead. If you understand, knock on the door panel.'

There was a pause, a susurration of sound and a sharp double rap. Chriswell had sprinted for the cover of the screen. He stuck his head over the top and shouted: 'Okay! One. Two . . .'

It was like a child's game, except that the Sons of Orion didn't keep to the rules. As Chriswell reached 'Three', the beautiful red doors were flung back on their hinges and five young Japanese, brandishing swords and screaming like Samurai warriors, leaped into the room. Instinctively my trigger finger tightened, but no attack materialized. The youths – they must all have been in their teens – blinded by the floodlights and finding no obvious enemy, were at a loss. Their sword arms drooped, their fierce cries subsided and they stood, blinking, in total disarray.

Chriswell, taking advantage of the moment, bellowed orders at them. 'Throw down your swords. Lie on your fronts, or you die. Hands clasped behind neck. Ankles crossed. Hurry!'

Four of them, in ragged disorder, started to obey. The fifth decided to be a hero. Teeth bared, he uttered a curious shout and sprang towards us. Two bullets with a single sound all but anticipated his intention. A hole flowered between his eyes and another in the middle of his chest. Only the impetus of his movement carried him to the foot of the screen.

His companions now lay in a neat line. They were as motionless as bits of board, and the sprays of red stars embroidered down the backs of their white jackets made me think of playing cards.

A security man emerged from his corner. Never letting himself obstruct the field of fire of the guns behind the screen, he manacled wrists and ankles. Then with a pull of his arm and a flick of his foot, not brutally but impersonally, he turned each youth on to his back and searched him.

'Nothing,' he said. 'Just a pack of kids with swords.' He sounded affronted.

'Get rid of them,' Chriswell ordered.

The four live Sons of Orion were heaped on the trolley. The dead hero was put in a sort of sack and also removed. This, it seemed to me, was done with extraordinary speed and efficiency but Chriswell, venting his irritation on his men, refused to be satisfied.

'Hurry it up!' he shouted at them. 'Hurry it up! We've not got all day to spend on this – this bloody hoax.'

'Hoax?' I said, startled. 'What do you mean?'

'I don't know! I wish to God I did. But I've a nasty feeling we're being led by the nose.'

He went across to the chest and glared at it. For a moment I thought he was going to kick it but, if that had been his in-

tention, he changed his mind. Instead he hoisted himself up
and sat on it, drumming his heels gently on its side.

'Could be the weapons are in here,' he said. 'The poor
bastards must have had something more than those goddam
swords, mustn't they?'

'Yes – I suppose so.'

'Suppose so? Piers, use your *nous*!' Chriswell swung himself
angrily off the chest and this time he did kick it, making a
brutal mark on the gloss of the lacquer. 'Look, chum, the Sons
of Orion – and don't be deceived by their fool name; remember
they're *Rengo Sekigun*, the Japanese Red Army – these Sons of
Orion have gone to immense trouble and taken great risks.
They've kidnapped Paul Paverton and killed indiscriminately.
Don't tell me they've done all this for fun. For Chrissakes,
Piers, these are the same people who master-minded the raid
at Lod Airport, who blew up the oil tank at Singapore, who – '

'All right, Tom! What are you getting at?'

He subsided like a pricked balloon. 'I don't know. I do not
understand. Those kids in the cabinet with swords! Not even a
grenade between them. And anyway they were so – so amateur-
ish! Can you see that lot leaping out of that cabinet and taking
hostages at the banquet tonight? Frankly I can't. The guests
would roar with laughter. They'd think it was some sort of
entertainment – a happening. But it's far from that. I'd stake
my life on it.' He shook his head slowly. 'Yes – what do you
want?'

The security man was holding out a bright, shining object
on a chain. 'We found this on the leader, sir, the boy we shot.
He was wearing it round his neck. It could be a key, though it's
an odd shape.'

Grunting his thanks, Chriswell took the shining bit of metal
and examined it carefully. 'Yes, it's a key right enough. It'll
be for the chest. Good. I was wondering how we were going to
open the blessed thing. Wouldn't do to blow the lock off if it's
stuffed with explosives, would it?'

'You think it might be?'

I stared at the beautiful, black-lacquered chest with a
mixture of curiosity, admiration and distaste. It was a very

fine piece of furniture. But I no longer coveted it. Although it was, in fact, too short and too deep I saw it now only as a coffin. And without warning I began to shake as I had done after my escape from the shambles at Colette's.

Chriswell gave me a hard look. 'No! I bloody well don't. I think the Sons of Orion have produced another funny ha-ha for us. Let's see what it is, shall we? Then, if we're not overcome with mirth, we can all go and have a drink.'

He strode angrily to the chest and, without any hesitation or precautions, thrust the bit of metal into the lock and turned it. There was a loud click. One of the security men shouted a warning, but it was too late. Tom Chriswell was grinning savagely when the booby-trap went off.

He died instantly. No one else was hurt.

# Chapter 8

It fell to me to tell Lady Paverton what had happened. Just as the Residence staff had been confined to their quarters and forbidden to go near the dining-room and its adjacent corridors, she and Margot had been told to spend the morning in Lady P's sitting-room, which was well-removed from the scene of operations. Until the last moment, Tom Chriswell had been very careful.

Lady P and Margot had heard nothing. The pistol shots had not been loud and the explosion small. When I went into the sitting-room I found them drinking champagne. They were watching television, the sound of which must have masked what noise there had been. They looked happy and relaxed.

'We were drinking to Paul,' Lady Paverton said. 'It's such marvellous news he's safe.'

'I – I'm very pleased for you and Sir Timothy, Lady Paverton.'

Margot heard the tightness in my voice. 'Piers! What's happening downstairs? What is it? What's wrong?'

Lady Paverton didn't wait for me to answer. She turned off the television sound, leaving the picture. The programme from the Elysée Palace hadn't begun yet, but the commentator was giving brief sketches of the VIPs. She poured me a neat whisky and thrust it into my hand.

'There you are, Piers. I'm sorry. I should have noticed. You look as if you need scotch more than champagne.'

She pointed to the sofa and I sat down beside Margot. I was grateful for the whisky. I drank half of it before I told them.

'Oh, poor Tom Chriswell!' Lady Paverton said. 'For God's sake! Why? Why would the Sons of Orion arrange such an elaborate set-up and then turn the whole thing into a – a kind of sick joke? It makes no sense.'

'But it must!' Margot said fiercely. 'It must. Maybe some of the Sons don't matter, but the Murasakis have taken a lot of personal risks. Presumably it was the two brothers who shot Jean and Johnny Rosemead, and one of them tried to kill Piers at the airport. Whatever this is about it has to be really important to them.'

I finished my whisky and began to walk about the room. I couldn't sit still. Margot was right. There had to be an acceptable, credible explanation.

I knew that Chriswell's second-in-command was trying to contact Le Gaillard; if anyone could make sense of this nonsense it was he, but I had little hope. Even if the DST had managed to grab the Murasakis – and by now I was so pessimistic that I was sure they had let them escape – I doubted we would get any information out of them. As for the Sons of Orion, some fairly rough treatment had made it clear that the youths who had leapt triumphantly from the red-lacquered cabinet had no information to give.

Reluctantly I faced the brutal truth. We were no nearer knowing the real aim of the *Rengo Sekigun* than we had been when Julian first produced his blackmail problem at La Perdrix d'Or on the Île de la Cité. Everything had led up to this extraordinary anticlimax.

I stopped dead in my tracks and stared at the picture on the television screen. I wasn't seeing the room at the Elysée where the cameras and equipment were being made ready for the press conference. I was thinking.

Was that what had been intended ? Were the British and the French meant to spend all their energies following a false trail? But that presupposed that H.E. had been expected to . . .

'There's Timothy,' Lady Paverton said, pointing at the screen.

And, as she turned up the sound, the announcer's voice supplemented my thoughts. 'The British Ambassador, Sir Timothy Paverton, who, during the years he has served in Paris, has done so much to make possible the new *entente cordiale* between France and the United Kingdom. His Excellency, a man well-known for his integrity and honest dealing . . .'

The key words were 'well-known'. I remembered the article on Lady Paverton I had clipped for Margot. Lady P had referred to her husband in terms that Margot had derided, but the fact remained. H.E. had a reputation for high principles.

'Suppose someone, someone with a devious mind, decided to take advantage of H.E.'s character,' I said. 'Suppose someone planned Paul Paverton's kidnapping not to blackmail H.E. but for a very different reason. Suppose the intention was to feed false information through H.E. to the British and French Security Services so that they concentrated all their attention on one place while the actual danger was elsewhere.'

'But – isn't there a snag to that?' Lady Paverton said.

I stared at her. I was scarcely aware that I had spoken aloud. 'What?'

'The somebody you're talking about would surely have planned this – this awful business at the Residence to coincide with the real attack. But that isn't what's happened. If you're right, Piers, they've given us an advance warning. And I can't believe they'd be as – as stupid as that.'

I didn't answer. On the television screen H.E. had been replaced by the French Ambassador to the Court of St James. I watched him blindly, my thoughts running like squirrels in a cage. I had already seen Lady Paverton's 'snag' and gone one stage beyond. And, as I tried to decide what to do, I let Margot put my fears into words.

Stammering in her sudden awareness of the danger, she pointed at the television. 'Wh – what's the use of a warning if it's only a question of minutes? You're still thinking of tonight's banquet, Lucy. But could be it's right now that matters. Perhaps – perhaps they've planted a bomb at the Elysée and it'll go off while – while thousands of people are watching on TV.'

'Oh God!' Lady Paverton said. 'No! Piers – '

'We may be wrong. I don't know,' I said, wishing she had someone other than myself to turn to. 'Listen, Lady Paverton, you and Margot go along to Chriswell's security room. Tell them what we've – we've guessed. If they're in touch with Le Gaillard, speak to him yourself. Warn him. But please – first, demand I be allowed to speak to Sir Timothy.'

'I will indeed. Margot – '

Margot had turned to me. In an involuntary gesture she held out her bandaged hands and then withdrew them. Our eyes met.

'You're going to the Elysée?'

'Darling – I must.'

'Of course.' She tossed back her dark hair and managed to laugh at herself. 'Okay, my love. But come back safely and I'll marry you. Lucy be my witness.'

'That's a promise. I'll keep you to it, darling.'

I kissed her hard on the mouth and ran. Behind me I heard the two women chorusing at me to take care. As I pounded down the corridor and took the stairs two at a time, a memory stirred faintly; Johnny Rosemead had told me to take care. 'Big bang, Da's friend. Take care.' And then some nonsense about Mike the peacock. I made an effort to clear my mind.

It was essential to get to H.E. and warn him. The responsibility would then be his; he could pass on my suppositions – and they were nothing more than suppositions – as he saw fit. At least he had the authority to ensure that the security people stayed alert. That was the best that could be done. The politicians would never agree to cancel their show, not now the cameras were on them. Why should they? They couldn't heed every vague warning.

Thankful that the Elysée Palace was only a stone's throw from the Embassy, I ran as fast as I could through the courtyard, past a startled guard at the gates of the Residence and along the Rue du Faubourg St Honoré. I had a sense of impending disaster. By the time I reached the Elysée my heart was pounding, my breath rasping in the back of my throat; after the events of the last few days I wasn't in very good shape. Nor was I exactly an imposing figure to demand an audience with the British Ambassador. I was wearing slacks and a sweater, suitable clothes for confronting terrorists but not for calling at the Elysée. And, if it hadn't been for Lady Paverton, I wouldn't have got across the threshold.

I was having a bitter, unproductive argument with two guards – the bitterness was all on my side since they were models of uncooperative politeness – when I heard my name called. Thanks to Lady P, help had appeared. The DST man who had been so efficient when Margot and I got back to the Rue de Longchamp after the bombing at Colette's greeted me like an old friend.

'Monsieur Tyburn, you wish to see your Ambassador at once. It's being arranged. Please come with me.' He gave me a sharp glance from under his beetling brows. 'Monsieur Le Gaillard should be here in a very few minutes. Meanwhile, have you any more to tell me?'

But there was nothing he didn't already know. Lady Paverton had been explicit and the DST was acting on the assumption that the danger was here and now, at the Elysée Palace.

'Naturally, monsieur, security is always tight at the Elysée and at the moment I would defy any unauthorized person to get in or out. Nonetheless,' he gave a shrug that could have been copied from Le Gaillard, 'I'm afraid we may not have done enough. These madmen who call themselves Sons of Orion are cleverer than we suspected. They've made us concentrate too much of our attention on the British.'

'Have you got the Murasakis?'

'The father, who is distraught – he is innocent, monsieur – and the two boys, who seem to be stricken dumb – yes. But, hélas, Madame Murasaki cannot be found.'

We had reached a long, narrow room that unfortunately reminded me of the ante-room at the Residence where I had spent the earlier part of this disastrous morning. Clearly it had much the same function. The DST man motioned me to a chair.

'Please to wait, monsieur. Someone will come. I myself have to supervise yet another search of the Palace. Not, you understand, that I have any great expectations. As from now, we're in the hands of le bon Dieu.'

He left me and I stared out of the window. It overlooked the garden and I could see across the lawns and beyond, through the trees, to the Champs Elysées. I wondered what on earth I was doing here. Lady P's telephone call had achieved everything necessary. There was nothing more that H.E. or I could do. The DST had been warned and had the situation under control, as far as was possible.

That, however, wasn't very far. We were all groping in the dark still. And somewhere, I was convinced, Madame Murasaki was waiting for God knows what plan to bear its revolting fruit. Nothing could have been more frustrating – or frightening.

Angrily I turned away from the window as the door opened. I was expecting H.E. but it was Charles Grail. He came purposefully into the room, and then stopped as if he had run into a glass wall. He swallowed with difficulty. I saw his Adam's apple working.

'Piers!'

'Hullo, Charles. I'm glad it's you and not H.E.'

'We – we thought you were dead, blown up in the explosion at Colette's.' He seized me by the shoulders and shook me roughly. 'My dear boy! I couldn't be more pleased. But where have you been? Why didn't you – '

'Charles, it's a long story and there isn't the time – '

'What about Margot? Is she all right too?'

'Yes. She's fine.' I suppressed my irritation. 'What's happening in the conference room?'

'The meeting's over. It went very well. They're walking around, chatting to each other, drinking champagne.'

'The President and our PM?'

'Of course. And the French PM and the Foreign Secretaries and H.E. and his French counterpart and all the support staffs. Why?'

I shook my head; I didn't know why I was asking these questions. 'What happens next?'

'This goes on for a while more. Remember, the media are there in force. The movie cameras are whirring. Other chaps are taking stills from impossible angles. Some of the more privileged pressmen are thrusting their mikes into the VIPs' faces and asking friendly questions; the tricky ones come later at the formal conference. I don't know how these politicians do it. If anyone ever pushes a mike at me, I – Piers! What's the matter?'

I stared at him. 'My God, that could be it! What Johnny meant. Mike. Big bang. Damjaps. He wasn't only talking about the peacock – though he mayn't have realized it.'

'Piers, you're not making any sense. I wish you'd tell me what this is all about.'

I ignored Charles. The door had opened again and there was Le Gaillard. I'd never been happier to see anyone. Le Gaillard would listen and trust my instinct and act.

'Monsieur Le Gaillard, you and Chriswell were sure I knew something – something I wasn't aware I knew – that could ruin everything for the Sons of Orion. I – I think you were right. It was something Johnny said while he was dying. There's no time to explain, but the bomb you're looking for – the device, whatever it is – it could be in one of the microphones or connected to a microphone – in a bit of equipment perhaps.'

'No, Monsieur Tyburn, I don't think that's possible. The microphones have all been checked.'

'Then check them again, for God's sake!'

'Monsieur?' He pulled at his carrot-coloured moustache.

'I'm sorry, Monsieur Le Gaillard, I apologize.'

With an effort I controlled my temper. Disappointed by Le Gaillard's response, I had seemed to give him an order. I had offended him. Now I would have to waste more time before I could convince him. And time was short. The explosion could come at any moment.

'Monsieur Le Gaillard, please be patient with me.'

'But of course, monsieur.'

'I repeat. Both you and Tom Chriswell were certain I had some information – nothing to do with the cassette – that was a real threat to what the Sons of Orion were planning.' I forced myself to speak slowly, reasonably. 'It was a threat they didn't appreciate until last weekend when – I would guess – they read or heard some inaccurate report of how Johnny died in my arms. Once they knew Johnny had talked to me, they had to assume he'd passed on whatever they'd said, even if in garbled form. And they had to kill me before I realized its importance.'

'But, monsieur, if Johnny had overheard some – some indiscreet remark, so would Madame Rosemead, and she would have comprehended it more clearly. Yet there has been no attempt to silence her.'

'It's possible they know she couldn't have heard it. Jean remembers nothing after the doorbell went. Perhaps she opened her mouth to scream and one of the Murasakis knocked her out. They could have been concentrating on her, arranging her "suicide", and not paying any attention to Johnny because they thought he was dead already.'

'Did Johnny tell you of the microphones, Monsieur Tyburn?'

'No. I doubt he knew what a microphone was. But he knew there was danger, there was going to be a big bang and it was connected with a – Mike.' I expelled a sharp breath; I couldn't start explaining about the peacock. 'Johnny wasn't completely witless, Monsieur Le Gaillard. He associated words and he made his own sense out of them. Don't you see? It was a risk the Murasakis couldn't take.'

'But would these Murasakis have spoken English?' Charles, who had been listening intently, interrupted.

'Why not? Their father told Lady Paverton they often speak it among themselves.' I was impatient; the seconds were ticking away. 'Look, why else should they have been so determined to kill me – whatever the cost, even if it meant blowing up Colette's? It must have been essential for them to get rid of me. Of course, if they could deny responsibility for my death, all the better. They were afraid H.E. wouldn't stand for much more. He'd made them swear to leave me alone. That's probably why the Murasaki woman insisted that President Kanudin was the intended victim.' I stopped. What was the use? My arguments were making no impression on Le Gaillard. 'Monsieur Le Gaillard, please. What have we got to lose?'

'All right then, Monsieur Tyburn. I'll have the microphones checked again – if it's possible, if the press conference hasn't started yet.' He was already at the door. I sighed with relief. 'Come with me and you can watch on the closed-circuit television.'

Waiting while Le Gaillard gave brief instructions to the

DST man who had been standing outside, Charles said: 'Piers, for heaven's sake, tell me what's happening.'

'It's probable that a cell of the *Rengo Sekigun*, called the Sons of Orion, is about to bring the new *entente cordiale* to a bloody end before it's begun,' I said bitterly. 'Where's H.E.?'

'Christ!' Charles was shaken. 'I – I left him drinking champagne. Everything's running very late. The press conference should have started ages ago.'

I nodded. This would explain the increasing time-gap between the end of the 'happenings' at the Residence and the disaster, still to come, at the Elysée. Chriswell too had probably been quicker and more efficient than had been expected – and I was meant to be dead. The Murasakis had under-rated us. Not that it was likely to do us much good. By now I was convinced that, miracles apart – and surely Paul Paverton had used up today's ration – the most senior political leaders of both France and the UK were likely to die in the very near future.

And since Le Gaillard had brought us to a room where a couple of his men were about to monitor the press conference, it seemed that Charles and I were to watch the whole catastrophe from a safe ring-side seat. Le Gaillard appreciated the point. Before he left us, he said:

'Messieurs, the press conference takes place on the other side of that wall.' He made an expansive gesture. 'However, it is a very solid and well-built wall.'

With his small, formal bow Monsieur Le Gaillard then disappeared, to reappear almost immediately, as if part of some conjuring trick, on television. I was already hypnotized by the two screens. Between them they enabled us to see the whole of the room next door. No corner was hidden from us and, in fact, we had a better view than if we had been present with the press.

Some twenty-five or thirty journalists sat in rows; each had an identity card with a photograph pinned to his jacket and had been thoroughly searched before being allowed to enter. In front of them was a long table, on which were glasses of water, five pads of paper, five pens and five individual microphones. Behind the table were five empty chairs. As we watched a nondescript-looking man turned away from the furthest mike and gave a single, infinitesimal shake of his head in Le Gaillard's direction.

'He's not found anything,' one of the monitors said, with regret.

'In that case there's nothing to be found,' the other was positive. 'They don't come better than Jean-Louis at this job, monsieur,' he added to me.

Beside me I felt Charles perceptibly relax. My reaction was the reverse. I had a wild desire to dash into the next room and, by some incredible act, render the whole press conference impossible. But I didn't have the moral courage. Instead I sat, goggling at the television screens, my knuckles white as I gripped the arms of my chair.

The President of France was taking his seat. On his right was the British Prime Minister, next to him the French Prime Minister. To the left of the President were the two Foreign Secretaries. The positioning was meant to be a visual demonstration of French and British solidarity. The press, who had stood for the entrance of these mandarins, sat down again. The conference was about to begin.

The President made a short statement: the *entente* was more *cordiale* than it had ever been and this meeting had ushered in a new period of cooperation which would be of inestimable benefit to both France and Great Britain. I scarcely listened. I was watching him and his fellow-politicians and wondering how, when they must know of their very real danger, they could be so calm. The press, I assumed, wasn't aware of any threat. Yet there seemed to be a certain uneasiness among them, at least in one section.

As the President finished speaking a camera panned in on the commotion and the reason for it became clear. A journalist was unwell, probably faint since a colleague was forcing his head between his knees. But it was nothing serious. Almost at once he sat up, then stood. Luckily he was at the end of the front row and it was easy for him to get out. He was a thin, narrow-shouldered man in a blue denim suit, with unkempt hair and tinted spectacles. Everyone felt sorry for him. Those nearest did their best to be helpful and many of the others gave him sympathetic glances. Even our PM paused before replying to the first question.

Only the camera was impartial. While a fellow-journalist explained the situation to the DST guard, it travelled slowly over the man who had fainted, as he leaned against the door-post. My attention divided itself between this group and the PM, who was giving one of his ponderous answers. Suddenly it was wholly focussed. A close-up of the sick man had filled the screen. I stared in utter disbelief.

The eyes, behind coloured glass, were hidden. The lack-lustre hair, badly-cut, was deceptive. The planes and hollows of the face were unfamiliar to me. But I recognized the mouth – small, prim and self-satisfied. I would have sworn to Madame Murasaki's smirk anywhere. Yet it was impossible. I was sure all the journalists had been vetted, photographed, authenticated. She couldn't have slipped through the security screen.

'Where are you going, Piers?'

Until Charles spoke I hadn't realized I was on my feet. I muttered something about the lavatory and made for the door. The two chaps monitoring the conference didn't look up. When I was stopped in the corridor outside I gave the same answer. The DST man directed me.

'It's nerves,' he volunteered, remembering he had seen me with Le Gaillard. 'Always go to the kidneys.'

Trusting he would put the same interpretation on my haste, I bolted for the cloakroom. As I had feared, it was empty. There was no journalist in a denim suit sitting palely on a stool or sicking his heart up in the loo. If he had been there, he had gone – via the open window.

The window was narrow and high. A small man could have climbed on the *bidet* and swung himself through without too much difficulty. It wasn't so easy for me, not because of my height but because of the narrowness of the aperture. I landed in a distorted heap behind a bush and lay, half-winded, on the ground. I peered through the foliage.

I was rewarded by the sight of a blue-denimed figure moving

cautiously between the trees.

Picking myself up, I hesitated. But speed seemed to me more important than silence – it was essential I didn't lose touch – so I set off in pursuit with only a minimum of stealth. Almost immediately, either hearing or seeing me, the figure ahead started like a deer, and bolted.

There must have been DST men in the grounds but, if there were, I didn't see any. Nor did it occur to me to shout for help. My one aim was to catch up with that swiftly-moving figure before it disappeared into some hiding-place. I had no doubt now that it was the Murasaki woman. And I was rapidly overtaking her, as she realized, because near the lake she stopped running and turned, her back to a tree. She waited for me.

'Who are you? You're not DST?' She was breathing hard.

'I'm Piers Tyburn, Madame Murasaki.'

Either she had already guessed or she hid her surprise well. 'You should be dead!' She spat the words at me. 'No! Don't come any closer. If you do I'll break your spine. You'll spend the rest of your life in a wheelchair.'

She held her arms loosely at her sides. She didn't have a weapon. But I believed what she said; my superior height and strength would be no match for her. The best chance I had was to distract her attention and somehow take her by surprise.

'The explosive's in a microphone, isn't it?'

'So that fool of a boy did tell you.'

'Yes, Johnny told me – after his fashion. I was his friend.'

'He was a little animal.'

I hated her for that and she knew it. She smirked at me, then looked at her watch. I edged nearer. Timing was important for her, and I could guess why.

'What are you waiting for, madame? Why don't you blow up the President and the PMs and the Foreign Secretaries right now? Because you do intend to blow them up, don't you?'

'Be patient, monsieur. The mike and the recorder I left on my chair are stuffed with *plastique*. In ninety seconds I'll be able to set it off – from here, with this transmitter. The whole room will disintegrate. The political leaders of France and Britain will be destroyed. The Sons of Orion will have struck a great blow against your bourgeois society.'

I was still ten feet from her but she held up her hand, warning me to come no closer. I stared her in the face and inched forward. I was willing her not to turn round.

'You've been clever, madame. How did you get the *plastique* through the Elysée security?'

She laughed. 'It was easy, monsieur. One of us – a workman – brought in the prepared microphone and recorder last week. He hid it in the washroom next to the press room with no trouble. Haven't you heard of deception, monsieur? The guards at the Palace were too busy worrying about our threat to the British Embassy. After I'd been searched with my equipment, I merely had to go to the washroom and make the substitution. No one would think of searching me again.'

She must have sensed there was someone behind her. She moved with extraordinary speed. Charles didn't have a chance. He was flying through the air and she had turned to confront me before I had done more than take the gun Chriswell had given me from my pocket.

'You fools! You stupid bourgeois fools! Did you think you could win because I'm a woman, because the DST seized my brother-in-law and I've had to take his place?' She looked at her watch again. 'Ten seconds. Then I'll be gone. Don't try to follow me, Monsieur Tyburn.' She glanced contemptuously at Charles, contorted on the grass, whimpering like a hurt dog. 'Your friend will recover, with luck, after a month or two of physiotherapy. But if you try to stop me I won't be so kind, I warn you. You'll never walk again. And forget that gun. You'd never have the guts to use it on a woman.'

She was wrong. I shot her without compunction. I was only sorry she died instantly and didn't suffer as Johnny had. I shot her because I had to prevent her from blowing the press conference and all those VIPs to hell or heaven. I shot her because of Jean Rosemead and Johnny, and the Pavertons, and Tom Chriswell, and Charles, and the innocent bystanders who had been killed and maimed. But primarily I shot her, emptying my gun into her, because it was the only way that Tyburn's war – the war I had unwittingly inherited from my old friend Julian Rosemead – could fittingly be won.